Skye

Rainbow Falls
Book One

HEATHER GRAY

Scripture quotations are from the ESV® Bible (The Holy Bible, English Standard Version®), copyright ©2001 by Crossway, a publishing ministry of Good News Publishers. Used by permission. All rights reserved.

Cover design by Paper & Sage.

Published in the United States of America by Heather Gray.
www.heathergraywriting.com

ISBN: 978-0-9981423-4-0

Rainbow Falls

Skye
Sunny (coming winter 2018)
Rose (coming summer 2019)

in celebration of my Savior
I know redemption only because He lives.
in memory of my daughter
She made my world brighter
and painted it with broad strokes of vibrant color.
with pride in my son
He stretches my understanding of life, people, and God
while filling our home with music.
with gratitude for my husband
I'm glad we've been able to walk this path together.

He has made everything beautiful in its time.
Ecclesiastes 3:11a

CHAPTER 1

March

Skye Blue was flying home.

Home.

What a strange word.

Too many years had passed since she'd last set foot in the vibrant but close-knit community of Rainbow Falls, Montana.

They hadn't been horrible years. Mostly. She'd had a roof over her head and food to eat. She'd gotten an education, been given a job. Life had been stable in Idaho, and that counted for something.

Then why, oh why, did leaving it all behind and running away from Boise to Rainbow Falls lift such a suffocating burden from her shoulders?

Or even better, why couldn't she breathe to begin with?

The only wrinkle in her escape plan was the man sitting next to her.

Her hometown was nestled in the Bitterroot Mountains of Montana, and those mountains — beautiful though they were — created some geographical limitations. As a result, Rainbow Falls boasted only a small airport. And small airports only took small planes. Small, as in seven rows of four seats divided by a center aisle – two seats on each side.

And because fate wanted to punish her for some unknown slight, Skye was trapped in a seat between the window and one of the most formidable people she'd ever encountered.

With one glance in his direction, her protective cloak of confidence fell away. She was once again the small girl watching in terror as police invaded her mother's home for the first time.

Prickles raced across her skin, heating it from the inside out.

Skye clenched her eyes closed. She could do it. She could block the image running rampant in her mind's eye. Her hands fisted around her seatbelt. It was the only thing she could hold onto, the only thing to anchor her to this moment instead of the past.

Eventually, her breathing returned to normal and she opened her eyes. The view outside the window drew her attention. The mountains. They had mountains in Idaho, but nothing compared to these. Mountains were vast and immovable. Which only served to remind her of the man sitting next to her.

"What brings you to Rainbow Falls?" His voice held the scratch of a smoker, but the telltale odor was absent.

"Um…" So much for avoiding conversation.

"I've never seen such a packed plane heading into our little corner of the world before. Rainbow Falls is growing and all, but still… Makes me wonder what's going on that I missed." His voice rumbled a bit too close to her ear for comfort.

Skye cast a glance at the man beside her. Ice blue eyes met her gaze. Wow.

Men were not supposed to be attractive and menacing at the same time.

Oh, who was she kidding?

Scary. He was scary.

Scary like he might, at any moment, whip out a butterfly knife and use it with lightning speed and deadly accuracy. Everything about his appearance screamed *danger*.

In fact, he probably wore an entire collection of knives hidden away on his person. How had he managed to sneak through airport security? What if he'd tucked a gun into the waistband of his faded jeans?

Of course, the weight of a gun would pull his pants down. Unless they were properly fitted. He wouldn't be able to wear saggy pants.

Skye stared at the floor in order to avoid examining the placement of his jeans. Talk about giving the wrong impression.

Was she honestly considering the possibility that the man sitting beside her had an arsenal of weapons stored on his person?

"Sorry. I didn't mean to intrude."

"I... You're not. I... I'm running away." She lifted her eyes to meet his again.

His eyes... What was it about them? Her earlier panic somehow became silly when she looked into his eyes.

A masculine eyebrow went up. Funny how she hadn't seen those brows before when she'd tried to determine his hair color.

He angled toward her and held out his right hand. "My name's Sam Madison, and I work with runaways for a living. In a way."

Sam. Hm. It suited him. But she would have named him 'Braxton the Butcher,' but then, what did she know?

She really should stop naming people before she'd spoken to them. Especially if her imagination had the man in question concealing guns in baggy pants and hiding knives in all his pockets. What was next? Toting a grenade launcher onto the plane?

She shook his hand. "Skye Blue. Nice to meet you."

His other eyebrow lifted. "So, you're from Rainbow Falls then."

Heat climbed her neck. "Guilty as charged."

"A Rainbow Girl. You can't hide it with that name."

Rainbow Girl. She hadn't heard that term in more years than she could say. "It's been a long time since I last visited the Falls. Do they still call us that?"

"A friend told me about the Rainbow Girls, but you're the first one I've actually met. Where did the nickname come from?"

Emmaline White… "Um, I'd rather not talk about it, if you don't mind." Not right now, anyway. "Why don't you tell me about your trip to Rainbow Falls. What landed you here on this plane with me?"

Huh. She was talking to the scary man. In a real conversation. With words and everything.

Going home might be good for her after all.

"Well, Skye Blue, like I said. I work with runaways. They wouldn't like being called that, but sometimes it's true. I manage a shelter for homeless military vets in Rainbow Falls."

"You don't look like…" Her words faded away as laughter flashed in his eyes. "I'm not sure what I intended to say, but I'm pretty sure it wasn't politically correct."

The corner of his mouth tilted up. "I won't take it personally. I'd always rather someone be honest with me than proper. So, I don't strike you as someone who helps the homeless? Or who can start and run a non-profit?"

A chuckle escaped before she could stop it. "Neither, I suppose. Does Rainbow Falls have a large indigent population? I don't remember it being an issue when I lived there, but… It's been a few years."

Sam's hands were clasped loosely in his lap. The way he'd angled himself in his seat gave her more room.

Skye breathed easier when she had more space in which to breathe.

And that made his answer a whole lot more interesting.

"The City Council has a whole slew of anti-vagrancy laws to discourage homeless people from staying too long in the area. Some outdoor magazine did a feature on us. Called Rainbow Falls 'The Hidden Gem of the West.' Talked about our hiking trails, waterfalls, horseback riding, fishing. And that was just the first paragraph. Next thing you know, we're packed to the gills with tourists who want to experience the Hidden Gem, and expedition companies who want to capitalize on them. The media attention has turned your hometown into a bit of a mountainside metropolis. And unfortunately, panhandlers would be a blight on the tourist-friendly atmosphere the Council wants to foster, so the homeless aren't exactly welcomed. I try to help make sure that they aren't just rounded up and shipped off to the next county. Or worse."

"Why only vets? They can't be the only homeless who show up in town."

Sam gave her a half-shrug. "There's another shelter on the other end of Rainbow Falls. They take men, women, and families. They were struggling to meet the need when I came along."

"That many homeless?"

"Now, yes. But when I started the shelter it was more about the other folks not being able to cope with some of the men who crossed their threshold. My desire to serve vets, and the other shelter's inability to provide the specialized services vets need and deserve, made the Falls a perfect fit for me."

Rainbow Falls had changed more than she'd imagined. "What drew you to vets?"

"My skill set makes me suited to helping vets, and that's where my heart is, too, so it works out."

The image of him holding a butterfly knife passed through her mind's eye again. She scooted closer to the window. "What skills would those be?"

Compassion rolled off him in waves, which didn't make sense. Barely one thought ago, she'd been imagining him flipping a knife around.

She was losing her mind.

"For starters, I served with the Marines, so I can relate to vets on a level not everyone else can. I understand combat and the scars it leaves." He touched a raised line of flesh near his left ear. "The physical ones, and the emotional ones."

"Shared history is important in business, but I'm not sure it counts as a skill."

His chin dipped the barest bit. "I don't think of what I do as a business, but you make a fair point. I'm a certified drug counselor, too, though the City Council passed a mandate prohibiting any addicts from taking up residence on the property."

"Can they do that?"

"It's their town. They call the shots. If I have a verifiable reason to believe someone's using, I'm allowed twenty-four hours to transport the individual to the nearest VA hospital."

"Yeah, but that's… I mean… It's been a while, but that's over three hours away, isn't it?"

Sam nodded. "I had to agree to their terms, or Samaritan's Reach never would have seen the light of day. And it's not as bad as it sounds. The hospital's decent and it's better than jail."

15

He was so unlike her. "You're not the type to worry, are you?"

"'And which of you by being anxious can add a single hour to his span of life?'"

Skye blinked. The words rang a distant bell somewhere in her past.

Sam Madison didn't look like a man who worked with homeless people, sure. But he looked even less like a man who quoted the Bible.

CHAPTER 2

Sam studied the woman sitting next to him. Straight dark hair, a shy smile, and a blue dress guaranteed to draw notice.

She obviously wasn't used to running away, or she'd have worn something a little more subtle.

"How long will you be in town, Skye? Maybe you'd like to come tour our facility. Not that it's huge. The tour might take ten minutes, if I talk slow."

Her honey-colored eyes filled with light. "I'm not sure how long I'll be around. I'm tangled up with responsibilities that might cut my visit short."

"You look a bit like you carry the weight of the world on your shoulders." Way to go. Tell a woman she looks tired and worn out. It worked every time.

"Not the world, no. A couple thousand employees, yes. So where is this facility of yours?"

Skye Blue acted like of some of the men he served at the shelter. She was neither inclined to smile nor to answer questions. He'd bet his left shoe she had scars of her own... and that she was hiding from them. "Do you know where the old Silver Heart Motel is?"

She nodded.

"It's now Samaritan's Reach, a shelter for vets in need."

"The Silver Heart was ancient when I lived in Rainbow Falls. I'm surprised it didn't get bulldozed a decade ago."

"Yeah, well, it's not the prettiest piece of real estate in town, but that's what made it affordable."

"How does running a place like that work?"

"It's a work in progress. For the most part, though, I provide residents with a safe place to stay and, in return, they help with the cooking, cleaning, and repairs."

"Do you have many... residents?"

This was a sore spot but she couldn't have known that. "Ten at the moment. Besides the City Council, the police don't seem to want us in town, either, so they're not particularly inclined to bring us the vagrants they come across. Whenever I ask about it, they claim there haven't been any, but that's not the story I'm getting from my guys. We go out from time to time and put up flyers where the homeless congregate. It can get discouraging when we arrive to find all our flyers from the last time gone."

Her brow furrowed. "What happens to them?"

Heat started to simmer in his gut. It wouldn't do to let her see his anger, though. She already had 'flight risk' written all over her. "The city takes them down. It's easier to run the homeless off if they don't know where to go for help."

"Is there anything you can do about that?"

"The Council is supposed to review the terms of my business license at the end of this year. I'm hoping they'll recognize the difficult position they've put me in and rescind some of the ridiculous ideas they've passed into law."

Her eyes widened. "Are you sure a review's a good idea?"

"Why wouldn't it be?"

She bit her bottom lip. "It's not nice to step into somebody else's sandbox and tell them how to play."

He chuckled. "I haven't heard that one before."

"It's your business, not mine. I haven't read any of the paperwork on it. I don't have a right to tell you how to do business."

"Sure you do. I'm giving you the right. Go ahead. Hop on into the sandbox. Maybe I'll learn something."

Skye nibbled on her bottom lip for a couple more seconds before nodding. "Review terms usually include a caveat allowing the granting party to terminate the business relationship if those terms aren't met."

His head tilted to the side. "This isn't a business contract."

"Of course it is. And as a businessperson, if someone I did business with wanted permission to do something I didn't like but couldn't legally block, I would give in with conditions attached."

"What kind of conditions?"

Skye frowned. "The kind that guaranteed failure. I might require a small business to show forty percent revenue growth in an industry growing by ten percent. Or I'd demand they meet a manufacturing quota of ten thousand units when they're currently producing only two thousand."

Sam frowned back at her.

"I'd lead them to believe I was doing them a favor, but instead I'd set them up for disaster. Then I'd tell them how sorry I was but that I was obligated to shut them down since they hadn't met the terms of the agreement."

His frown deepened. "My lawyer would have checked for something like that. He would have warned me if that's what the paperwork said."

"If he's a corporate lawyer and good at his job, probably."

Sam heart dropped to his stomach. "He's a divorce lawyer. We used to serve together. He did the work pro bono for me."

Her lips drew into a grim line. "Tell him to reread the contract."

"You're an attorney, then?"

"Heavens, no. I do enough business with them, though, to know a few things."

It seemed she had more business know-how in her right earlobe than he had in his entire bald head. Despite having scripture in his heart and on the tip of his tongue, he struggled not to worry about Samaritan's Reach. Did the City Council want him to fail? Their growing anti-vagrancy reputation didn't bode well for him. He would call his lawyer once he got home.

"I hope I didn't overstep." Her voice carried an apology. But why?

"No, no overstepping. I want this shelter to succeed. It has the potential to change lives, but only if I can take advice from people who know more than me. Besides, I don't think it's an accident we ended up sitting next to each other."

"I wouldn't say I know more." The corner of her mouth tilted up a scant couple of millimeters, but she didn't respond to the rest of his words.

The pilot came over the speaker. "We will be landing in Rainbow Falls shortly. Please make sure your tray tables are in the upright position and that any carry-on bags are properly stowed."

The lone flight attendant made her way down the aisle, collecting empty cups and dirty napkins with a garbage bag.

Once she passed, Sam returned his attention to Skye.

"Come by for a tour. No pressure, but you might be able to offer other suggestions once you see the place."

Skye stared ahead, gripping the armrests in silence. Her posture told a story, as did the fear that had been plain as day on her face when she'd first looked at him.

Maybe she'd take him up on the offer of a tour.

A woman who wore a show-stopping blue dress to run away in was a woman worth getting to know.

This couldn't be the last he saw of Skye Blue.

CHAPTER 3

Skye disembarked from the plane with her one carry-on bag, an old battered leather suitcase that had belonged to her dad. She stepped out of the small, single-story airport, breathed in the brisk air that teased with her with its hint of spring, and approached the lone waiting cab.

"Rainbow Heights, please."

The driver nodded to her in the rearview mirror before pulling away from the curb. "What brings you to town?"

Questions from a cabbie, she could handle. They were easier to deflect. "I have business nearby, and this looked like a decent place to rent a room while I'm in the area."

"No rental car?"

He had her there. So much for her great powers of deflection. "I might get one later. For now, I just want to settle in at the hotel."

"Must not be planning to stay long. You don't have much luggage."

Small-town cab drivers were clearly more intuitive than their big-city counterparts. She forced a small smile. "I have everything I need."

Skye turned her head and stared out the window. In the city, this action would have passed for a semi-polite *don't talk to me*. Hopefully, it meant the same thing here. Otherwise, it was going to be a short but tedious drive.

When the cabbie refrained from more chatter, Skye breathed out a sigh. Maybe she should have used the same trick when Sam had first spoken to her. Then again...

He'd proven to be an interesting diversion.

The cab pulled up under the hotel's portico, and Skye passed the appropriate bills to the driver. Most people paid with credit cards these days, but the lessons drilled into her by her grandfather lived strong despite his death.

Never give another person access to your financial information.

Don't trust technology.

Pay cash and protect your privacy.

Grandfather. A twinge hit Skye in the general vicinity of her heart, but she ignored it, climbed from the cab, and pushed her way through the hotel's front entrance.

Rainbow Heights used to be as close to a resort as Rainbow Falls offered. That wasn't its selling point, though. Seclusion was its biggest appeal. That, and locals didn't frequent it, which made it the perfect place to hide away.

"Skye? Skye! Skye Blue, is that you?"

Her head snapped up to catch sight of someone running toward her. A trail of long, wavy brown hair was all her numb mind registered before slender arms wrapped around her.

"Skye! I never thought I'd see you again. How are you doing? Where did you come from? When did you arrive in town? Say you'll stay with me. I've missed you so much!"

The arms — and the person attached to them — held on longer than was strictly comfortable, so Skye did the only thing she could think of. She lifted her hands and patted the woman's back. That must have been some sort of signal, because the woman finally released her and retreated a step.

"Tawny…?"

The woman's eyes widened. "You didn't know it was me?" Then she burst out laughing. "No wonder you didn't want to hug me. I suppose it's not every day a complete stranger accosts you in the lobby of a hotel and wraps you up in a hug." Another giggle. "Yeah, it's me. Tawny Brown at your service."

Tawny executed a bow with a flourish of her hands.

"Um…hi."

Tears in her eyes, Tawny pulled her into another hug. "It's so, so good to see you. I thought we'd lost you forever."

When had someone last hugged her like that? Her grandparents hadn't been huggers. Affection hadn't been a priority. The last time someone had cared enough to push past her barriers to hold her close like that… Could it be? High school? In Rainbow Falls? That was over a decade ago. Surely, someone had embraced her since then…

Skye returned the hug. On purpose. "I think I've missed you, too."

Tawny pulled back and linked her elbow with Skye's. "You *think* you've missed me? Oh, sweetheart, we've got a lot of work to do. What did that city do to you? Please tell me you'll stay with me."

Skye tugged the woman in the wine-colored broomstick skirt toward the front desk. "I'm only here for a few days, and I've already made a reservation."

"Cancel it."

"Skye Blue to check in."

The man behind the granite counter started typing on the keyboard.

Tawny didn't let go of her. "The hotel's overbooked. There's no room for you. Stay with me."

Skye plucked her arm free, smoothed her hair, and looked her friend in the eye. "Tawny, we haven't seen each other in over ten years."

"Twelve. Graduation was twelve years ago."

Skye blinked. Why had she let her grandparents keep her away so long? "What if we end up having nothing in common? What if you're a vegan, and I can't live a day without a rare steak? I think it would be better if I stay at the hotel. Besides, I…" Her words stumbled to a halt. Could she speak her mind, or did it show too much vulnerability? The truth was, she wasn't used to being around people, at least not ones like Tawny.

"I'm sorry, ma'am, but according to the computer, your reservation is for next weekend, not this weekend."

The desk clerk's apology did little to calm the churning in Skye's gut.

Tawny clapped her hands and cheered. "I knew it!"

Was there a polite way to ask if they still had any rooms left for this weekend? Skye stared from the man behind the counter to the exuberant woman by her side as the jaws of a steel trap closed around her. She wasn't going to be able to escape this, not without serious emotional injury to either her or Tawny.

"Um, okay. I guess I'm staying with you. Only if you tell me what you're doing here, though."

"Don't worry. I didn't know you were coming. The mixed-up reservation isn't my doing." Tawny waved a careless hand in the direction of a frosted glass door labeled *Spa*. "I provide the hotel with some naturopathic products for their clients. Facemasks, scented lotions, stuff like that. I run my own business. Nature loves you."

"Oh, no. You actually *are* vegan, aren't you?"

Tawny pulled Skye through the hotel's front entrance in a manner only slightly more ladylike than dragging. "Yeah, but don't worry. I still like carnivores. I just don't cook the meat. So if you want any while you're staying with me, you'll have to prepare it yourself."

Skye shuddered. She and cooking didn't get along. Then again, she'd never bothered trying to learn. "Maybe I'll just order in."

Tawny squealed, whipped out her phone, and pulled Skye close. The selfie was accomplished in an instant. Who knew whether or not Skye even had her eyes open for the shot?

A couple more steps, and Tawny opened the trunk to a small electric car. "Here. Put your baggage in. How long are you staying, anyway? Because that's not a very big bag."

Skye stowed her suitcase and, as she walked to the passenger door of the car, allowed herself a small smile. A woman she hadn't seen in more years than was forgivable had invited a guest to stay at her place without any idea how long she planned to be there. Tawny hadn't changed.

But Skye had. Her smile slipped. She wasn't the same girl who used to live in Rainbow Falls and run with the Rainbow Girls. Did she even know that girl anymore?

CHAPTER 4

Sam's gaze swept the parking-lot-turned-courtyard. It was an old motel, but it belonged to Samaritan's Reach. And the bank, of course. The mostly U-shaped structure allowed him to accommodate up to twenty-two men easily, more if he put two to a room. That would take time, of course, but the goal was to eventually have thirty men on a regular basis.

The leadership program was key to the success of Samaritan's Reach. It made them unique among shelters, but that wasn't why he'd started it. He'd wanted to make a lasting difference in the men's lives. He'd wanted them to leave not just full and rested, but able to function and thrive in society as well.

His stride purposeful, Sam marched to the room next to his and pounded on the door. "Up and at 'em, Franco!" He moved down two more doors. "Come on, Gid! It's time to get a move on."

Today was going to be an exceptional day. Sam could feel it in his bones the same way he used to instinctively know a scouting mission would end well back when he'd been on active duty.

Franco stumbled out of his room, pants and shoes on but hair in disarray. He was buttoning a shirt over a sweat-stained ribbed tank.

Gideon, eyes bright, opened his door and stepped out. Wire-rimmed glasses would have made him look studious if not for the beard that was just a little too long to be considered conventional in the world of academia. "What's up, Boss?"

A smile pulled at Sam's mouth while he drew in a deep, satisfying breath.

Not my will, God, but Yours.

Both Gideon and Franco had taken to calling him *Boss* once they'd entered the leadership program. It might have started because they'd been willing to do whatever it took to stay off the street and keep a roof over their heads. Now, though, it was more than that. It was about the roof, sure, but not due to a desperate fear of being kicked out. Instead, it was out of gratitude for the chance they'd been given. They showed him honor when they called him *Boss*, kind of in the same way — but on a much smaller scale — that he showed Jesus honor when he called Him *Savior*. Not out of fear, but out of gratitude.

These men looked up to him. His influence on them never failed to remind him of Paul's words in 1 Corinthians. *Be imitators of me as I am of Christ.*

May he never forget the importance of leading these men in the right direction.

"I have coffee and breakfast in the office. After that, we're going to hit the road and go to every known homeless site in and around Rainbow Falls."

Both men nodded to him as they ambled toward the siren call of caffeine.

Sam followed them and appreciated the improvement they'd shown in the months they'd been with him. Their clothes had seen better days, but they were clean. The same could be said for the men. Shadows still lurked in their eyes, but those same eyes got a bit clearer each day. Some of the shadows came from their time in the service, and some came from their time on the street. Both were war zones in their own right.

Franco's yells had woken Sam twice the night before. His nightmares were getting better, though. Less frequent. Maybe even less ferocious.

Sam empathized. He still sometimes went to war at night, too. There had been days when the nightmares had been so vivid he would wake up hoarse from all the screaming he'd done while asleep.

Only twice was a remarkable improvement for Franco. His first two weeks at the shelter, they'd all crawled out of bed in the mornings with bags under their eyes.

The intense need for privacy because of those nightmares was one of the reasons he put new residents in a room with an established resident — and held out the promise of a private room after three months if the new resident attended all the assigned classes and counseling sessions.

Sam nodded to the man sitting behind the office's only desk. "Baxter. Thanks for coming in."

The retired Gunnery Sergeant acknowledged him with an absent-minded wave. "Gotta love this online school stuff. Can keep an eye on your sorry place while I earn my master's degree."

Sam snorted. Sure, Baxter would spend an hour or two doing his schoolwork, but he'd pass even more time playing solitaire. Assuming none of the residents needed him. "You've been working on this degree since you left the Marines what, eight years ago? Are you sure it's supposed to take that long?"

Baxter quelled him with a single glance. "Don't mock your seniors, son. Especially when they're volunteering their time to help you out."

"You know I appreciate it." Sam stretched an arm across the desk to fist bump his longtime friend. He had paid staff, but the volunteers were the lifeblood that kept Samaritan's Reach running.

Even when all the residents were off-site, the city wanted the shelter manned. It made sense, in case they got a walk-in. It wasn't always convenient, though. On days when they were short-staffed, for example. Mack Baxter made a great volunteer. He'd put in over twenty years with the Marines before calling it done and heading back to civilian life. Like too many vets, though, he'd found ordinary life harder to adjust to than he'd expected. It didn't help that his wife wasn't ready to retire. Spending day after day kicking around his house with no one to talk to had headed him in the direction of stir-crazy.

Come to think of it, a lot of Sam's volunteers were former military. Their boredom benefited him.

Sam, with Franco and Gideon close on his heels, entered the fifth homeless camp of the day. This one was ten miles west of town and hidden far off the beaten path. The only way to find it was on accident. Or by getting directions from someone who'd been there before.

Each camp they'd visited that day had been abandoned... until now.

Eyes watched them warily from every direction as the trio stepped around the men and women. Sam climbed up on a rickety picnic table. He looked at the crowd, took a deep breath, and sent a quick prayer heavenward. Then he spoke.

"My name is Sam Madison. I run Samaritan's Reach in Rainbow Falls. We help homeless vets get off the street. I have room if anyone would like to come with us. Whether you want to stay for a night, a week, or longer, our doors are open."

Sam had learned early on that telling people about the leadership program and educational opportunities didn't matter. People cared about their immediate needs and what would be required of them in return. Interest in the other programs didn't come till much later.

"We provide two squares a day and hook you up with the food bank so you can take care of the third meal. You have to share a room, but the bedding's clean, and the roof doesn't leak. All we require in return is that you attend a daily Bible study. It's forty-five minutes out of your day, tops."

Sam nodded to Gideon and Franco before continuing. "My men here are handing out sandwiches and water. Please take them. No strings attached. Taped to the outside of each sandwich bag is a business card that lists the location of our shelter and includes all our contact information. We'll be down by our van..." He indicated the direction they'd hiked into camp from. "...for an hour. If you'd like to come to Samaritan's Reach, be at the van before we pull out. Even if you don't want to come, though, or you can't because you're not a vet, please keep the business card. Use it or pass it on to someone else who can."

He started to climb down but paused. "If you're not a vet, or if you're a woman, you can't come to our shelter, but we can drop you off at the other one in town. They'll feed you and put a roof over your head, too." Sam stepped off the table and watched his men at work. Franco passed out the water bottles, avoiding eye contact, and hurrying from one person to the next. Gideon, on the other hand, chatted with each individual as he gave them their sandwich. Some of his words carried across camp enough for Sam to catch bits and pieces. "Hot water... Shower... Three squares... Washer machine..."

For a man normally reticent to speak, Gideon said plenty to the people in camp. One of these days, Sam would ask Gideon about what he'd done in the service. The shadows in his eyes bore a distinct texture. Franco had seen action. He'd been in firefights and had witnessed the devastation of IEDs. Gideon, though... There was something different about his scars.

Like Skye. Shadows haunted her eyes, too. He doubted she'd ever been in the service, but she carried herself like someone battle-weary. She never did clarify what she was doing in Rainbow Falls, but her answer of 'running away' had stayed with him.

Was she running from someone? Or something?

Her ring finger had been empty, but that didn't mean she wasn't fleeing a spouse. Her story might remain a mystery to him, but he could still talk about her to someone in the know.

I don't know what the deal is with Skye, Lord, but please watch over her. Whatever she's running from, work it out for Your glory. Help her find her way through the darkness.

CHAPTER 5

April

She'd done it.

After her brief visit the previous month, Skye had packed up the important parts of her life in Idaho and had hauled them back to Rainbow Falls.

Now she stared at the front door of the house she'd once shared with her mom. Her grandparents had owned it, and Sky had come across the deed and other paperwork in their belongings. The home must have been their way of controlling the environment in which their granddaughter grew up. It hadn't worked out as they'd hoped, though. The building might not have been in the middle of a drug-infested neighborhood, but that hadn't stopped the dealers from coming by whenever her mom had called them.

Had the neighbors ever realized what went on in the quaint, middle-class home so close to their own? Or had the fact that it looked just like theirs blinded them to the terrible things happening within its walls?

Why?

Why had her grandparents kept the house all these years? It made no sense.

Once her mom died, they should have sold it and put that chapter of their lives behind them. They hadn't, though. They'd kept it and paid someone to care for the yard. Receipts indicated a handyman had been hired on occasion to make exterior repairs, too. As far as she could tell, though, no one had stepped one foot inside the house since the police technicians cleared the scene after the discovery of her mother's body.

Wait. Someone must have been in the house at some point. Otherwise there would be fingerprint dust somewhere under the layers of regular dust. The house had been cleaned up after the police, but that was probably the last time. It didn't look like anyone had been in there since.

Today would be no different. Skye turned back to the car sitting at the curb, the one she'd loaded down with luggage and memories before driving it up through the mountains from Boise to Rainbow Falls.

Thirty minutes later, she parked at the curb of another house. This one displayed a *Just Sold* sign in its front yard.

When she'd bought that plane ticket and run away to Rainbow Falls, she had never expected it to turn into a permanent situation. Here she was, though, and her entire world was different. Hopefully, it wasn't insanity that had brought her to this place.

A smile forced its way out even though Skye's heart stuttered as she studied the front of her new home.

She was broken. She was too smart to deny it but too tired to do anything about it.

She carried deep wounds, and changing her zip code wouldn't change who she was. Removing herself from the suffocating cloud of her grandparents' memory, though... getting far enough away to breathe... If she could accomplish that, she might find a way to be okay someday.

Skye made the trek to the front door, key in hand. The sun was warm enough to make winter a memory but not so hot that summer felt close. And for the first time in more than a decade, her heart wasn't a heavy rock in her chest. Instead, it felt almost light.

Was that what peace felt like?

"I realize the transition is going to create more work for you in the short term, but I don't believe your long-term duties will change much. You're being compensated for the time, too." Skye sucked in a lungful of air. She shouldn't have to convince her assistant to do her job.

Charlotte sighed. "It's not the extra hours. You said you'd pay me, and that's all the thanks I need. The thing is, there are a lot of rumblings around the office that you're going to sell the company, and it's making people uneasy."

Skye chewed on her bottom lip. At least she was on a phone call and not a video call. Moving her personal office to Montana, while leaving the corporate headquarters in Idaho, had created more strife than anticipated. Of course people didn't like it. Change made people antsy. Her Board of Directors was in an uproar, though, and their attitude was spilling over to the rest of the employees. Yet everything in her screamed that this was the right move.

She released her bottom lip and used her commander-of-the-boardroom voice on her assistant. "I can send out memos until the Internet takes over the world, and nobody will believe me. They'll believe you, though. So I'm telling you. I have no imminent plans to sell. I needed a change of scenery, and the company practically runs itself. Nobody needs me to tell them what to do. All my duties can be accomplished long-distance, and I trust you to keep me informed of anything requiring my attention. I will be back quarterly to check in with everyone and show my face. In the interim…"

Charlotte sighed again. "I'll try to make sure I'm getting my coffee while Jimmy Malone is in there."

Jimmy was the office's biggest gossip. A casual mention in his presence guaranteed the entire company would hear it by day's end.

"Thank you, and if that's not enough, do let me know. But I think all the fuss will die down within a week or two."

"I hope you find what you're looking for. I can't imagine leaving the city for some tiny little town out in the wilds of Montana, but I've seen how much your grandparents' legacy weighs on you. I want you to know…" Charlotte's voice trailed off, and she cleared her throat. "I want you to know that nobody here blames you for wanting to distance yourself from them or their memory. People get scared when they think their jobs are in trouble, but there's not a soul in this company that doesn't want you to be happy."

"Thank you." The two words weren't nearly enough, but they were all she could force out through the tears clogging the back of her throat.

Once Skye hung up from her call with Charlotte, she glanced around her living space. The furnishings were sparse. In fact, her office consisted of a barstool left by the previous owner and the peninsula separating the kitchen from the living room. It wasn't much, but there were people in the world with a lot less.

She snatched her keys off the pegboard where she'd left them and pulled her purse from the front closet. She should furnish her new home. She needed a dining room table, not to mention a desk, television, and couch. New curtains wouldn't be a bad idea, either. The ones hanging in the house now didn't do justice to her new life of freedom.

Buying furniture wasn't supposed to be so difficult. A couch shouldn't be such an impossible decision. Skye didn't have a lot of rules. No sectionals and nothing white. Simple, right? Yet in the whole world of non-sectional, non-white couches available in Rainbow Falls, not a single one held any appeal.

Gah.

There was something wrong with a woman who couldn't decide on something as simple as a couch. Wasn't there? She left the store empty-handed and headed home.

She spent so much energy mulling over her couch-buying failure that she missed her turn... and the next four turns she could have taken. Which landed her smack-dab in the middle of the old part of town. Not the historic-and-preserved section, either. She was in the used-and-abused part of Rainbow Falls. She spotted a place to make a U-turn in front of a sagging sign for the Silver Heart Motel.

The Silver Heart Motel.

Definitely not where she wanted to be.

Skye pulled over to the side of the road.

What was she thinking?

She climbed out of her car.

Forget thinking. What was she *doing*?

On the sidewalk now, there wasn't much choice. What if she'd been seen? Getting back in her car would be insulting. With a touch of cowardly. And cowardice was something she'd determined to leave behind in her old life.

The partially blocked-off driveway up into the motel's courtyard was steep. Skye climbed it in her strappy sandals. Hiking boots would have been better. The climb itself didn't warrant boots. They would have delivered a much-needed boost to her confidence, though. Hiking boots were like battle armor to someone accustomed to wearing heels all the time.

"Uh…hello there." A sandpaper voice came from her right.

Skye turned to a man with yellow teeth and straggly brown hair that pointed in every direction as though it were trying to escape his head. He waved to someone on her left. Another man walked toward her across the former parking lot with its worn expanse of faded asphalt broken up by grass and weeds sticking haphazardly through its cracks.

The new man on the scene sported trim hair with a scraggly beard, a worn shirt, pants with a patch over one knee, and wire-rimmed spectacles. He took one look at her and hollered. "Boss! You're needed in the courtyard!"

A door to Skye's left squeaked open, and a voice she recognized from the airplane greeted her. "Skye, right? This is a nice surprise."

"You said I could stop in sometime."

"Indeed I did. I didn't expect you to still be in town."

"I haven't been. At least, not this whole time. I went back and tidied up a few things so I could make the move permanent. I, uh…" She stared at her feet. "I live here now."

"Rainbow Falls is lucky to have you. And if I'm being honest, I'll tell you I'm surprised you took me up on the offer of a tour — but I'm glad you did."

"Me, too."

His eyes crinkled at the corner. "Which? Surprised or glad?"

She took in his earring, bald head, and faded goatee. Then her eyes wandered to the scar by his left ear, and from there to the tattoos covering his arms. She hadn't seen *those* on the plane. "I'm not sure."

CHAPTER 6

Sam kept his distance. Skye looked like she might bolt at any minute. Whatever had brought her to the Samaritan's Reach, she definitely wasn't there because she'd decided hanging out at a homeless shelter would be a fun afternoon outing. The vein in her neck pulsed at breakneck speed, giving away more than she likely realized. Her mile-wide eyes were another clue.

"Would you like to tour the facility?"

She looked from him to the ragtag group of men who'd gathered around. Then she took a step toward him.

Sam waved the men away. "Go back to what you were doing, gentlemen. No need to crowd our visitor."

In any other situation, he would put his hand on the woman's back and guide her in the direction he wanted to go, but Skye still had the shell-shocked look of someone fresh from the battlefield. There was no telling what she'd do if he touched her. So instead, he walked ahead to the office and opened the door for her. She slid through with a demure *thank you* before coming to a stop in the small thirteen-foot by four-foot space.

"Being an old motel has some advantages and some disadvantages." He pointed to the half-door that led behind the front counter. "The office is through here. It's small, and there's not much to see, but at least you can get an idea of the scope of what we're doing."

She leaned over the counter without touching the surface and took in the clutter covering every square inch of the office. "Did you talk to your attorney about your business license and the City Council?"

On a normal day, Sam would sit down and try to have a casual conversation. That was how he connected with people. Nothing about Skye said casual, though. Not the stiff way she held herself, nor the orderly fall of nearly black hair over her shoulders. "I did. The day our plane landed. You were right. The terms of my original agreement with the City Council allow them to not renew my business license if I fail to comply with any new regulations they implement."

"Did they make it impossible for you?"

He tried not to scowl, he really did. His failure was etched into her ever-widening eyes, though, and accompanied by her quick intake of breath as she backed away from the counter.

"I... I should go."

The problem finally registered. There were plenty of problems, but one in particular he'd been too dense to catch right away. She hadn't made eye contact with him even once since she'd arrived. Every time she looked at him, her eyes went straight to his arms.

Sam reached for a wrinkled long-sleeved t-shirt draped over the back of his desk chair. He yanked it over his head. "Is that better?"

He was so used to living in his own skin and being around men, that he'd forgotten his tattoos weren't exactly genteel. Not to mention, there was a segment of the population who disapproved of tattoos no matter what the ink depicted.

Her gaze lifted to his, and the air left his lungs. *My word.* Her eyes were even more beautiful than he remembered, but they still had the look of delicate porcelain, as if they might shatter with one wrong move.

"You scare me." She covered her mouth with a hand as soon as the words escaped, and color climbed her cheeks faster than a desert wildfire. "I didn't mean…"

"You meant it. You just didn't mean to say it."

She gave a single nod, and her gaze flitted from him to the front door.

He wouldn't let her escape that easily, though. He needed to say something first. "I was in the Marines for several years. I did a lot of living in that time. I'm not proud of some of the things I did back then." Sam took a breath and ran a hand over his bald head. "I'm not proud of most of the things I did, at least in my personal life. But then one day I met this guy, and everything changed."

She wasn't running away. That had to be a good sign, right?

"His name is Jesus. The guy I met. I didn't literally meet him." Sam stared out the window to where the men were still all gathered together and trying to act like they weren't staring at the office. He turned back to Skye. "I'm doing a bad job of this. Sorry. It's just that the tattoos are who I used to be, but I met Jesus and He showed me something better. I wanted what He showed me, and here I am."

Skye held her purse in a death grip. "I'd like the rest of that tour now."

Women.

Could they be any more confusing?

Sam slipped out from behind the counter and again pushed the office door open for the enigma that was Skye Blue.

She followed as he showed her the storage room, then the motel room they'd converted to a kitchen. "We provide lunch and dinner here."

"What about breakfast?"

Sam pointed to a corkboard with some information pinned to it. "We have an arrangement with the local food bank. The men are given vouchers they can exchange for a week's worth of breakfast items plus a few extra snacks. Control over their food, even if it's limited, gives the men a sense of security."

"I've heard people who live on the street start to hoard things like food. Is that ever a problem?"

Sam shrugged. "Like I said, the food bank is valuable. The men crave control, enough to give them a sense of security at first. Then, as they learn to trust us to give them two meals every day, they begin to relax, and soon they're rationing their food wisely. To make it in life, these men need to develop the ability to be frugal with their money and to make their funds last until the next paycheck. What we do with the food bank is a microcosm of that. It helps them develop some foundational skills they can draw on later down the road in much bigger ways."

Skye didn't argue the point, which she could have. His approach to dealing with these men — growing them, really — was somewhat nontraditional. It worked, though, and he would defend it if called upon to do so.

Next, he led his guest out of the kitchen and into the laundry room with its one working washer. Thank goodness they had two dryers. Today was laundry day, and each of the men had their basket of clothes lined up against the wall in there. Strips of masking tape with names scrawled on them marked each basket. The men were responsible for doing their own laundry, but they had the whole day, so nobody worried about it too much. One basket sat there waiting for its owner to claim it and fold his clothes. A load of clothing was in the dryer, and another was in the washer waiting for the dryer to be emptied.

After the laundry room, he showed her the motel room they'd transformed into a learning center. "We're working on getting more computers, and hopefully a higher-bandwidth internet connection. We have good service as long as only three of four people use it at a time. But anyway — the men can take online college and vocational courses here. The goal is to help them get the education they need so they can find sustainable employment."

The computers were so old that one still had a monochrome monitor. Not exactly impressive, but she didn't comment on it.

"Do all the men take classes?"

Sam shook his head. "Anyone in our leadership program is required to work toward a degree or certification of some sort. Outside of the leadership program, though, it's optional. We try to get a feel for what will work best for each man and help point him in the right direction."

"Sounds like a lot of effort." Her eyebrows rose, but was it admiration or skepticism?

"A high school guidance counselor from Waschak Falls comes over once a month to work with any of the guys that are interested. He helps them fill out the paperwork, secure scholarships and other funding, gives them aptitude tests, and stuff like that. He's skilled at narrowing down the options and helping the men figure out where they're most likely to excel. No point in working on an accounting degree if you hate numbers, right? But if you were trained by the Air Force to handle payroll and loved what you did..." It sounded easy enough when he said it, but there were a lot of complex moving parts involved in getting the men into the right classes, let alone finding the funds to pay for it.

From the learning center, Sam led Skye to the outdoor picnic bench that sat in a back corner between the two segments of the motel. "I'd say the property is U-shaped, but since this one corner doesn't connect, that description doesn't quite do it justice. We've managed to make use of all the space we have, though, so I can't complain. The men hang out and relax at the table here, and the courtyard — what used to be the parking lot — is where we do everything from daily Bible study to exercise classes, depending on the weather."

"What about during the winter?"

"We move everything out of one of the empty rooms and use it. Eventually I'd like to build a gym that could double as our main meeting room."

"Why a gym?"

It was an easy enough answer, but it might not be one she was comfortable with. "The men who end up at Samaritan's Reach are here for a reason. They each come with their own set of issues. For some, it's anger. For others, it's fear, or PTSD, or even something like insomnia. A gym would give them a safe and controlled environment to work out some of those issues. Or just make them tired enough to sleep."

She pursed her lips as though deciding what to say.

"Boss!" Gideon's voice came from over by the office.

Sam pointed toward the front of the property where the courtyard met the driveway. "Today is haircut day. Rainbow Falls has a barber who's a Desert Storm vet. He comes once a month, brings some equipment along, and gives each of the men a wash, cut, and a shave if they want it. Let me go get him settled in. Make yourself comfortable anywhere you'd like. Just don't go into any of the men's rooms."

He jogged toward the van inching its way into the courtyard. They kept the driveway blocked for a reason. The courtyard was usually in use, and they didn't need vehicles driving into that space at random. The partition that blocked it could be moved, though, as was always the case on haircut day. Harry gave the men a full-service treatment, and that meant equipment that nobody wanted to haul up the steep driveway.

"Good to see you." Sam greeted Harry with a firm handshake. "We've got a sizable group for you today."

"Sam, my man. Long time. Help me get this unloaded?" Harry unfolded the ramp at the back of his van and opened the swinging doors.

Together, they rolled the haircut station onto the ramp and lowered it to the ground.

Gideon and two other residents climbed into the back of the van and began pulling out the items Harry used whenever he stopped by. In no time at all, a wash sink — complete with swooped headrest rim — was set up in the middle of the courtyard, with buckets of water sitting beside it and an array of supplies spread out on a folding table. Rather than pipe water over to the portable sink, residents filled the buckets with warm water from their rooms. It wasn't a perfect system, but it worked.

Just as Paul sat down to get his hair washed, the office phone rang. Sam unhooked it from his belt. "Samaritan's Reach, this is Sam. Can I help you?"

"Sam Madison?"

"Speaking."

"Mr. Madison, my name's Conway Schneider. You served with my sister in Afghanistan. Ginger Schneider."

Sam's heart dropped. "Is she okay?"

"Oh… I'm sorry. She's fine. Deployed right now, but fine."

Sam took a breath and blew it out. "Whew. You scared a year off my life."

"Sorry, Mr. Madison. Didn't think."

"Call me Sam, give Ginger my best the next time you talk to her, and don't give it another thought. Now tell me what I can do for you."

"Sure, if you call me Conway. And I'm calling because Ginger mentioned you'd set down roots in Rainbow Falls. You're not from around here, right?"

Sam strode toward the office so he could get away from the men's chatter and better hear Conway. "No, I'm not. I'd seen it on a map once. Then Ginger started talking about her hometown, and it caught my interest. I thought I'd go visit for a spell after I got out, but when I saw it, I knew this was where God wanted me. So here I am. Are you still in the area?"

"I am. In fact, that's why I'm calling. I talked to Ginger last night, and she mentioned what you were doing and that you bought the old Silver Heart Motel. I haven't been out to that part of town in a few years, but if I remember, it's in need of repair."

"You could say that. We've done a lot to it, but it's a constant project."

"I own a small construction company. Not big enough that I could send you guys to work for free, but big enough that I could probably give you a day or two of labor at cost. If you're interested, I can come on by, take a look at what needs doing, and put together an estimate for you."

Sam took a deep breath. "There's a lot more than a day or two of work to be done, but I'll take whatever you can afford to give."

Conway chuckled. "Yeah, I kind of figured it wouldn't be a small task. But if I can get an idea of everything that's in need of attention, we can weigh cost and need before we prioritize accordingly. Does tomorrow afternoon fit your schedule?"

"Yep. I'll be here."

Sam had no sooner hung up the phone than a shout out in the courtyard drew his attention. He ran out of the office. Gideon was holding Alan, one of their newer residents, in a headlock.

CHAPTER 7

Skye ran.

Sam's voice bellowed behind her. "Somebody had better tell me what's going on, and I mean *now*."

She sprinted past the picnic table, around the back corner of the building, and doubled over. There wasn't much in her to come up, but her body didn't seem to understand that as she heaved over and over again into the grass.

Another voice reached her. "I don't know what started it, but it might have something to do with your lady friend. She's puking her guts out behind the building."

Sneakers slapped pavement, then crossed over onto dirt before they came to a skidding halt behind her.

Large hands gripped her shoulders with a soft touch. "Skye, are you okay?"

The spasms in her stomach stopped long enough for her to gulp down some air. "I'm fine."

Sam guided her upright as she wiped the back of her hand against her mouth.

She'd already told him he scared her. Now he'd seen her throwing up. She was earning top points for making a lousy impression.

"Look at me, Skye."

She couldn't. The ground was so much easier to stare at. "I said I'm fine."

He released her shoulders, and she shivered as her inner chill replaced the warmth of his touch.

Sam bent down and got directly into her line of sight. "I need to know what happened. I can't let my residents fight, but I need to know what went on out there before I take action."

"I…" She swallowed then grimaced. She needed some mouthwash.

"If I let you freshen up, will you be able to tell me what started the fight?"

Skye nodded.

"Alright then. Follow me."

Sam led her past the picnic table and into the courtyard. His steps were slow, and she kept up easily, but she refused to lift her eyes and meet the gazes of the men. The jittering emotions in her middle were too mixed up for her to tell them apart. Was she embarrassed or terrified?

Sam opened a door across the courtyard from the office and waved her in. "The bathroom's on the left. Help yourself to anything you need."

She squeezed past him to get into the room, his room by the looks of it. It had all the ambiance of a hospital room that had been stayed in too long. Or a motel room that someone tried to make feel like home.

Skye hurried through the space — a bedroom — and slipped into the bathroom, closing the door behind her. She slid down, her back against the door, until the cool linoleum of the floor welcomed her. Skye pulled her knees up to her chest, wrapped her arms around them, and buried her face in her cocoon.

No tears came, but sobs shook her body until she had to fight to get any breath into her lungs. Her body's battle for air won, beating back the icy fingers of terror that had her curled up on the floor of a virtual stranger's bathroom.

Using the sink, she pulled herself up and looked in the mirror. A cool washcloth against her face would feel sublime, but she didn't have her cosmetics bag with her. She couldn't repair any damage she did, so she skipped the washcloth and instead reached for the tube of toothpaste. She squeezed a generous dollop onto her finger and rubbed her teeth. She rinsed, spit, and wiped her mouth on a nearby towel.

There wasn't much more she could do. She wouldn't be able to hide out much longer, either, without Sam coming to look for her. Getting stuck in the small confines of the bathroom with him was a bad idea. Her nerves still jangled from passing him in the doorway to his room. Another reaction she'd rather ignore. Had it been fear? Or...?

Her head dropped forward. She needed to get control, to rein in her thoughts. Her questions. Her feelings.

"Skye?" A light tap on the door accompanied Sam's voice.

Drat. She'd waited too long.

Skye took a deep breath, reached for the doorknob, and twisted. The door opened inward toward her and revealed Sam standing a few feet back, giving her some much-needed space. She flicked off the bathroom light and moved past him and back into the sunlight.

This time she walked ahead, allowing him to follow her. She returned to the laundry room where she'd been killing time while Sam had handled whatever he'd needed to do earlier.

He followed her in and looked around the space.

Skye had folded the laundry in the two baskets with clean clothes. She'd emptied the dryer onto the room's small counter, moved the items from the washer machine to the dryer, and begun a new load of wash. She turned away from Sam and started folding the clothes still piled on the counter. The laundry basket they belonged to sat at her feet, its masking-taped name — Alan — glaring up at her.

Sam crossed his arms and leaned against the doorjamb. "Everyone's been sent to their rooms until I can get this sorted out, and I had to send Harry home, too. Are you ready to tell me what occurred?"

Skye folded a worn t-shirt with meticulous care. Concentrating on each crease and fold allowed her to breathe. It gave her the control she craved when so much around her was spinning out of control. "You were busy, and I was bored, so I thought I'd help. I don't know how to do much, but I can handle a washer and dryer. So I folded the clothes that were waiting to be picked up and started a new load of wash. I wasn't bothering anybody, but all the sudden, a man came in, and he kept yelling at me."

"Who?"

"He was one of the guys standing by me when I first got here. Not the one who called you. The other one. His breath…"

Sam didn't move or speak.

Skye began pairing socks and rolling them together. "He got in my face, but I couldn't understand anything he was saying. His eyes were dead, and he was yelling at me, and his teeth were rotting, and I couldn't get away from him because he was blocking the way to the door."

"Then what happened?"

Skye slipped the socks down into the basket with the shirt and picked up a pair of pants. "The man who called you *Boss* grabbed the angry man from behind and dragged him out of the room."

"Anything else?"

She glanced over at him. He hadn't budged. Not a single muscle had moved. "As soon as the door was clear, I ran. Then you found me."

"Did the first man touch you?"

Skye stared at her hands. "No. He might have. He kept getting closer, but then that other man came along."

"Stay right here."

Sam disappeared.

She jumped as knocking rang on a door somewhere.

Sam returned a minute later, another man in tow. "This is Franco. He's going to stand right outside the door to the laundry room. He won't let anybody in, and if you go anywhere else on the property, he has to go with you."

Skye's eyes flitted from Franco — another imposing man — to Sam. "That's not necessary."

Something flashed in Sam's eyes. Was it pity? She clenched her jaw and glared.

"It is. You can't leave until you get apologies from the men involved, but I want you to feel safe in the meantime."

Sam's words swirled around in Skye's mind until they were twisted up in knots.

You can't leave. I won't let you, and you're too weak to make me.

The line between what he'd said and what she'd heard was getting blurrier by the second.

"I can leave if I want to."

Sam blinked before his eyes widened. "Of course. I didn't mean you're not allowed to. I would appreciate it, though, if you could stay until the men apologize. Do you think…?"

Skye nodded. "Franco and I will do nicely together."

Her heart should be pounding. She should be trembling.

But she wasn't.

Was it Sam's calming presence or Franco's intimidating one that made the difference?

And when had Sam gone from threatening to calming? Not that he'd ever actually *been* threatening. She couldn't forget the impression he'd made, though, when she'd first met him.

Skye could speak to a boardroom full of people without a moment's panic but had completely taken leave of her senses when that man had come rushing at her. She didn't want to think about the reason just yet. So, like any mature adult, she focused on the task at hand and shoved her jumbled-up reaction down deep inside where she couldn't see it well enough to analyze at present. She could take it out for a closer look after she was far away from this place and the tattooed man with the ice blue eyes.

A stranger approached the door and spoke in hushed tones to Franco. Then he poked his head inside the door. "Name's Matt. Sam sent me to pick up my laundry."

Franco stepped far enough into the doorway to glower at the man while Skye pointed to the basket with Matt's name on it.

"Thank you, Miss Skye."

The man disappeared out the door, his basket in hand.

A couple of minutes later, another head popped around the door following a short conversation with Franco. "My name's Benjie. I'm here for my clothes."

Skye pointed to the basket, and Benjie picked it up and gave her a half-bow. "Thank you for folding my laundry, Miss Skye. It's been a long time since anyone's folded anything for me."

He left as quickly as he'd come, and Skye finished the clothes she'd been working on. Alan's. She put the basket full of folded clothes on the floor and slid it into the spot where Matt's had been.

"Hey, Franco?"

The bulky man stepped partway into the doorway.

"Is he going to be coming for his laundry?" She pointed to Alan's basket.

Franco crossed his arms and shook his head. "Not until he's ready to apologize."

Skye swallowed. "Is he the one who came to my rescue?"

Franco shook his head again, and Skye shivered. Obviously, Sam had insisted she needed someone to keep an eye on her for a reason.

CHAPTER 8

Sam knocked on Alan's door. When the man didn't answer, he knocked louder. "I have the master key, so you might as well let me in."

Alan finally yanked the door open, but then stormed across the small room to the table and single chair on the other side of the bed.

Wisdom, Father.

"Do you want to tell me what set you off?"

Alan crossed his arms and tipped the chair back on two legs. "That woman was folding my clothes."

"She was trying to help."

"No one touches what's mine."

"First off, she was being helpful. She wasn't harming you or your clothing. Secondly, I don't care how you think she wronged you. You have no right to speak to anyone the way you did to her. You're being written up."

"Whatever. You don't want me here anyway."

Sam looked around Alan's room as he leaned against the wall and sank to the ground. "This is your second write-up in the ten days since you arrived. One more and you will be asked to leave. I don't want it to come to that. If I kick you out, you won't be allowed back here for ninety days."

Alan huffed.

Sam took his time stretching his legs out in front of him. "You need to get your act together. Terrorizing people isn't the way to make friends, but that's not the point. Even if you don't want friends, I can't let you threaten people who are trying to help this place be successful."

"Whatever."

"I'm walking you over to the laundry room, where you will collect your folded clothes. You will apologize for frightening Miss Skye, and you will thank her for the effort she put into your laundry. Then you will come right back here to your room where you will remain until dinner."

"I ain't apologizin'."

"You are if you want to sleep in that bed tonight."

Alan glared daggers at him.

Sam remained seated.

Alan grumbled a bunch of words.

Sam frowned. He was better off not understanding.

Alan thumped the front legs of his chair down on the floor. "Fine."

Sam bit back a smile as he followed Alan out his door.

Franco held his position by the laundry room as they approached. His stance would have intimidated even a battle-hardened leatherneck. Sam smirked when Alan's steps faltered.

Sam nodded to Franco, who moved aside to let Alan pass.

The smaller man sauntered into the laundry room, snatched his basket off the floor, and started stomping his way out. Franco blocked his exit.

Familiar tension coursed through Sam's body, the same as any time a conflict was at hand. Of course Alan wasn't going to be compliant. The man had a hefty chip on his shoulder, and it spilled over into his attitude and actions the way hot lava spilled out of an exploding volcano.

Sam held his position at Franco's elbow. Tension or not, he wouldn't give up on diplomacy just yet. "Alan would like to say something."

Alan groaned before following through with gritted teeth. "I'm sorry for scaring you. Thank you for folding my laundry."

"Apology accepted." Skye's voice was stronger than Sam expected. "And you're welcome."

"Hmph." Alan rushed through the now-clear doorway and back across the parking lot.

Sam nodded to Franco before heading over to Gideon's room. What a day for his intern, Lance, to be gone. Another pair of eyes sure would have come in handy.

Gideon opened the door before Sam finished knocking. "Come on in, Boss."

Like all the other men, Gideon only had one chair. He offered it to Sam and sank to the floor opposite it.

Sam tapped his leg. "Rules are rules."

"I'd do it again."

"I know. You should have come and gotten me, though. I have to write you up. No fighting. It's a big one here. These men look up to you, and you can't behave like this. You might have done it for the right reasons, and I might even be glad you stepped in when you did, but I still can't let it go without some sort of consequence."

Gideon nodded. "I got no problem with that. I know the rules. I chose to break them, and I'd do it again. My conscience is clean in this."

Sam frowned at the other man. "I can respect — appreciate even — your desire to step in and protect Skye. If something like that happens again, though, I need you to come get me."

Gideon returned his frown. "Who knows what he would have done to her?"

"It would have taken you thirty seconds. Or you could have sent one of the other men for me while you tried to verbally diffuse the situation. Force is never the right first choice."

He didn't say the words, but Gideon clearly didn't agree.

"Having said that, it didn't go unnoticed that you used a headlock on him." He could have gone for a chokehold. Gideon knew how. He'd opted for the less lethal – and more legal – headlock, though. Which meant he'd been in control of his actions, and that was big. Not just big — huge. The choice of headlock also meant Sam didn't have to call the police and report the incident. Had it been a chokehold, no matter how much he hated it, the results would have been out of his hands. They would have all been forced to say goodbye to Gideon.

The man in question grunted. "I wanted to restrain him. Not kill him."

"I need you to apologize."

"Sure thing." Gideon hopped to his feet with more agility than his grey hair would have indicated.

Sam followed him across the parking lot and nodded to Franco, who stepped aside and allowed Gideon to pass. Not that he expected Gideon to act like Alan, but he still listened in on the conversation as Gideon approached Skye.

"I'm sorry about what happened. We're not all like that. Alan just has some demons riding his back. Makes him hard to be around, but we've all been there at one time or another. It might not seem like it at the moment, but this is the safest place for him to be because we understand him. We've been where he is."

Skye's words reached Sam through the open door. "Thank you for coming to my rescue — and for the explanation. I hope you didn't get reprimanded."

"Everything's fine."

"What's your name?"

"I'm Gideon. Sorry. Should have introduced myself."

"You're a good man, Gideon. I appreciate what you did for me."

Gideon left the laundry room and went back to his room. Sam nodded to Franco, who headed across the courtyard. His chair sat out by his door, and he settled into it. Even sitting down, he was an intimidating figure.

Sam poked his head around the doorframe. Skye was a woman who dressed like she'd had an easy life. Sam would bet money she wore only designer labels. The outfit she wore must have cost at least as much as his entire wardrobe. But she'd been gracious to Gideon. Gideon was more genteel than most of the men in residence, but he was still homeless, and she knew that. This wasn't the first thing about Skye that didn't jibe. She was a walking, talking contradiction.

Skye leaned against one of the dryers.

"Doin' all right?"

Her eyes lifted to him, and she gave a small nod. "There's not much to do but wait for the next load to finish. This would be faster if you owned another washer and dryer."

He nodded. "Those things cost money, and our funding is keeping us up and running for now but not doing a whole lot to provide for luxuries like extra washers and dryers."

"Everybody has to start somewhere."

For her wellbeing, he should broach the subject with her, but everything in her demeanor said she wouldn't welcome the intrusion. "Do you want to talk about what happened?"

"I told you everything."

"You told me the facts, and I appreciate it. You didn't tell me what made you run." Or throw up.

She shrugged.

"Please."

Her eyes snapped to his, hot with anger. As soon as their gazes connected, though, the heat seeped out of her eyes. She took a breath. In the millisecond before her eyelids slid down, those captivating golden orbs radiated a depth of pain few people showed, one she couldn't have intended for him to witness.

Her words came out in a murmur, and he leaned in close to catch them. "It's like I got tunnel vision. All I could see was that man's face as he yelled at me. I just stood there trying not to duck and cover."

"Duck and cover?"

"Yeah, you know. When you throw your arms up and cower to protect yourself from a blow."

He knew what duck and cover meant but, in his world, it had more to do with incoming artillery fire than with protecting oneself from an angry man. Sam's heart twisted. There was a lot she wasn't telling him, a past she wasn't yet willing to share. "Can I give you a hug?"

Her eyes grew wide. "What kind of hug?"

"How many kinds are there?"

"There's the creepy kind that lecherous old men give, the I-want-things-I-shouldn't-want kind that men who think they're better looking than they are give, the..."

"Comfort. A comforting hug. I feel bad this happened, and I just want to give you a hug and make sure you're okay."

"Oh. Well, that kind of hug is acceptable, I suppose." Her voice was anything but certain.

CHAPTER 9

She talked a good talk, but the truth was Skye didn't come from a family of huggers. Her mom had been a hugger, but she'd been gone far too long for those memories to be fresh.

Skye held herself still as Sam put his arms around her.

Hugs were supposed to be two-way interactions. But she just couldn't...

She'd already admitted her fear out loud once that day. She couldn't very well say it again. And pity had flashed in his eyes the last time. She didn't *do* pity.

For a man who looked like he ripped the heads off stuffed kittens for fun in his spare time, Sam had a tender way of looking at her. His tall, broad form, earring, scar, and tattoos said he could snap her like a brittle twig if he ever decided to. His eyes, though, said he wanted to cocoon her in cotton batting to keep her safe.

How was Skye supposed to know who he really was?

Especially when she didn't even know who she was.

Sam released her from his platonic hold and took a step back. She hadn't gotten around to returning the hug. She'd been too busy living inside her head, trying to sort out who this man was and whether or not to trust him. Oh well. She'd never see him again, anyway.

"I don't suppose you'll ever want to come back for another visit after today…" He let the words hang between them.

Skye stared at her sandals.

"For what it's worth, I think you'd be a great addition to our volunteer staff. Having you around might inspire some of the men to work on developing their civilized manners again. When you live away from women for a long time, you kind of forget how to treat other people. That's part of what makes it hard for men to acclimatize back to civilian life after serving."

"Women, too." Her voice was small.

"Yeah, women, too. I don't have the facilities or staff to take this place co-ed, so I get single-minded sometimes."

Skye nodded.

Would she come back? Not likely. Sam scared her, Alan terrified her, and all the men had heard her heaving behind the motel. They'd eat her for breakfast if she ever returned.

She stuck her hand out. "Thank you for showing me around today. I wish you all the best with what you're doing. There's an evident need. I hope you can meet whatever demands the City Council makes so that you can keep your doors open."

Sam took her hand in his large, warm one and shook it. His grip was firm, strong. Those stuffed kittens didn't stand a chance.

When she got around to meeting his gaze, though…

Those stunning eyes of his… Why couldn't they be cold, hard, or unfeeling?

Instead, they had so much emotion in them that she couldn't sort out all the strands. Sadness, compassion, tenderness, concern, and a dozen others she couldn't begin to name. Not pity this time, though. That was weird. After the twenty different kinds of sideways the day had gone, shouldn't she be on the receiving end of an unwanted pity fest?

Skye broke the handshake, collected her purse, and slipped past Sam to get out the door.

No pity. Huh. Her estimation of Mr. Sam Madison went up.

Gritting her teeth, she took a peek back.

Sam stood in the doorway to the laundry room, his eyes following her. A dozen men gathered in groups of two and three around the parking-lot-turned-courtyard. None of the men bothered to soften their words with a whisper. Their voices carried easily across the battered asphalt.

"Think she'll come back?"

"We didn't scare her off, did we?"

"That one's a keeper, Boss."

Skye climbed into her car and pulled onto the street, making a U-turn and heading back the way she'd come.

After the day she'd had? No. She wasn't going back. A herd of wild unicorns couldn't drag her back to Samaritan's Reach.

Cringe? Or cry? Skye stood, lost, in the middle of a department store.

Granted, she had zero intention of ever going back to Samaritan's Reach, but that didn't mean she couldn't help them. Those men were in dire need of some of the basic creature comforts of everyday life.

Socks.

Underwear.

She shook her head. That was what she got for folding laundry. If she hadn't taken it upon herself to do that, she wouldn't have discovered the deplorable condition of most of the men's clothing.

She couldn't block the mental image of the men's clothes. It taunted her, distracting her from the other things she ought to be concentrating on. Like doing her job. And furnishing her home.

She'd managed to resist the urge for a while, but she'd finally given up. Or given in. None of those men could go for a job interview anywhere. Not even a fast food restaurant would hire them if they showed up dressed in the clothes they currently owned.

"Skye!"

She braced herself and pivoted toward the voice of her old friend. Tawny wrapped her in a quick but fierce hug. There were few things Tawny did by half measure, and hugs were no different. A hug from Tawny required bracing oneself or risk toppling over.

"Hi, Tawny."

"What're you doing here? This can't be the sort of place you normally shop, not with all your fancy labels and dry-clean-only clothes."

Was that a compliment? She was better off not asking. "I thought I'd buy some things for the men at Samaritan's Reach."

Her friend's eyes widened. "You know about our local vet's shelter? Look at you, getting out and about and plugged into town politics." Tawny pulled her into a side-hug. "I'm so glad you're home."

Home.

The word warmed her heart.

Even so, adjusting to Tawny's exuberance was going to take a while.

"They need things. Like socks and underwear and stuff. So I was going to buy some, but I didn't know what kind. I've never purchased clothes for a man before."

"What about your grandpa?"

Skye shook her head. "Heavens no. I bought him a new watch every Christmas and a new pen for each birthday."

Tawny crossed her eyes. "Bo-oring. Why the same gift all the time?"

"That's what he wanted."

"You weren't allowed to buy him anything else?"

Skye shrugged. "It never occurred to me to try."

"Never mind that, then. We'll figure it out as we go." With those words, Tawny hooked her fingers through the end of Skye's shopping cart and towed it along behind her as she ventured into the men's underwear aisle.

"Are you sure you know…?"

"You worry too much." Tawny tossed a glance over her shoulder. "I know exactly what I'm doing." She started grabbing packages off the hooks and tossing them into the cart.

"Um… I'm glad you know what you're doing, but do you think you could clue me in?"

"You have lots of men. Socks don't come in that many sizes. You can buy socks in bulk and let the people there sort them out, or write names on them, or whatever they do. No need to get different socks for everybody. Plus, if the socks are all the same and you lose one, you can hold onto the remaining one until you lose another. Then you'll be back to having a matched pair."

Skye inched the cart forward as Tawny moved down the aisle. Men's underwear. Skye glanced over at her friend. "This part's not as easy as socks, is it?"

The two women stood side-by-side, taking in the display.

Tawny shook her head. "Not easy at all. I didn't know they made so many different kinds. Boxers, briefs, boxer briefs, super briefs, sport briefs, low-rise briefs, bikini briefs, g-string…"

"Not those. Categorically. No. Not those." Skye cut her friend off before she could name any of the other options further down the aisle.

"Can you imagine buying these for your grandfather?" Tawny held up a package of red, sparkly, barely-there underwear.

Skye fanned her heated face as she took the package from Tawny and hung it up on one of the hooks. Backwards. So she didn't have to look at it. "Which of these do you think men wear the most?"

Tawny rolled her eyes, but her cheeks had a touch of flame to them, too. "It seems like the ones they have the most of would be the most popular ones, right? Half of this aisle is boxer briefs, so I'd say those."

"They don't look like what I folded, though."

Tawny spun around to face her, brows arched. "You what? What did you fold? When? Why are you folding men's underwear?"

A man who had started down the aisle toward them backed his cart out before spinning it in the opposite direction.

"I went to Samaritan's Reach."

"You?"

Skye pursed her lips. "I'm not a terrible person, you know."

Tawny's mouth dropped open. "I didn't mean it like that. Please know that. I just… You're just…"

"Afraid."

Tawny's eyebrows rose. "I was going to say classy. Why would I think you were afraid?"

Where was a good, old-fashioned sinkhole to open up and swallow you whole when you needed one? Skye reached both arms up, wrapped them around as many packages of underwear as she could manage, yanked them off their hooks, and dumped them into the cart. "There. Lots of sizes, and I think I got a couple different kinds, too."

Tawny's mouth quirked up as she stared from Skye to the shopping cart full of men's undergarments. She reached down and pulled a package from the pile. "What about this one?"

If Skye could chant that sinkhole into existence, she would. "I don't know how that got in there."

Tawny waved the package clearly labeled bikini briefs, and burst into laughter. "They have…" She could barely get the words out between her gales of laughter, but she wasn't one to give up. "They have flowers on them."

Skye leaned in to get a closer look. Sure enough. Skimpy men's underwear with flowers on them. She would never be able to fold laundry again without blushing if those ended up in one of the baskets at Samaritan's Reach. Not that she planned on going back and folding again. But still…

Skye grabbed the package from Tawny, tossed it in the general direction of where she thought it was supposed to be hanging, and dragged her friend out of the aisle while manhandling the cart like a pro.

Skye was laughing by the time they left the underwear section.

Not a little chuckle, either, and not the kind of laugh made when trying to humor someone else who is laughing. She was laughing so hard her sides ached. "I'm never... going shopping... with you... again."

Tawny poked at one of the packages of underwear. "Oh, yes you are. Shopping without me will be boring from now on. You'll be begging me to go with you."

Skye slapped a hand over her eyes. "I can't stop laughing if you keep touching the underwear."

CHAPTER 10

May

Two weeks slipped by without another visit from Skye.

Alan had stayed out of trouble, for the most part, but Sam wasn't quite ready to let his guard down where that particular resident was concerned.

"Hey, Boss, you got any rules about long distance calls?" Gideon leaned over the office counter.

"As long as it's not international, have at it."

Gideon came through the door and into the back-office space, picked up the phone from Sam's desk, and stood there.

Sam looked up from the spreadsheet consuming his attention. "Need something else?"

Gideon stared over Sam's shoulder. "I…uh… Miss Skye got me to thinking. About who I am and who I used to be. She thinks I'm a good man."

Sam leaned back in his chair but didn't say anything.

"I used to be a respectable man, but then I ran away, and I think maybe I left some hurt people behind. If I'm going to be that kind of man again, I…" Gideon pushed his spectacles up before meeting Sam's eyes. "I need to call my sister, let her know I'm alive, and apologize for making her worry all these years."

"How many years since you talked to her?"

Gideon studied at his shoes. "Twenty, give or take."

Sam stood, cupped a hand on Gideon's shoulder, and nodded toward the outer office. "I'll give you some privacy. Would you like me to pray with you before you call her?"

"No, that's okay. But feel free to say a prayer for me."

"You got it, but do me a favor and stay in the outer office. Nobody's allowed back here unless I'm present."

"Sure thing, Boss. Thanks."

Sam stepped into the sunshine and stretched his arms high over his head. He needed to find someone willing to do the paperwork free of charge. Sitting at a desk was miserable.

He took a couple steps away from the office door and glanced over at the laundry room.

Would Skye come back?

And who had he seen that day as she left?

Nothing had seemed unusual as he'd talked to her that day, but when he'd stepped out of the laundry room to watch her walk away, he'd caught sight of someone out of the corner of his eye. A lot of the men were standing around watching her go. So it shouldn't have struck him as so odd. Something in his gut, though, had put him on edge. The feeling of being watched had followed him afterward, too, but none of the men had reported seeing anyone unregistered on-site.

Sam headed toward the back of the property to check on the men and their chores. Aside from the basics, like doing their own laundry and taking turns with dishes and cleaning the kitchen, the men had taken on a variety of tasks from the list Conway had compiled.

Ginger's older brother was a class act. Conway Schneider had made a list ten pages long of what needed to be done around the place. He'd marked everything that could be handled by unskilled labor so Sam could hand out those jobs out to the men. He'd given estimates on all the rest. The big one would be the roof. Its replacement became more urgent with each passing week. Conway was checking around, trying to find a supplier willing to donate shingles. Hopefully he would find one before winter hit. Sam had spent a little too much time on the roof last winter shoveling snow and patching the bald spots left by missing shingles.

Sam needed to court a construction-conscious donor. An education-friendly donor, too. Or donors in general. He wasn't exactly swimming in funds.

Several of the companies supporting Samaritan's Reach had pulled their funding once they'd realized the city hoped to shut him down. Nobody wanted to dump money into a sinking ship. He probably should have kept his troubles with the City Council to himself, but he'd thought sharing the prayer needs of Samaritan's Reach would help unify the shelter's donors. Boy, had that backfired.

Sam was ten feet away from the chess game when Franco pointed behind him. "Miss Skye."

He twisted around and, sure enough, Skye walked into view in a navy-blue, tailored lady-suit and close-toed shoes. They were a far cry from sensible shoes, but at least they weren't the hand-tooled sandals she'd worn last time.

Skye stood beside a woman wearing a billowy skirt, one of those loose, flowy-type shirts, and brown hair that reached almost to her waist.

Sam ran a hand over his hairless head.

Skye's companion had a look about her. Earthy.

Each woman held a dozen or more bags from the local big box store. He never would have pegged Skye as the sort of person to set foot inside one.

He jogged over to meet the women and relieve them of their load. "Can I help you with that?"

"Just tell us where to put it." The brown-haired woman eyed him, and he got the feeling not much had escaped her inspection.

"Depends on what it is, I suppose."

Skye took a step toward him. "Some clothing and personal hygiene items."

Sam turned toward the supply room behind the office as he reached for his keys. "Follow me, ladies."

He opened the door and pointed to a large empty table against the far wall. "Set everything there. I need to sort and inventory before I can put any of it away."

The women stepped through the door. The brown-haired one dropped her bags on the table easily, but Skye struggled to lift hers. Sam moved in to help, but the other woman took the bags instead and lifted them to the table. "How'd you end up with all the heavy ones?"

Skye shrugged. "I grabbed them to hand to you, not to haul up the driveway. You were already reaching for the other bags, though, so…"

The brown-haired woman threw her head back and laughed while Skye gave an impish grin.

Huh. Skye wore the smile well. She should wear one more often.

"I'm Tawny." Skye's companion offered her hand like a woman used to being in charge.

Sam took it and returned the firm handshake. "Sam Madison. I run this place."

Tawny's eyes traveled him up and down, and she shook her head. "You're not quite what I pictured."

Color stained Skye's cheeks.

He held Tawny's eye, though, and addressed her. "What did you expect?"

She clucked her tongue. "Suit and tie, clean-shaven, preppie type."

Skye's blush intensified.

Sam nodded sagely. "I can see how this might be a disappointment then." He wore faded jeans and a button-up denim shirt cut off at the shoulders. His ever-present goatee, bald head, tattoos, and single earring pretty much guaranteed no one would ever call him preppie.

Tawny clapped her hands together and changed the subject. "Are you going to show me this place of yours, or is the supply closet the highlight?"

The tour complete, Sam led both women into the office. Gideon had finished his call, so they had the space to themselves.

Sam was less than stellar at this part of the job. He needed to learn to close the deal. He hadn't even tried the last time Skye visited. Of course, those circumstances had been unique, to say the least.

"So tell me, ladies, do you have any interest in assisting Samaritan's Reach or the men we serve?"

No was on the tip of Skye's tongue. She hadn't said it, but the twitch of her lips tipped him off to the words' effort to escape.

Tawny jumped in. "We'd like to give a helping hand. We're not sure how just yet, though. We'll talk it over, pray about it, the usual."

In other words, don't call us; we'll call you. The volunteer kiss of death.

Sam gritted his teeth. "Of course."

Skye's flinch was almost inconspicuous.

Sam flexed his jaw and counted to ten before making a conscious effort to soften his voice. "When my donors became aware of the City Council's intentions, several of them pulled their funding. People don't generally like betting on a horse when the odds are beyond long."

Tawny frowned. "Skye told me about what the Council is doing."

Sam tucked his hands in his pockets. "Losing donors meant cutting back on staff."

"What staff?" Skye glanced around. "You were the only one here last time."

"I had a part-time administrative assistant and a part-time fundraising coordinator. Without them, I'm the one who answers the phone, files the taxes, and comes up with inventive ways to get volunteers and donors. Unfortunately, I'm not particularly skilled at any of those things. I have interns who help out on a regular schedule, too, but they work with the men, not in the office."

Tawny looked from him to Skye, then back to him. "Like I said, we'll discuss it."

As sure as the sun had come up that morning, an undercurrent swirled around his legs. He just couldn't tell if it was trying to pull him down or keep him afloat. Tawny was as much of a mystery as Skye, but maybe she would end up on his side. And she might be able to talk Skye into coming back.

Skye tugged on her friend's arm. "We should get going. I didn't plan on being away from the office so long."

Tawny raised an eyebrow. "You work from home. It's not like the office is going anywhere."

Skye's chin jutted forward, and her eyes managed a half-roll before she tugged again. "We're in a period of transition. I told them I'd stay available."

Tawny's eye-roll didn't stop halfway. "'Available' is not the same as chained to your computer. You have a phone. They can call you if they need anything. Being the CEO should come with at least a few perks, don't you think?"

Skye shook her head and gave up on her friend's arm. "Bye, Sam."

She slipped out the door, abandoning her friend. Tawny didn't waste the opportunity, either. She gave Sam a hard stare. "We just got her back. Don't you dare hurt her."

Then she was gone too, the glass door swinging closed behind her.

What on earth had just happened? And why couldn't women talk straight and make sense?

Yep. The undercurrent was pulling him under.

If only it was as simple as knowing how to swim.

CHAPTER 11

June

Skye's glare would have drilled holes into the clock if she could have managed it.

Friday evening had arrived.

Most people didn't worry about Friday nights. They either went out or stayed in. No major decision.

Skye wasn't most people, though.

Back in the day, all the Rainbow Girls got together for dinner on Friday. In high school, they'd met up at someone's house. When everyone grew up, they switched to a favorite restaurant. That was what Tawny had told her when she'd invited Skye to join them. For the umpteenth time.

Skye'd been back in town for over a month, closer to two, really, and she'd scrupulously avoided the rest of the Rainbow Girls. Not that she didn't like them. She did. She loved them. At least, who she remembered them to be. Was she ready to face them *en masse*, though?

Another look at the clock. Dinner started in fifteen minutes.

If she stayed home, if she kept avoiding the people who had once been her friends, then she was handing the victory over to her grandparents. They might be dead, but they weren't gone if they still dictated her actions.

Her whole reason for coming back to Rainbow Falls had been to escape their memory, the control they'd exerted over her life, and the sadness and sense of failure that pressed down on her for letting things continue on the way they had for such a long time.

Staying home allowed them to keep control.

She needed to be able to face herself in the mirror.

Skye snatched her purse from its hook inside the closet and went to her car. She hit the button to open the garage door and, with shaking hands, started the ignition.

She could do this.

She couldn't do this.

Skye sat in the parking lot, staring at the entrance to Italita.

If she leaned just right, a glimpse of a broad corner booth off to the side came into view. Several women sat in the circular seating section. She counted six, but part of the table was shielded from her sight. They laughed together, talked at the same time, and ate. They grabbed food off each other's plates, waved their hands around to emphasize whatever they were saying, and... looked happy. They were family.

Why was the idea of having family again frightening?

Any thought of the Rainbow Girls opened a pit of sickness in her stomach. The sweet memories of their days together were all colored over with the pain of having lost them. Having people who loved her just the way she was — and having those people ripped from her life — had hurt. She'd lost more than just Mom when she'd been taken from Rainbow Falls.

Skye jumped at a tap on the window. She fumbled with the keys that lay forgotten in her lap, stuffed them into the ignition, and clicked it over it far enough to allow her to lower the window.

"I'm running late, too. Want to walk in together?"

Skye stared at a woman with exotic features and straight black hair. "Jette?"

The woman tipped her head toward the front door. "I had a deposition, but I couldn't stay away. They have the best tiramisu here. Sometimes I can't help but miss dinner, but it'd take a herd of raging bulls to keep me away through dessert. Come on, walk with me."

"Um, sure." Skye rolled up the window and scrambled to collect her keys and purse, resisting the urge to check her makeup in the mirror. She climbed from the car and followed Jette.

Unlike Tawny, Jette didn't pull her into an exuberant hug or talk nonstop. In fact, Jette didn't say a word once Skye got out of her car.

Instead, Jette employed a familiar and useful technique. She walked off without looking back.

Skye couldn't very well make an excuse or say she'd changed her mind if Jette wouldn't speak to her.

Then again, maybe Jette just wasn't a talker. Or happy to see her.

Stones rolled around in Skye's stomach as the table came into view.

Then Tawny saw her, and her whole face lit up. As long as Skye only looked at Tawny, she'd make it through.

"Scooch, scooch." Tawny was on the end of the horseshoe-shaped booth. She pushed all the other women to the side, then grabbed Skye's hand and pulled her into the booth. Jette slipped in after her and exchanged a look with Tawny.

Hm. Jette's timely appearance in the parking lot might not have been a coincidence after all.

The group that greeted her included sisters Rose and Ruby Rhed and two of the Green girls — though which two? Tawny Brown was present, obviously. As was Jette Black and another woman... Did Skye even know her?

Rose gave a small finger wave. "It's good to see you, Skye. Tawny told us you were back in town, and we've been hoping you'd join us one of these Fridays."

"Here, have some chips and salsa." The food was shoved in her general direction.

"If you want to skip dinner, at least order dessert. The tiramisu is to die for."

Um... Something was wrong with this picture. "Tortilla chips? And tiramisu?"

The stranger at the end of the table laughed.

Ruby leaned forward. "Italita. It's an Italian-Spanish restaurant."

Tawny bumped her shoulder. "Makes for an interesting menu."

One of the Green sisters pointed to Skye's menu. "But seriously. Skip dinner if you want, but don't miss out on dessert."

Skye picked up her menu, and conversation burst out around her as if held back too long by a leaky dam.

"We're here every week. You should come."

"You look fantastic. Life has treated you well."

"Love your purse. Where'd you get it?"

"I wish I could tame my hair to look like yours."

"That guy over there's trying to flirt with one of us."

"Yeah, but which one?"

The words came so fast and from so many different directions, Skye couldn't keep straight who was saying what. It was a lot like she remembered. Everyone talked into and over each other, yet everyone understood. Except her. She'd been away too long.

Her chest tightened, and each breath came faster than the one before it.

Everyone around her was sharing conversation and camaraderie.

So why did she want to climb over Jette and bolt for the front door?

Jette leaned close and whispered in her ear. "Smile. You're safe here."

Skye glanced over at the dark-haired beauty whose eyes brimmed with understanding. How much Jette knew, or how she'd come to know it, remained a mystery. Regardless, Skye's breathing slowed, and the steel bands loosened their hold on her chest. She gave a small nod to Jette as the mystery woman stood in her spot dead-center at the bottom of the horseshoe, stuck two fingers in her mouth, and whistled loud enough to crack glass.

"Sunny, get down from there!"

The Green sisters, one on each side of the whistling woman, yanked her back onto the bench before giving Skye an apologetic smile. "Her parents own this place, so she…"

Their words halted as a waitress arrived at the table, pad and pen in hand. "No shoes this time, I hope…?" Acting as though nothing was out of the ordinary — and maybe it wasn't — the waitress turned her attention to everyone else. "Alright ladies, what'll it be tonight?"

Five orders of tiramisu later — some people planned to share — the waitress left, and all eyes swung to Skye. She took Jette's advice and smiled. Hopefully it didn't come across as forced as it felt.

One of the Green girls leaned forward. "Tawny tells us you're running a company. CEO or something. What does it do?"

Skye nodded. How should she answer?

"I'm Fern, by the way. We were lab partners in…"

The pieces fell into place. "...in sophomore biology."

Fern grinned at her. "Yeah, that was a fun class, wasn't it? Talk about eye candy."

They'd been two of four girls in the whole class, and underclassmen to boot. The rest had been upperclassmen, including the entire starting lineup of the football team. How something like that had happened, they never did figure out. They hadn't cared, either. They'd spent too much time giggling behind their hands and staring like love-struck teens.

Skye was still smiling, but it wasn't as forced anymore. "I inherited my grandparents' chux manufacturing company."

"Chux?" Several voices chimed in at once, and curiosity lit everyone's gaze.

Tawny reached over and gave her hand a quick squeeze under the table, and Skye started answering questions. "Chux are absorbent pads that go under bedridden patients or seniors who struggle with incontinence during the night. They absorb any leaks or spills without letting the fluid soak into the bedding — or the bed. We sell to hospitals, assisted living facilities, things like that. We're breaking into the pet market, too, but that's a long story."

"That sounds..."

"Um..."

The other Green sister — Olive? — voiced the thought showing on everyone's face. "That's an old-people product. You're too young to be doing something like that."

Skye pushed the chips away to make room for the tiramisu she was going to share with Tawny. "Patients of all ages use chux in the hospitals. You can find our products in the neonatal unit, the geriatric unit, and everywhere in between. But, yeah, this company was my grandparents' baby. I inherited it, but it's not exactly what I pictured myself doing in life."

"And you can work from home? You don't have to be at headquarters or anything?"

Skye shrugged. "I don't want to run the company, but I can't sell it, either. Working from home is my compromise."

Jette vocalized her thoughts for the first time since her whispered comment earlier. "Why not? Was it a stipulation in the will?"

"Legally, I can do what I want, but morally... A lot of people depend on this company for their livelihood. It puts food on their families' tables. If I sell, whoever buys it will move production overseas."

Jette, again. "How do you know that? You could put a stipulation into the sales contract to prevent that."

The waitress approached with a large round tray and five servings of tiramisu for the crowded table.

Tawny dug into their shared piece while Skye answered the question. "I've received a couple of offers even though I haven't gone looking for them. People either tell me outright that they plan to move the manufacturing overseas, or they refuse to allow any stipulations about keeping the current employees employed."

"Do you need to work?" This question came from the new girl, Sunny. "I mean, if you sell it, will you look for another job, or did you inherit a boatload of money to go along with the company you don't want?"

Tawny pushed the plate toward Skye. "Here, eat before there's nothing left."

Skye savored a bite of the espresso and cream dessert before answering. "Wait a second, Tawny. You're vegan. How can you eat tiramisu?"

"Oh, that's easy. I'm only vegan Saturday through Thursday."

"Um?" Skye took another bite. "How exactly does that work?"

Fern laughed at her. "You've tasted the tiramisu. *That's* how part-time veganism works."

A glance at her plate confirmed that she had polished off the rest of the piece she'd been sharing with Tawny. "Ha. I guess I can understand."

Tawny pulled the empty plate back over, picked up her fork, and scraped every last morsel of flavor off of the plate. "Mock me all you want. Just come back next Friday. Oh, and answer Sunny's nosy question. She's waiting."

Skye glanced over at Sunny, who watched her with lifted eyebrows and eyes that danced with mirth. Skye shook her head. "What was the question again?"

"Do you need to work, or are you set?"

"I need to be smart about my money, but I won't be flipping burgers anytime soon. Although I wouldn't mind working here. They could pay me in desserts."

Ruby leaned forward. "You have to ignore Sunny. Her mom's Italian, and her dad's Spanish."

Sunny laughed. "Yeah. They say I inherited the Italian passion for life and the Spanish temper. Not sure where the lack of tact comes from, though. Both my parents are appalled by it."

CHAPTER 12

Sam stepped out of the shower and used the towel to clear a spot on the fogged-up mirror.

Today was Sunday. He loved Sundays. Today, though...

He'd found a small church on the outskirts of town that welcomed them. New Hope Church of Rainbow Falls. Before showing up with the men in tow, he'd thought it prudent to make sure they would be well-received. New Hope had been the most amenable to the shelter's presence in their service.

He'd been honest. He'd told them the men had no money to give, might at times cause distraction, and sometimes might not smell all that fantastic.

Taking the men to church with a brand-new resident always added a little extra stress, though. Jack had walked onto the property late last night. His body odor could have knocked out an elephant. He'd had nothing but the clothes on his back, too. Sam had been able to offer him clean socks and underwear, thanks to Skye, but the few bits and pieces of clothing left in the supply room had all been ludicrously big on the skeletal man.

Which meant that, for the first time since they'd begun attending church services as a group, he would be showing up with a man who truly looked and smelled homeless.

It shouldn't bother him. Sam's job — by his own choice — was to help these men. Today would put the church's commitment to the test, though. This might end up being the day they asked Samaritan's Reach not to return.

Before Sam's mind wandered too far down that road, the shelter's phone rang.

"Samaritan's Reach. This is Sam."

"Hey Sam. Conway Schneider here."

"Conway. Good to hear from you. What's on your mind? Any luck with those shingles?"

A heavy sigh came across the line. "I found a distributor over in Waschak Falls who's willing to give us the shingles at cost. It's not the same as a flat-out donation, but it's still something. There's a catch, though."

Lead settled in Sam's stomach. "What's that?"

"Whatever the City Council is doing, word's gotten around. My guy wants to hold the shingles till things are resolved. He doesn't want to lose potential profit by donating shingles to a business that might be shut down in a few months. He wants to know you'll be around long enough to use the shingles first."

Sam's hand tightened around the phone. "Makes sense."

"I know it's not what we hoped for, but it's the best I've found so far."

"I appreciate it, man. So how's Ginger doing? Hear from her lately?"

A smile filled Conway's voice. "She's great. Hoping for furlough sometime this summer. Says she'll even help me do your roofing if the timing works out."

"Ginger? Up on a roof?" The girl was tiny. But she was a Marine, too, so if anyone could pound nails on a sun-drenched rooftop, Ginger could.

"She used to work summers for me before she went into the Corps. It'd be fun to have her on a crew again, and I know she wants to do something to help Samaritan's Reach."

A brief exchange of small talk, and Sam was ready to end the call. One more mention of what the City Council was trying to pull, and... One hand balled into a fist while the other held the phone in a death grip. "I...should go."

"No problem. I'll let you know if anything changes with the singles."

"Sure. Thanks. Have a good one."

Conway was trying. It wasn't his fault. The City Council was bent on destroying Samaritan's Reach, though.

Did Sam have any chance of stopping them?

His shoulders slumped as he set the phone down.

Sam strolled past the picnic table to the gravel strip beyond. The Samaritan's Reach fifteen-passenger van sat there in all its beat-up, rusted glory. A quick walk-around showed that all the tires still held their air from its last use. That was an encouraging sign.

He returned to the courtyard and knocked on each door. Then he headed up the stairs to make sure those men were awake and moving as well. They needed to be on the road in twenty minutes if they were going to make it to church on time.

They didn't attend Sunday School, but he did try to get the men there in time for the doughnuts and coffee that were served in the foyer ahead of the worship service.

Men streamed out of their rooms. A few looked like they'd been up for hours. Some looked like they hadn't gotten much sleep at all. Alan's hair, combed for once, was a nice change.

And Jack… Wait a second. Clean clothes? If Sam wasn't mistaken, the pants belonged to Gideon, and the too-large shirt was Rafael's.

A smile split Sam's face. His men did him proud.

As for the church… One of these days, he was going to show up with a resident sure to clear all the surrounding pews. He needed to stop worrying about it, though, and trust God to be as present there as He was at the shelter.

The men all crowded around the doughnut table. Whether he had three men with him or the twelve he had at the moment, they easily cleared out two dozen doughnuts. No matter how many his men ate, though, the church always seemed to have another dozen to put on the table. Except for a few months back, when they'd gone two weeks without any doughnuts at all. The sermon both of those weeks had been about gratitude. Had the loss of morning carbs prompted the sermons, or had it been the other way around? The men were all convinced it was the former.

As the men moved on to the coffee, the pastor sidled up to Sam. "Seems like you're growing."

"God is good."

"That He is." The pastor nodded before fishing a piece of paper out of his shirt pocket. "I was asked to give this to you."

Sam took it and glanced at the name and phone number written on it.

The pastor tapped the paper. "Rebecca coordinates the doughnuts each week. She'd like to chat with you."

A smile pulled at Sam's lips. God's grace never failed to amaze. Here he'd begun the day worrying they might get kicked out of church. "Are my men eating all the doughnuts? Point her out to me, and I'll go talk to her now."

"No can do. Rebecca is eighty-four and laid up with a broken hip that's not healing as well as the doctor wants. She's on bed rest till further notice. But I doubt your men are the issue. Rebecca's not shy about voicing her opinion, but she's also the first to extend a hand of friendship and grace."

Sam stared at the phone. His options for convincing the City Council to keep them open were running out, but an idea had struck while talking to the pastor.

He took a deep breath, sent a prayer heavenward, and dialed.

"Hello?"

"Hello, Miss Rebecca. My name is Sam Madison, and I'm with Samaritan's Reach."

"Well, hello, young man. How are you doing? Did Pastor Dennis finally give you my number? I've been after him for weeks, but he's forgetful like that."

Sam smiled in the empty office. He liked her already. "He did. What can I do for you?"

"I wanted to ask you to text me each Saturday and let me know how many men you have. It'll help me plan doughnuts."

"Of course. Not a problem. Tell me, though, how are you able to get the doughnuts if you're laid up?"

"I used to buy the doughnuts every Sunday, but when I fell, that all went to pot. Nobody thought to fill in for me. You might have noticed the dry spell there for two weeks. If you ever want to see the senior Sunday school class mutiny, take away their coffee and sweets. You'd have thought the rapture had come and gone and we'd been left behind with all their hollering, bellyaching, and carrying on. So I made some calls and rounded up volunteers to pick up the doughnuts. I just have to tell them how many dozen and make sure they save a coconut one for the pastor. Those are his favorite, and if he doesn't get his coconut doughnut, his preaching isn't the same."

"I thank you for thinking of my men. It means a lot to them, and to me."

"It's my Christian duty to think of others. Besides, we were all getting a little too set in our ways. Having Samaritan's Reach come in has shaken up the whole congregation, gotten them to being more thankful for what they have and a little more concerned with doing for others."

"Hopefully without too much hollering or bellyaching."

Miss Rebecca hooted. "Oh, you're still wet behind the ears, aren't you? Either a babe in the faith or too young to grow your own whiskers. Which is it?"

Sam tugged on his goatee. He'd been going to New Hope for a while now, but his focus had always been on the men. He'd probably met Miss Rebecca before and just didn't remember. In a church as small as theirs, though, surely she knew who he was. "Young in the faith, I suppose, at least compared to you by the sound of it."

"Let me tell you something, Sam Madison. I was a pastor's wife for forty years before my Charles went home to be with the Lord, and if there's one thing I learned during that time, it's that people like to bellyache. They complain when summer gets hot and when winter gets cold. They complain when the church shrinks, and they complain when it grows. But most of all, they complain when God is growing them. Because, let's face it, sometimes those growing pains hurt. I expect your attendance has led to a fair amount of grousing, but that doesn't mean it's not the right thing for all of us."

Sam leaned a hip against the wall, his spirit settling. "I have a proposition for you, Miss Rebecca."

CHAPTER 13

"You missed church yesterday."

Skye blinked at Tawny. "Nobody told me it was a requirement."

"It's not. You know that. It sure would be nice to see you there, though."

Skye shrugged and stepped back to let Tawny enter. "I was busy."

Tawny clapped her hands together, something she did whenever she was trying to convince people to agree with her. "I have a fantastic plan for today, but you need to get dressed in something serviceable. Nothing that requires dry-cleaning and nothing you won't mind getting ruined. Just in case."

"Just in case what? What are you planning that's going to ruin my wardrobe?"

Tawny gave her a wide grin. "It's a surprise. You're going to love it, though. I promise."

Skye glanced at her laptop. She'd been in the middle of composing an email to her board of directors. It wasn't urgent, though. Things were going fine without her. Like she'd told her assistant, the place practically ran itself.

Guilt might have wanted to tug at her, but she shushed it with a quick text to Charlotte. *Away from computer rest of today. Text if anything comes up.*

She tromped to her bedroom in search of something that didn't require dry cleaning.

"When are you going to buy a dresser?"

Skye turned. Tawny stood in the doorway. "I don't remember asking you to follow me."

Tawny winked at her. "You sent me a telepathic message and asked me to check out the rest of your place. Don't you remember?"

"Um. No. I'm fairly certain I'd remember that."

Her friend's eyes swiveled across the unmade bed, scattered clothes falling out of multiple suitcases, and a closet packed with plastic-wrapped outfits. "So, are you planning on sticking around? Because this looks like you're prepared to make a quick getaway."

Skye wrenched a pair of jeans from one suitcase. "I'm settling in."

"People who are settling in usually have a dresser. Or a couch."

Skye avoided Tawny's probing eyes and dug for socks in another suitcase.

"When you left the last time, you didn't have much of a choice. We all understood." Tawny's voice was void of its usual chirp and bluster. "If you leave again, though, it'll be your choice."

Skye frowned and searched for her favorite flannel shirt. It was worn too thin to be warm, and she mostly slept in it these days, but the shirt was still good enough for whatever Tawny had in mind. As long as it wasn't yard work.

Hm. Maybe a t-shirt underneath would be a good idea.

"Promise me you won't disappear without a trace. Promise I'll be able to check on you from time to time and make sure you're well."

Skye clutched her clothes, her chest burning from the inside out. "I promise."

Tawny's brown eyes brightened, and her smile returned. "Now that that's settled, you can get dressed. We leave in five minutes."

Tawny didn't bother with the front door of her own home. She went around to the side and threw open oversized French doors. "Welcome to my kingdom."

Skye entered into the industrial kitchen built into a home whose outside resembled a beachfront bungalow. "I'm still stunned by your house. It's quaint on the outside and then — boom — a kitchen bigger than the old high school cafeteria's."

Her friend grinned at her. "Yeah, well. Got to make my soap somewhere."

Skye followed as Tawny unlocked a room she hadn't noticed before right off the kitchen. Clear plastic bins stacked floor-to-ceiling filled the space. Each was labeled with a different product name and scent.

Lotion – Grapefruit

Lotion – Honey Verbena
Liquid Soap – Peppermint
Liquid Soap – Cinnamon
Sugar Scrub, Salt Scrub, Bar Soap…

The totes went on forever.

Skye picked her jaw up off the floor. "That's a lot of stuff."

"I get orders of all different sizes. Sometimes someone orders one of three different kinds of soap. It's not very time-effective to make a whole batch just to sell the one bar. So I keep a stock on-hand for most of what I sell."

"It's all so organized. I never would have thought…"

Tawny stuck her hands on her hips. "Now listen here. Liking nature does not make me a flake. There's nothing wrong with not wanting to put chemicals in or on my body."

Where had that come from? "Is that what people think?"

Tawny shrugged. "Small-town Montana."

"Rainbow Falls isn't *that* small anymore."

Tawny pulled Skye back into the kitchen. "True. Old attitudes are hard to change, though. If you don't support the logging industry, they call you a granola. If you aren't ready to wrestle a bull to the ground with your bare hands, you're a…"

Skye flicked the end of Tawny's braid. "That just makes you an entrepreneur with eclectic taste in friends."

"I suppose…"

"But you have to admit. You're not the most organized person in the world. I've seen your refrigerator. And your sock drawer — the one that's full of hair ties."

Laughter lit Tawny's eyes from within. "All my organizational molecules are invested in my business. The rest of my life is a mess by comparison."

Skye surveyed the kitchen until a corkboard snagged her attention. "Nature Loves You. Is that the name of your business?"

Pink colored Tawny's cheeks as she dipped her chin before turning to the massive island in the center of her kitchen. "Today I'm teaching you how to make liquid laundry soap."

"You said that to me the day you found me at Rainbow Heights. I just thought you were being Tawny."

"What? You think I go around walking up to people and telling them that nature loves them? I might be offended if that weren't so stinking funny."

Skye rolled her eyes. "That was a pun, wasn't it? Stinking?"

Tawny chuckled. "Nah. That was on accident, but I'll have to remember it for future use."

"That corkboard wasn't here when I stayed at your house. I'd have noticed it."

"I might not have had it up yet. It's supposed to help keep me inspired and organized. Instead, it collects odds and ends of information. To the point of clutter."

Skye snorted. "I can't believe I thought you were telling me that nature loved me."

"See? Small-town Montana. You probably thought, 'What a granola.'"

What was Skye going to do with her? She shook her head. "So... laundry soap. Whatever for? And how on earth?"

"Samaritan's Reach needs help, and laundry soap is simple enough to make. Cheap, too, as long as we don't try to hide the soap smell with some frilly scent."

"I can barely brew coffee. I'm not sure you want to set me loose in your kitchen."

"I don't set anybody loose in my kitchen. You'll be closely supervised the entire time."

Skye rolled up her sleeves. "It's a good thing you had me change clothes."

Tawny placed a couple of large boxes of white powder on the island and several bars of some sort of soap. She started pointing to different things and ordering Skye around. "Get the tall pot from over there... Put that water on to boil... Measure out eight cups of each powder... Chop the bar soap."

Two hours later, Skye wiped the sweat from her brow as Tawny handed her a tiny white plastic scoop. "What's this for?"

"That's how much soap you use in each load."

Skye looked at the buckets on the kitchen floor and sputtered. "But we made enough for like a thousand loads. How am I supposed to lug this stuff over to the shelter?"

"Hm. You might have a point. I didn't think of putting it into smaller containers. I just multiplied the recipe by ten and got something big enough to hold the finished product." Tawny snapped her fingers. "Never fear! I have exactly what we need."

A couple minutes later, Tawny rolled a dolly into the kitchen. "This should do the trick."

The ladies manhandled a bucket onto the dolly. They ran into a small problem, though. The dolly was designed to hold something square or rectangular, and the bucket was round. Every time they tried to move forward, the bucket rolled from side to side.

It was Skye's turn to put her hands on her hips. "Unless we come up with a better solution, our hard work is going to end up all over your kitchen floor. Maybe your driveway, if we can get it that far."

"Somebody needs to invent a rounded dolly, don't you think? There'd be money in that for sure."

Skye shook her head. "Not my department. Maybe... Um... They make these stretchy doohickeys. Like rubber bands but with hooks on the end. People use them to secure things or hold them down. I think."

Tawny ran from the room and rushed back in seconds later, holding up the items in question. "These?"

"Yes. What're they called?"

"Bungee cords. They're perfect for the job."

With both five-gallon buckets loaded into the trunk of Tawny's electric car, the friends climbed into their seats and headed down the road.

They came to a stop sign and Tawny peered over at Skye. "How are we going to haul them up that driveway?"

Skye burst into laughter, the kind of spontaneous laughter that surprised the one doing the laughing. She laughed until tears collected in the corners of her eyes. "We're never going to be able to lift these buckets out of the trunk, let alone up the drive. One attempt, and we'll drop them, the lids will come off, and soap will go flying everywhere. With my luck, I'll have my mouth open when it happens."

Tawny laughed with her. "We'll slip in it and fall, and every time we try to get up, we'll go splat all over again."

"What did you get me into?"

Tawny made a left turn onto the old highway that headed out to Samaritan's Reach. "Like I said, my ability to organize and think ends with Nature Loves You. Had this been a business order, I'd have thought through the whole packaging thing better. You're buying me an iced coffee, by the way. After all this, you owe me."

"I owe you? I would have been perfectly happy getting already-made soap from the store. In normal-sized containers, too. You're the one who forced us to make giant-sized tubs of soap that guarantee we'll be bathed in the stuff when we try to unload it."

They were still laughing as they pulled into the drive-thru at the Coffee Barn.

Two lattes and the latest scoop on an orienteering outfit moving into town, and they were back onto the highway. Tawny threw a smile at Skye. "It makes my heart happy to hear you laugh like that. I've missed the sound of it."

Skye took a sip of her drink. "I think I've missed it, too."

"If you ever want to talk, you know I'm here, right?"

"I'm not much of a talker."

Tawny nodded. "Still, the offer's there."

Skye reached a hand over and brushed it against Tawny's arm. "Thank you. You have no idea how much that means to me."

They pulled up to the curb in front of the shelter.

Tawny opened the trunk, and the two women stared at the buckets of soap. They both looked over to the steep driveway they would need to hike.

Skye tapped her toe. "I'm beginning to understand how Sam bought the motel for such a low price."

"Oh? How much?"

"I don't know, but it had to be cheap. The driveway alone has probably been scaring away buyers for years."

"Try decades." Tawny leaned into the trunk and started maneuvering the unwieldy buckets. She managed to lift the edge of one bucket so it partially rested on the lip of the trunk's opening.

Skye should probably do something to help...

A yell from the direction of Samaritan's Reach sent her nerves into jangle overdrive.

Alan jogged down the incline from the motel. What had he said? Had there been words, or had it been an inarticulate, angry shout? Skye backed away from Alan and pulled closer to Tawny, who was trying to climb into the trunk.

A line-dancing ten-step polka took up residence in Skye's belly as Alan came to a stop about fifteen feet away. She wasn't alone this time, and wasn't afraid. Okay. So the last part was a lie, but she wouldn't let the fear win. "Wh-what did you say?"

Alan didn't move any closer. "I was just sayin', you can't be movin' that on your own. Let me help. I don't know what it is, but I don't want y' gettin' hurt."

"Oh." He was being cordial. How was she supposed to respond to that?

"'Sides, if you're hurt movin' it 'cause I didn't help, I'll prob'ly get kicked outta here."

Tawny, apparently a contortionist in her spare time, hopped down from the trunk to the asphalt.

Skye took a deep breath and stepped onto the sidewalk so she no longer stood between Alan and the car. Her stomach settled to a quiver, and her nerves calmed to a slow rev.

Alan reached into the trunk, pulled a bucket up and out, and deposited it on the sidewalk next to Skye. Then he grabbed the other one with a grunt, his attention on Tawny. "What's in these things, anyway?"

Without a blink or a hint of fear, Tawny smiled. "Laundry soap."

"In buckets from the hardware store? What kind of laundry soap do they sell?"

Tawny ignored the question, popped the trunk closed, and hooked her arm through Skye's. "Lead the way, good sir."

Alan picked up one bucket in each hand, grunted again, and started the climb.

His back was to them, but that didn't stop Tawny from calling after him. "You ever yell at my friend again like you did when you charged my car, and getting kicked out of here will be the least of your problems."

Alan halted and swiveled his head around in their direction.

If he were to drop a bucket, it would roll back down the hill and flatten Skye and Tawny in the process.

He didn't drop one, though. His gaze flicked back and forth between the two women. He gave Tawny a hard look before turning to Skye. "I was plannin' to say this after I got to the top and set the buckets down, but I'm sorry about the other day. Genuinely, not just because I'm being forced to say so. I got..." His Adam's apple bobbed. "I have some issues, and sometimes things set me off, and I can't always explain what the trigger is. It's kind of like... It's kind of like that tunnel vision you talked about."

Tunnel vision? He'd overheard her conversation with Sam.

They were still a fair distance from him, but Skye took a second to look at Alan. There was something in his eyes that she'd missed the last time. His anger had clouded her ability to see anything beyond her own fear. Today, though, his eyes weren't angry. They were sad, a little embarrassed, and...broken. It was a bit like looking in a mirror. "Do you have a last name, Alan?"

He turned back toward Samaritan's Reach and resumed his slow trek, but he called back over his shoulder, "Just Alan."

CHAPTER 14

"Hey, Boss!"

Sam was in the middle of helping newcomer Jack fill out some paperwork when Alan's yell reached him.

His most cantankerous resident stood outside the office's glass door with two giant orange buckets at his feet, Skye and Tawny behind him. "Jack, I need to go take care of something. Do you want to finish this together later or do it on your own?"

Jack grunted with his usual lack of cheer. "Don't matter to me."

The paperwork, if completed correctly, would garner Jack some financial assistance to help him out while he continued his life skills classes and worked on getting a job.

Sam opened the top drawer of his desk and slid the paperwork into it. "We'll do it later." He followed Jack out of the office and locked the door behind him. "What's in the buckets?"

Alan scowled. "Laundry soap. Heavy laundry soap."

"From the hardware store?"

Tawny gave an exasperated huff. "Looky here, people. We made it. It's homemade soap. You have enough for twenty-five hundred loads of wash, it's better for the environment, and the buckets are reusable. Keep them, and we might be nice enough to fill them up again.

119

Oh, and it smells clean in case you care. So get over yourselves and put the soap in the laundry room."

Skye stared at her friend.

Tawny, usually a laid-back person, shrugged. "I'm annoyed that so many people are questioning my intentions."

Sam nodded to Alan. "You heard the woman. Laundry room."

As Alan sighed and picked up the heavy buckets again, Sam gave the women his full attention. "I didn't properly thank you for the items you brought last time. They were much-needed."

Color climbed Skye's cheeks. Huh. So she didn't want to talk about men's underwear. Understandable, but still funny.

Sam tucked his hands into his pockets. "I have coffee in the office, if you'd like."

"No, thanks. We should head out." Skye started tugging her friend back toward the downward-sloping entrance, her eyes glued to his tattoos much the same way they'd been last time before he'd donned a long-sleeved shirt.

Tawny pulled free. "Skye is looking for somewhere to volunteer. How are Tuesdays and Thursdays for you?"

Sam wasn't sure who was more surprised — him or Skye. "Those days work just fine. Today's Monday. Does this mean I'll see you tomorrow?"

Skye, eyes wide, shook her head. No.

Tawny nodded. "She'll be here at eight in the morning. You probably need help on Sundays, too. She can come in then, too."

He wouldn't have thought it possible, but Skye's eyes widened even further.

"Sundays are fine. I could use an extra pair of eyes when I take the men to church. I've never had any problems, but we're starting to grow. Safe is better than sorry."

"Good, then. Anything else she should know?"

Tawny stood, the picture of feigned innocence, while Skye looked like she was still working up the nerve to spit nails.

Sam pulled on his goatee. "I have my quiet time at eight in the morning here in the office. I wrap up around half past." He directed his next words to Skye. "You're welcome to come then, just know I won't be the most talkative, and don't take it personally."

Skye nodded, her eyes still wide, before following the exiting Tawny back down the slope to her eco-friendly car.

"Uh, Boss?"

Sam's gaze remained with the departing women. "What do you need, Alan?"

"I might have scared Miss Skye again."

"Tell me about it."

"The brown-haired one was trying to finagle those buckets out of the trunk, and I ran down to stop her. I wanted to offer to help, but Miss Skye... She, uh...

She saw me running toward her and got all panicky looking."

Hm. Something had happened, and Alan was telling him of his own free will. Sam decided to enjoy the victory and let tomorrow worry about itself. "How did you handle it?"

"I stopped a ways off as soon as I saw the look on her face. Then I just talked and explained what I was doing. I also told her I was sorry about the last time, but the other lady told me if I ever yelled at Miss Skye again, I'd have bigger problems than you."

Sam chuckled. "Her name's Miss Tawny, and I think her super power is mind control. She gets people to do what she wants without any bloodshed."

Worry still creased Alan's brow. "I can't afford to get kicked out of here."

Progress. It was satisfying.

Sam clapped a hand on Alan's shoulder. "Thanks for letting me know what happened. I'm sure everything's fine, but if for any reason it's not, I'll give you a fair chance to explain yourself."

Alan nodded before ambling away toward his room.

Sam was up before the rooster. The roosters two time zones to the east weren't even crowing yet. His tossing and turning through the night had mocked his decision to let the next day worry about itself.

Today was Tuesday.

Skye was supposed to arrive at eight-thirty, but would she? Tawny had volunteered her, and Skye had stood by and let her. Most people would have told their friend to butt out, but not Skye. Her aversion to confrontation ran deep.

Either that, or she actually wanted to be at Samaritan's Reach.

Long before eight o'clock, Sam stepped into the office. The space always felt small, but part of the problem was its current state – messy beyond messy. Papers and boxes covered every surface — and most of the floor — with their scattered mess. Little room remained for Sam to fit his long legs and broad shoulders.

Somewhere in the chaos were the forms he would need Skye to fill out. She had to be vetted, references checked and all the rest, just like any other volunteer.

Once he found the right papers — in a box labeled *Miscellaneous* — Sam settled down at the desk and pulled out his Bible.

He was ten minutes into his reading when someone knocked at the glass door out front. Skye held two steaming cups, a much larger purse than he'd ever seen her with before, and a look that said she was ready to run.

Sam flipped the deadbolt on the door and held it open for her.

"I brought you coffee." She offered him one of the cups.

He hated to do it, but... "I don't drink coffee, but I'm sure one of the men will appreciate it."

"But you make coffee. You offered us coffee yesterday."

"I make it for the men. Some of them have coffee running through their veins." He pointed toward the back office. "I'm still having my quiet time, but make yourself at home."

He opened the vertical blinds on the window to his back before retaking his seat and staring at the Bible page he'd been reading just moments before. Sam had a dozen reasons for not putting his quiet time aside to welcome Skye, but they all tasted like sawdust in his mouth. The rules were in place for a reason, though, as much for the men as for him. He needed to protect Skye, too.

Whether she realized it or not, she was fragile, and if he didn't keep his distance, he'd spook her.

Sam could feel her eyes on him as he stared at the same page in his Bible. His concentration had abandoned him with her first knock, so he closed his eyes instead.

Father, be with the shelter today. Give me wisdom. Guide the men. Bring us more volunteers. And be with Skye. Give her courage.

Courage. Where had that come from? He hadn't intended to pray that, but the petition was there anyway. Sometimes God gave him words when he prayed and revealed things to him he wouldn't have otherwise noticed.

Skye struggled with fear. He'd have to be blind to miss that.

The way she'd hid behind the motel to throw up because Alan had yelled at her was just one of the many things that had tipped him off. She'd come back, though, and that showed courage. After all, fear and courage weren't mutually exclusive. Courage was about marching ahead despite the fear.

Hm. He needed to think about that one some more, talk it over with God again when he had more time.

Sam closed his Bible, pushed it to the side of his desk, and looked to where Skye sat in the small foyer of the office.

"Do you drink *anything* with caffeine?" Her eyes widened as she clapped a hand over her mouth.

CHAPTER 15

Do you drink anything *with caffeine?*

Skye reached forward with her empty hand as though she could catch and retrieve the words.

She should have asked what he was studying. Or what he'd learned during his time with God. At a minimum, her words shouldn't have come out sounding as though she thought he was the slime on the bottom of the scum underneath a rusted, leaky sewer pipe.

Sam sat back in his chair and laughed. The sound pushed out from him until it filled every crevice of the office.

The laugh lines at the corners of his eyes came readily, and his laughter was full-throated and came from his core. Somehow those things worked together to make him less intimidating, a little less fierce.

Her lips twitched as she hid behind her coffee.

Sam's laughter quieted to a rumble in his voice. "Too much caffeine makes me jittery. I love coffee. Cream, no sugar. Feel free to bring me a cup anytime, as long as it's decaf."

"I didn't mean…"

He cut her off. "Don't ever apologize for saying it like it is. In private. When talking to the men, a little tact can go a long way. With me, though, you can speak your mind. I prefer honesty, even when it's awkward."

Skye took a deep breath, and the air was sweet. Boise air hadn't tasted this exquisite, not once in all the years she'd lived there. "I'll try."

Sam pushed open the little half-door that separated the foyer area from the actual office. "The place is a mess. I don't know what half this stuff is. I had an admin assistant who insisted we needed all these things, but when my budget got slashed, I had to make cuts, and… I've never caught back up."

She eyed the mess — a generous word by far — then gave her attention back to Sam. "Are you asking me to organize this chaos?"

Sam's eyebrows lifted and drew together. "Would you mind?"

This might not be the best time to tell him he looked like a puppy dog. "I think I can manage that. Is there anything I should know? Anything I can't toss?"

He reached for some papers on his desk. "This is the volunteer application. Fill it out so I can talk to your references and run the criminal check. If we can knock that out this morning, then I'll be able to give you access to our files and the computer. Until then, you can work on the physical mess in here, but I can't let you near the virtual one."

"Hm. I'm not sure if I should be thankful for the reprieve or worried about what's to come."

He handed the application to her. "In the spirit of transparency, a little of both would be appropriate."

Skye set her coffee on the counter between the two rooms, plucked the papers from his hand, pulled a pen from her purse, and began filling out the forms.

Name, Date of Birth, Aliases, Social Security Number, Address...

The questions were all basic, as was the authorization for the background check.

Sam took the forms from her when she was done. "We also do random drug testing. Employees, volunteers, and residents."

"I saw that on there."

He gave her a quick look as he booted up his computer. "People don't always read the fine print."

She couldn't argue. The years at her grandparents' company had taught her that and many other valuable lessons.

Sam waved in the general direction of the back wall. "Feel free to start wherever you'd like. Hopefully I can wrap this up pretty quick."

Skye turned her attention to the back wall. It was hideous. The boxes were bad enough. The pressboard bookshelf with pealing wood-grain-colored paper on it was worse. The faded gold lamé wallpaper with a balding red velvet design, though? It had to go. Period. "Your wallpaper belongs in a fifty-year-old brothel."

Sam glanced up from the computer and grimaced. "I want to take it down and paint, but a hundred other things keep getting in the way."

"Can I grab some of the men and get them to help me move the boxes out of the way and strip the wallpaper?"

"Residents aren't allowed behind the counter unless one of the staff is back here, and today that's me and Lance. Or you, once I've talked to your references."

"Background check done that quick?"

"Yep. Modern technology at its best."

"How should I go about collecting some men?"

"Grab Franco or Gideon — whichever one you see first — and tell them to pick one other person. I think two's the most you'll fit in here."

Skye walked around the counter to the foyer and peeked out the front door. Gideon was nowhere to be seen, but Franco sat in a chair outside one of the rooms.

She pushed the door open and marched right up to him. Granted, she kind of thought of Franco as her protector, so it was a relatively safe march, but still.

Her words were sure, steady. "I need help in the office. Can you grab another person and come on over?"

He flexed his large fingers. "What kind of help? I'm no good at typing."

And just like that, she smiled. Skye didn't smile around people she didn't know well. In fact, prior to her return to Rainbow Falls, she hadn't been in the practice of smiling much at all. So why did someone who looked like the cross between a heavyweight champion and a bouncer make her smile as she stood in the middle of a faded former parking lot peppered with weeds?

Huh. Why care about the why? Some gifts didn't need to be examined too closely.

"You'll be moving boxes and taking down wallpaper."

"Seriously? The boss is gonna do away with that classy wallpaper in the office?"

Maybe it wasn't too late to find Gideon instead. "Um, classy?"

Franco laughed. "I'm just joshin' ya. We'll all be glad to see that stuff go. Makes us feel like we should be puffing on cigars and playing poker whenever we walk into the office."

Thank goodness. She might be brave enough to cross the parking lot and talk to Franco, but she wasn't ready to go toe-to-toe with him over wallpaper.

"Getting the paper down might take more than a day."

She rested her hands on her hips and flared her elbows out. "It's not a very big wall."

"Yeah, but that stuff looks like it's been up there since the Kennedy administration. I think it's petrified."

Skye shook her head. "So, are you going to help or not?"

"Lemme grab someone. We'll be there in a minute."

"Alright then." She headed back to the office and, even though it didn't make a bit of sense, she could have sworn she'd just grown an inch.

Skye took in the disaster in the office. It could be worse.

Sam came through the glass door in the foyer behind her and let out a low whistle. "I thought you were supposed to make things better."

"It's always darkest before the sunrise."

"You're not quoting song lyrics at me, are you?"

Skye looked over her shoulder at him. "Only if it helps."

He shook his head as he stepped through the half-door into the office. "So, what's your plan for fixing this?"

"You've been working in this pig sty so far. A few more days won't hurt you."

"What's going to happen in a few days?"

"Paint."

She caught his wince in the reflection on the computer monitor where she'd temporarily moved it. "About that…"

Skye ignored him. "One gallon ought to do it. Maybe a quart for some of the trim work."

"Listen…"

"A tarp or two. Brushes. Some of that painter tape, right? Anything else?"

"Skye, we can't afford it." He wasn't going to drop it gracefully.

"It's on me. I should be able to buy everything for around fifty dollars. Give or take. The labor will be free. Franco said he's lousy with a paint brush, but he thinks Alan worked as a painter sometime in the past."

Sam frowned at her. "I can't be in the office. I need to be out there facilitating the classes and other things we're doing with the men."

"I understand."

"You won't be comfortable in here alone with Alan."

"What about Lance?"

"No can do. He's on driver duty the rest of this week. We have some men with appointments over in Peterman Falls."

"Appointments?"

He shrugged. "A couple for the doctor, one for social security, a financial aid visit to the community college. The basics, but it'll take up his whole week."

Skye took a step back, put her hands on her hips, and straightened her spine. "Well, as it happens, you don't get to tell me what I am and am not comfortable with. Nobody gets to tell me that."

Sam tucked his hands into his pockets, leaned against the counter, and sighed. "Fair point. So I'll ask instead. Skye, are you sure you'll be at ease if you're in here alone with Alan?"

Her breath came faster, and her midsection wobbled like a too-warm gelatin mold. She almost backed down. It was so temping. She couldn't do it, though. She couldn't give up the ground she'd gained. "Comfortable or not, I'm a volunteer at Samaritan's Reach, and I have a job to do. If you don't think a resident should be in here alone with me, then you should make that clear and apply the same rule to all the residents."

A look flashed through Sam's eyes, gone faster than a bolt of lightning. Skye wasn't a pro at deciphering enigmatic men, but if she wasn't mistaken, that look had been admiration.

He gave her a nod. "You should read our Operations Manual when you get a chance. A female volunteer is never to be alone with a resident."

"That day I folded laundry?"

"I didn't know you were in the laundry room that day, not until it was too late. The door was open the whole time, though, and the room has windows in it. Even if you were in the room with a resident, you were never alone."

That made sense, but... "If a female volunteer can't be alone with a resident, what good are they?"

Laughter lit his eyes. "You really need to read the OM. As long as a third party is present, you're good."

"Like another volunteer?"

"Or resident. It just needs to be a third party."

"How are two residents safer for a female volunteer than one resident?"

Color climbed his neck. "It's the state's rule, and the way it was explained to me, it's the same rule that applies to a gynecologist. If he's a guy, you need a third party in the room. Doesn't matter who or what gender."

Her cheeks heated. She couldn't very well question him further on the subject. He might use the world 'gynecologist' again, and she couldn't very well have that. Not if she wanted to avoid a fire-engine-red blush. "So... Alan and somebody else for the painting."

Sam nodded. "I'll talk to Franco. He'll either be able to recommend someone, or I'll ask for a volunteer."

"Okay. I can live with that."

"Excellent, because you don't have a choice. You'll need to keep the blinds open, too."

She glanced to the vertical blinds pulled wide to let sun stream into the office space. They weren't open for the light, though. "That's why you always open them whenever I come into the office. Because I can't be alone with a resident... Or with you."

"Can't very well ask the men to follow rules I'm not willing to follow, now can I?"

She gave him her best frown. "Makes sense. But why did you even ask if I'd be comfortable? With Alan, I mean."

He gave a half-shrug. "I was trying to let you reach the right decision on your own."

"That doesn't seem to match your honesty policy very well."

Sam winced. "You have a point. I'll try not to do that again."

Good. See that you don't. She stopped the words before they came out. She might be brave enough to call him on it, but giving orders to the man who had terrified her at first sight not too many months ago? She wasn't there.

Yet.

CHAPTER 16

Sam thrived on high-pressure situations. A worthwhile challenge got his adrenaline pumping.

Skye was a whole new kind of challenge, though.

He understood vets. He worked with them. He could interpret the shell-shocked look in their eyes. He knew how to counsel them. Move slowly, talk softly, and call it like it was. Until the situation demanded something else, which it sometimes did.

"Do you mind what colors I choose?"

Sam looked at the wall. It shouldn't have been possible, but it was just as ugly without the wallpaper. "Not red. Not gold. No bodily fluid colors."

Skye made a choking sound. "I was thinking soft and soothing. Blue that looks like the morning sky over the ocean. And a shimmery wet-cement grey."

Wet cement made him think of a mafia hit, not something calm and relaxing. "Blue for the wall or the trim?"

"Walls."

"I can live with that."

Skye collected her purse from behind a box. "I didn't want to pick colors that might agitate any of the residents or cause them to…"

The light bulb went off. "Ah. That's why you thought I'd have an opinion about color. So… Avoid black and red, and soft colors are generally better than dark, bright, or loud colors. I'd skip anything in the beige family, too. Just a personal preference there, but some of the men might share it. I'd be hard-pressed not to go crazy if I had to stare at walls that reminded me of the Middle East sandscape."

She started for the door, and Sam had every intention of letting her go. The words slipped out, though, despite his best effort to hold them back. "I didn't think you'd come today."

"I didn't think I would, either."

"What changed your mind?"

Skye pursed her lips and waggled her head back and forth.

Sam tried to interpret. "Not sure?"

"I would have stayed away because of how Tawny forced me into volunteering, not because of how I felt about it. I guess that's what it came down to. I realized I actually wanted to see if I could do some good here." She took another step toward the door before she stopped again. "The truth?"

"It's always my preference."

"I wanted to see if I could learn not to be scared."

"Of?"

"You, this place, these men, all those tattoos, the unknown, and maybe my own success or failure, too."

Sam tucked his hands into his pockets. "Tattoos aren't so scary."

"One of yours is a skull with a knife through its eye socket."

He chuckled. "Okay, I'll give you that one. But it's just ink. It can't hurt you."

"It's ink that tells me who you are."

He shook his head the smallest bit. "It's ink that tells you who I used to be."

"I know, and I know most of these men are tattooed, too. It's funny. Gideon has some, but his don't bother me. Maybe you're the problem more than the tattoos."

Now he was getting somewhere with her. "How so?"

"If you were some scrawny little five-foot-six guy with skull tattoos, I wouldn't give it a second thought."

"There's not a lot I can do about my height."

"You should go on a hunger strike and drop about forty pounds of muscle. Three or four inches, too, if you don't mind." Her eyes glinted in the glare coming through the foyer's glass door.

"That might be a little tough."

The hint of a smile touched her mouth. "Then I guess I'll have to adjust to you, your tattoos, and those ridiculously muscled arms."

Sam held his arms out in front of him. "Ridiculous?"

Color stained her cheeks. "Now you're fishing for compliments, and I have better things to do than feed your ego."

In the blink of an eye, she was gone, and Sam was left staring at the door as it meandered its way closed behind her.

Skye was different than the men he worked with, sure. She was also different than any woman he'd ever met, too. Until today, every time he'd spoken to her, her eyes had shown him the fractures in her soul. He could move slowly. He could talk softly. He could tuck his hands into his pockets so she wouldn't feel threatened. He could do those things — but he couldn't talk to her the way he would a man. He couldn't just call her out. The straight talk that served him well with the men would only push Skye away.

He didn't know much about how women thought, and when it came down to it, he had no idea what she'd been through. He identified with the vets. He'd been there. Whatever haunted her, though, remained a mystery. It might not be anything he could relate to, and he wasn't prepared to step out into that minefield when a misstep might mean blowing her world to kingdom come.

Sam had all the certifications. He was licensed. He had worked himself nearly into the ground taking graduate classes while still serving with the Marines. He'd been forced to leave his doctorate until after he'd left the service. Practicums and all that. Sitting in an office and working with patients under the supervision of a psychology professor was a little tough to accomplish when you were eating dust in Afghanistan. So he'd had to leave the job he loved to finish the education he needed in order to launch a new career to which he was called.

And he had zero regrets.

Patience. It was a lesson he'd learned in his military career that also served him well at Samaritan's Reach.

"Hey, Boss!" Gideon stood in the doorway.

"What?"

"I only called your name like three times."

He ignored the jibe. "What do you need, Gideon?"

"You said something about helping some lady from the church. The doughnut lady?"

Sam nodded. "She's laid up with a broken hip and needs some yardwork done, among other things."

"How many men are you taking?"

"Four, I think. I was still deciding. Why?"

"You said Thursday?"

"Yeah. While Skye's here to hold down the fort."

Gideon frowned. "I'd normally jump at the chance to do something outdoors. Yardwork, anything. I'd rather be outside than inside anytime. You know that."

"Sure."

"I gave this some thought, though. It might not the best idea to leave Alan here with Miss Skye unsupervised."

Sam looked over at the man with the spectacles. "Can you paint?"

Gideon shrugged. "Never done it professionally. I don't have to be in the office. I just think I should be nearby."

"Franco's going to keep an eye on things."

Gideon grunted. "Don't trust me around Alan, huh?"

Sam cast a sideways glance at him. The man was in a mood about something. "It's not that. I know you like the outdoor work, so I'd already planned on you being part of my crew."

The resident grunted again.

Sam fixed his gaze on the other side of the courtyard. "How'd the talk with your sister go? It's been a while."

Gideon's shoulders slumped. "Number's been disconnected. I tried information, too, but couldn't find her."

Sam contemplated his next words.

Gideon needed to know he had a place, a family.

"It's time to increase your responsibility. That's part of being in the leadership program. I'm putting you in charge of the learning center. Technology's not your favorite thing, but you're smart, and the men who are struggling with college classes could use someone to help them study. You can work out a schedule with some of the volunteers to cover the times you can't be in there. That way you're not completely tied down."

Gideon's eyes widened the tiniest bit before he averted them. "Part of me thinks it's time to move on."

"I'm not sure you're ready to go, and I'd hate to see you leave here without having a job lined up somewhere."

"I've been trying."

Sam couldn't argue that. "I'm not saying you haven't been. The City Council seems to be going out of its way to make sure none of our men find jobs locally. They can't put a stop to education, though, and I could use your help."

Gideon crossed his arms. "I suppose I can give it a try. I've been considering changing my major."

That gave Sam pause. "Oh? To what?"

"Business."

"Two year, or four?"

Gideon shrugged. "Probably two."

"What would you do with it?"

Gideon stared off to the side, not meeting Sam's gaze. "Thought I might be of use here. Or someplace like it."

That didn't mesh with Gideon's seconds-ago comment about moving on. The guy was torn, obviously, and his sister's disconnected number hadn't helped.

On the solid footing he had with the men, Sam pushed ahead. He knew Gideon well enough to be able to sidestep the confusion and get to the heart of things. "I might be able to track down your sister. If you want my help. Otherwise, say the word, and I'll leave it be."

Gideon's sucked in a quick breath. "You won't contact her?"

"Nope. I'll try to find an address or phone number. The rest will be up to you. I can't promise it'll work, either."

The other man blinked a couple of times before he agreed. "Give it a try. Can't hurt, right?"

It could hurt a lot, depending on how things went.

CHAPTER 17

"You're doing it all wrong."

Skye peered over her shoulder at Alan, who was correcting her taping methods. "Nobody told me there was a right way or a wrong way."

He huffed and took the painter's tape from her. "Let me show you."

She stepped back and watched as he deftly put tape into place, protecting the trim from the Robin's Egg Blue that would shortly go up on the walls. She wasn't convinced the blue was actually the shade of a robin's egg. It still looked like a sunrise over the ocean to her. She'd never seen a real, live robin's egg, though, so it wasn't worth arguing the point.

"There, like that. See?"

The tape didn't look any different to her. "Maybe you should do it? I'm not sure I'll get the hang of it before this room's done."

Alan ignored her remark and went back to taping. "I was visiting with the lady over at employment services the other day."

The Alan she'd met the first day at Samaritan's Reach was gone. Maybe he'd had an attitude adjustment. Maybe he'd been cloned by aliens. Either way, the new Alan was proving to be a keeper. "Oh?"

"She told me about all you Rainbow Girls. Said there were Rainbow Guys, too, but they hate the name and don't use it."

Skye chuckled. "Yeah. The boys never much cared for being called Rainbow anything. Not enough testosterone in the title or something. What brings that up?"

"I looked at the paint you brought. A grey called Cloudy Sky on a Drizzling Day — whatever that means."

It definitely looked like wet cement, but nobody had asked her what to name it.

"And Robin's Egg Blue. Made me think how funny it would have been if you had a sister named Robin. Poor kid might've gotten stuck with a middle name like Egg."

"Y'all need to quit your yammering and get back to work." Jack groused from his ladder-top spot on the other side of the small office.

Franco poked his head in the foyer door. "How's it goin' in here, Miss Skye?"

Sam had given her a watchdog. She could live with that. "So far, so good. Who knows? We might even get some paint on the walls today."

"Anything's better than bloody-fur wallpaper." Franco disappeared from view, and Skye went back to loosely supervising the other men's work.

Her role was more like babysitting than supervising since she'd contributed nothing other than the color choices and the necessary supplies. Even then, Alan had informed her she'd bought the wrong brushes.

146

Next time she needed to go to a hardware store for anything, she might need to make it a field trip and take some of the men with her.

"Lunch time, everyone. Jack, Alan, go grab your grub." Sam stood aside as the two men exited the office. Then he stepped through the half-door and set two plates on the desk. "I made you a sandwich. I hope that's all right."

He stepped back around to the foyer, grabbed another chair, and brought it into the cramped space, leaving the more comfortable desk chair for her.

"Thank you." Skye nodded to the food before she slipped into the office's miniscule half-bathroom so she could wash her hands. "We're almost done. Provided you don't mind supervising them, Jack and Alan should be able to finish up tomorrow. If not, it can wait till Tuesday when I'm back."

"Tomorrow should be fine, but we'll see."

She settled into the desk chair. "I never knew taping to paint could take hours instead of minutes. Or that you had to wait such a long time in between colors so the paints wouldn't blead into one another."

"Letting one color dry before you do the other is pretty standard. The fastidious taping, though? I'm pretty sure that's an Alan original."

She reached for her sandwich.

"You mind if I bless the meal?"

"No. I mean, yes. Or no."

His left eyebrow lifted the tiniest bit, drawing Skye's gaze to the raised scar near his left ear.

She pinched the bridge of her nose. "No, I don't mind. Yes, go ahead and pray."

Sam bowed his head and Skye studied him.

"Father above…"

He used the same voice with God as he used with her. Close, personal. Intimate. Personal, at the very least, but… Yeah, intimate was the word that came to mind.

"…Amen."

Skye blinked. She'd completely missed his prayer. She'd been too absorbed with looking at this man who had made her think of a thug when she'd first met him, especially in the close confines of the airplane. How could someone who'd once seemed so frightening turn out to be so humble? How could someone covered in tattoos with skulls, and other images of death, be so meek?

"Is everything okay?"

She forced a smile and took a bite of her sandwich, hoping there was no mustard. When her mouth didn't immediately start to burn, she sighed.

Thank you.

Whoa. Where had that come from?

"Skye?" Sam hadn't taken a bite of his sandwich yet.

She nodded to him and reached for her napkin. Had she just prayed? Had she thanked God for not putting mustard in the first bite of a sandwich she'd forgotten to inspect? Where had that come from? It had been a long, long time since she'd talked to God.

Not that she'd been angry with him exactly. She'd allowed considerable distance to grow up between them, though. Skye had done a masterful job of holding God at arm's length, much the way her stern grandfather had always kept her at bay.

She put her sandwich down. Where had that thought popped in from?

Sam continued to watch her.

She had to say something so he wouldn't pry. "Mustard. I'm allergic. I usually check first, but I forgot."

The worry lines on his brow eased. "No mustard. Turkey, bacon, lettuce, tomato, and mayo."

"A club."

He nodded.

"That was my dad's favorite sandwich."

Sam's gaze remained riveted to her face.

He could probably see all the way to the toenail polish inside her new tennis shoes.

"I'm sorry for your loss."

She shot to her feet. "I just remembered that I need to be somewhere."

Her purse was in hand before his voice penetrated the fog. "...the truth..."

Her heart raced, her breath came faster and faster, and her hands started to tingle. "Wh-what?"

"You can leave. I don't mind. Tell me the truth first, though. Remember? I don't care what you have to say, as long as you're honest about it."

Skye pulled her hands into tight fists. She would *not* let this panic overtake her.

In that moment, she might well have hated Sam. She wasn't typically a hateful person, but how else could describe the burning heat ripping through her middle like cut glass? "You look at me as if you can see everything. Every hurt I've ever suffered, every moment of insecurity, all my confusion and uncertainty. And I wish you'd stop. You don't know me. You don't know anything about me. You need to stop acting like you do."

Her hands crossed from tingling to numb. She pried her fingers apart by sheer power of will.

"Thank you for being honest."

"Whatever." She pushed her way into the foyer and out the glass door. She had to force herself not to run to her car at the curb.

Friday evening was upon her. But was Skye looking forward to it?

She'd had a busy day of teleconferences with the main office in Boise and was ready for some down time. The night wouldn't be her own, though.

Jette had texted to say she'd pick her up on her way to Italita for dinner.

On a scale of one to ten…

She wasn't as ambivalent as the week before, but neither was she thrilled at the idea.

A honk sounded in the driveway, and Skye picked up her purse and keys.

Deciding how ambivalent she was about the evening would have to wait.

Locking the door behind her, she walked to the passenger side of Jette's sports car and climbed in. "Nice wheels. Suits you."

Her long-ago friend smiled. "My brother wanted me to buy a truck the size of a small house, but I told him to take a hike. A girl ought to have a few luxuries in life, and this is mine."

Ooh. A safe subject. "How's Cole doing these days, anyway? What's he up to?"

Jette tossed black hair over her shoulder before easing back onto the road and gunning it to the corner. "He's up in Alaska doing something with the pipeline. I don't ask, and he doesn't try to explain."

That didn't sound like the Jette and Cole she'd spent time with in high school. "Aren't you guys on speaking terms?"

Jette laughed. "I'd say he's my best friend if I weren't worried about offending the other Rainbow Girls. Nah, we're great. It's just that I went to law school and he became an engineer. When it comes to work, we don't speak the same language. I use words, and he uses numbers."

"I can believe that. Remember when you blackmailed Cole so he'd tutor me in Calculus?"

Jette took the next corner at warp speed. "That was priceless. He was almost done with college before he found out I didn't actually have any pictures of him making out with Sienna."

Skye braced herself against the door as Jette whipped the car into the parking lot. "Is he still the wild child, or did he finally outgrow that?"

Jette snorted. "Not only did he outgrow it, he went to seminary."

"Seminary?"

"Yep. He's not a pastor or anything, but he went to seminary and got himself a Doctorate of Divinity. Go figure."

"But he's not a preacher?"

"Nope. I think he simply needed to understand God, you know? He's always seen the world as a puzzle. That's the way his mind works, but he wasn't getting the kind of answers he wanted in church. So he took his pursuit for answers to the next level, and something he learned there changed him. He's still the same Cole, but he's different, too. He grew up good. Not everybody gets to say that about their big brother, but he's turned into this man I'm proud to call family."

Jette couldn't realize how much those words hurt. Skye was all alone in the world. She'd never had any siblings, and everyone else was dead. "I'm glad."

Jette climbed from the car before leaning back down to peer across at where Skye still sat. "You have family, too. Even when we didn't know where you were, you were our family. We prayed for you, talked about you, remembered you, and loved you. Now that you're back... We're all a little afraid of smothering you and pushing you away. We're trying to give you space. Because that's what people do with family."

Skye released her seat belt and got out of the low-slung car. She considered Jette over the roof, nodded, and headed toward the restaurant's entrance.

Family.

The word sent a chill through her veins at the same time that it warmed her heart.

CHAPTER 18

Impotent.

It was an ugly feeling. Sam would rather be out-arm-wrestled by an Airman.

Sunday morning came, and he watched the sun lighten the sky. A little more sleep wouldn't have gone amiss, but it hadn't been possible, not with all his tossing and turning.

He'd confronted armed gunmen before. Why did facing Skye this morning have him tied up in knots?

He scrubbed a hand down his face. He needed to relax. Going muscle group by muscle group, he tightened and released each one in turn. As he reached his calves, the answer hit him in the solar plexus.

Sam owed her an apology.

Try as he might to be an approachable and humble guy, apologizing was near the bottom on his list of fun things to do. Hauling a guy off to the state hospital was right below it. Being wrong — about anything — was just above it.

The aroma of coffee reached him just before the tingle of the bells on the outer door.

"Decaf." Skye set the cup on the counter.

She'd come. Good. That was a start.

"Thank you."

"Hey, listen."

"I'd like to say…" They both spoke at the same time.

Sam took a whiff of his coffee, and his lips curved into a smile. "I'd normally say ladies first, but I need to say something if that's okay?"

Skye bit her bottom lip and nodded.

"I apologize for other day. And any other times I've made you uncomfortable. I'm…" Words were easier with the men. "I'm more or less a social worker here. I help the men get back on their feet and out into the world. Most of them need to talk. They need counseling, but they don't want to see a counselor. I've learned to build that into the way I interact with them. The things I say, the questions I ask, the way I react. Counseling kind of comes out of my pores now whether I want it to or not. It spilled over onto you, but you didn't ask for it. You're not in my care. You're not one of the men here. I need to learn to do a better job of turning that part of myself off and not pushing in where I'm not wanted."

Skye sipped her coffee. "I'm sorry, too. After I got over being upset, I realized I wasn't angry so much as I was defensive."

"Still, I'm sorry."

She met his eyes, and her golden gaze was clear. "You are who you are, and the thing that sent me over the edge on Thursday is one of the things I most admire about you. You have a way with people, an approach that's both soft and hard at the same time. It's one of your strengths. So I won't accept your apology. You can't apologize for being yourself. I'm not sure why I reacted the way I did. I…"

"I was poking at sore spots."

"Maybe so." She put her coffee down. "So, when do we leave and must I ride in that big, ugly van with you, or can I drive myself?"

He rolled with the change of subject. He'd had his say, and she wasn't holding a grudge. "You can drive yourself, but it would mean a lot to the men if you rode with us."

Her eyebrows scrunched together in silent question.

"Some of these men are used to being shunned and ignored, or worse. Riding separately sends a message to them whether you intend it to or not."

Skye's lips thinned as she reached for her coffee again. "There are all kinds of silent rules here I don't know about or understand."

Sam choked down his laughter. She'd pretty much just explained every single man's first interaction with someone of the opposite sex.

"Hm."

Sam looked over at Skye. "It's not that bad."

"It looks like it should have been in the van graveyard twenty years ago."

"Load up, everyone!" The men wore their expectations on their faces. They were waiting for Skye to change her mind. He could almost taste it on the air. They were anticipating her rejection. Her comment about the van hadn't helped, either.

She swung open the passenger door, though, and climbed up into the seat. "If it breaks down, I'm not getting out to push. Let's just clarify that here."

Franco called from the backseat. "That's fine, Miss Skye. I can push enough for both of us."

She wiped a hand across her brow. "Whew. Thank you, Franco. I knew you'd have my back."

The tension in the van broke, and the men relaxed. Their smiles came easier, too, as Sam shifted into gear.

"This way, Miss Skye. They have doughnuts."

"The coffee's over here, Miss Skye."

"You can't take food into the sanctuary, Miss Skye, so you have to eat out here."

"The restrooms are over there, Miss Skye. There's a drinking fountain, too."

Sam stood back and observed as his men herded Skye through the doughnut and coffee lines. She'd gotten a little bit of that deer-in-the-headlights look as he'd pulled into the parking lot. She never had anything to say when he mentioned God, but if the expression on her face had been any indication, church wasn't exactly where she wanted to be on Sunday morning.

"Running a co-ed facility now?" Pastor Dennis Diangelo shook Sam's hand.

Sam took a draw on the now-cool decaf coffee Skye had brought him. "She's a volunteer."

"She volunteered to help you at church?"

"Let's say she got volunteered, and she's too much of a lady to back out."

Pastor Dennis chuckled. "Must be some friend if she didn't feel she could back out."

"Tawny. Her friend's name is Tawny."

The pastor let out a soft whistle. "My kid brother got volunteered to run for class president his freshman year in high school. Lost by a landslide, too. Thank you, Tawny Brown. She was on a tear about social inequality, and my brother took one look in her eyes and forgot how to say no."

"Sounds about right, except I doubt it was her eyes that convinced Skye."

Pastor Dennis sucked in a sudden breath. "Wait a second. If her name's Skye, and she's a friend of Tawny's…"

The incomplete question had a dangerous feel to it, sharp and jagged somehow.

The pastor's voice dropped to a whisper. "Is that Skye Blue?"

Sam nodded, trying to gauge the man's bizarre reaction.

Pastor Dennis excused himself and headed toward the office rather than the sanctuary. Sam stared after him for a minute before Skye's voice reached him. "We're ready to go in, Sam. Are you joining us?"

Sam's attention was equally split between the pastor and Skye.

"…boldness as we approach those who are different than us."

Her brow wrinkled.

"…tempered with compassion and love…"

She bit her bottom lip.

"…about grace…"

She frowned.

"…and in joy…"

She glanced down.

"…we're all called…"

She tucked a lock of hair behind her ear.

Sam closed his eyes. He needed to focus. He led the Monday Bible study each week, and it was supposed to be a follow-up to the sermon so he could answer any questions the men had. At this rate, the answer to every single one of their questions was going to be, "Skye."

CHAPTER 19

Skye sat in the sanctuary of a small church. Several Samaritan's Reach residents were in the pew with her. Sam sat in the pew behind, with the rest of the residents.

The men were all bathed and in their Sunday best. Their clothes were decent enough. Not fantastic, but not worn-through. Their shoes, on the other hand, were a real problem. Some had holes big enough to see through. On the bright side, she could see the shiny white brand-new socks they wore.

Skye hid a smile as she stood with the rest of the congregation for the first song. Some of the men were clearly more comfortable in church than others. A few of the ones in her pew kept casting furtive glances her way. They seemed to be watching her so they'd know when to stand, sit, or pick up the hymnal.

That was okay.

Church was familiar.

It was like an old pair of jeans discovered in the back of her closet, worn so often that the denim was soft. When she pulled those old favorite pants on, one of two things happened. Either they fit perfectly, and she let out a sigh of joy at the way they welcomed her body back like a blue cotton hug. Or they were uncomfortably tight and made her wish she'd never found them because they'd once been her favorite and could no longer be worn at all.

Skye stood again, this time for the closing song. Church was familiar, like it fit well, but it pinched, too. Why? Her breathing came faster, and her heart started to rev up for a full-on race.

Everyone began to exit, but Skye cut around the line and skipped the whole hand-shaking thing. She just couldn't do it. Not today. Maybe next Sunday. Or she could just volunteer Tuesday and Thursday.

"Hey, Miss Skye, what's the rush?"

She slowed her escape to the van, allowing Gideon to catch up. "No rush. I think I got a cramp from sitting so long."

Harumph. "And I'm a twenty-year-old swimsuit model. You lit out of there like you were being chased by a spider."

"No spider. It's just been a while since I've been in church."

"Was it like you remember?"

"Yes and no."

"Which is yes, and which is no?"

He wasn't going to let it go, was he? "The music was familiar, and the routine of it all. But my friends weren't there, and the world's not as simple to me anymore."

They'd reached the van, and Gideon stood with her and watched the other men approach. "I get the feeling your world was never simple."

Skye shot him a back-off-and-don't-pry glare, but he gazed off into the distance. Had his words even been intended for her?

They returned to Samaritan's Reach, and Skye wandered toward the office.

Sam's question stalled her. "You gonna stick around or head home?"

"I don't know. I guess I thought I'd do my regular time. Why?"

"Baxter will be by in about fifteen minutes to go with some of the men to the flea market. The rest of us are going to have lunch. Why don't you join us? The mess in the office will still be there when you're done."

Alan, who had been heading toward the room they'd converted to a kitchen, halted his steps. "Jack and I are cooking today. He cooks better'n he paints."

Half the men had stopped and trained their eyes on her.

She hadn't eaten with them yet, unless you counted that morning's doughnut. "Sure. Lunch sounds good."

Jack had already headed into the kitchen, but Alan gave her a smile and tilted an imaginary hat to her. "Sure thing, Miss Skye. We did the prep work this morning, so the meal should be done in about twenty minutes."

The rest of the men wandered over to where the picnic table sat in the back corner. They needed another table. Or a whole row of them. Funds, though.

Skye still had so many questions about Samaritan's Reach and how they functioned. "What's at the flea market?"

Sam pulled on his goatee. "People donate things to us now and then. We keep a table at the flea market each weekend to sell those things. The men work the table on a rotating basis. It's a good experience for them."

A flea market in Rainbow Falls wasn't exactly prime real estate. It wouldn't bring in much in the way of funds. "After I'm finished going through all those boxes, I should look into doing some fundraising for you."

Sam leaned against one of the painted metal poles that held up the built-in canopy that kept the motel room doors in the shade. "I was hoping you'd untangle my books for me."

"How badly tangled are they?"

He let out a weary sigh. "The software I use got some sort of upgrade patch about six months ago, and I haven't been able to get anything to balance since. I've looked and looked for the problem, but it's hiding."

"Is the software installed on the computer or in the cloud?"

"Cloud, I guess. I pay a monthly fee for access. It synchs with the bank and is supposed to make all my accounting headaches go away."

"How long have you been using it?"

"Since we opened. It's only been the past six months that it's been a problem. I should call their tech support, but I haven't been able to cut enough time out of the day to sit in the office on hold."

"What on earth is all this stuff for?" Covered in dust, Skye stood in the middle of the office and pointed at a pile of boxes in the foyer.

Sam looked at the boxes. "My last admin assistant wanted to have hard copies of everything.

Tuesday afternoon was upon them. She was over tidying the office the way a teenage girl was over the previous year's boy band or the previous week's hair style. If she never saw it again, she'd live a happy life. Had she realized how all-consuming the mess had become, she might not have volunteered so readily. "Yeah, but you can store these forms on the computer and print them when the need arises. You don't have to keep all these hard copies."

"Are you volunteering to run the office?"

"No, but I'm willing to work in it when I'm here, and I'm willing to upload all the documents into an orderly, virtual filing cabinet so you can easily find them."

Sam stared at the boxes. "What happens if I end up hiring another admin, and she wants hard copies of everything?"

"She can print them from the computer files?"

"Paper and ink that I don't want to have to pay for again."

She'd gone through and sorted everything. The shelves in the office were full. These five extra boxes needed to find another home. "You either let me toss them in the recycling, or you provide me another room in which to store them."

Sam cringed. "Recycling it is."

Skye opened the foyer door. All the men stood in some weird position out in the courtyard. She let the door fall closed but couldn't tear her eyes away from the sight. Men of all shapes, sizes, and ages squatted as though sitting on an invisible chair with knees bent at a ninety degree angle while holding their arms out straight in front of them. It was *almost* familiar. "Um... Are they doing yoga?"

He answered without looking at her. "Probably."

"Seriously? Yoga?"

"We offer yoga and aikido on a rotating schedule. The men have to participate in at least two exercise classes each week. The yoga was a bit of a fluke. I didn't think any of the men would be interested."

"What's aikido?"

"A form of martial arts. I've adjusted it to fit our demographic here. At its heart, though, aikido is about learning to defend yourself without harming your attacker."

What a novel concept. "But wouldn't most people want to harm their attacker?"

"Disable, yes. Harm? I hope the aikido teaches them a different approach."

"Do they spar? Is that even a good idea? You've said it yourself. Some of these men have PTSD."

Sam glanced up from his paperwork. "Like I said, I've adjusted it for our demographic. We don't use weapons. No sparring outside of class. And even in class, sparring is rare. We focus on the tenets that teach self-control and discipline."

"Sounds like you've thought it through."

He grinned. "That's why I earn the big bucks."

The men moved into what she was pretty sure was a variation on the warrior pose. "I should probably wait till they're done."

"Nah. Go for it. Not everyone's doing yoga. Someone will answer the call."

Skye took a deep breath and opened the foyer door again. "Anyone want to volunteer to haul some boxes for me?"

Rafael and Matt, who'd been watching the yoga class but not participating, jogged over. "Sure thing, Miss Skye. Which ones and where to?"

She pointed to the boxes. "The recycling bin, please."

It took the men a couple of trips, but the foyer carpet was soon visible in all its worn, threadbare glory.

Triumph!

"Wipe that silly grin off your face. Now you can start looking at the accounting." Sam's voice held laughter.

Skye spun from the foyer to the inner office. "Bring it on."

Sam glanced at his phone. "You only have an hour left. Are you sure that's enough time?"

"I'll familiarize myself with the software. It'll be fine." On those words, she slipped through the half-door into the now-tidy inner sanctum. "Write down any passwords I'll need."

"You know I'd rather you memorize it."

"And I will, but I memorize a lot better if I can look at it."

Sam scribbled a string of characters onto a piece of scratch paper. He handed it to her as the foyer door opened again.

CHAPTER 20

July

"Hey Boss. Jack said you need me." Gideon leaned on the counter between the foyer and office.

Sam didn't get a chance to talk to him, though, before a man in a brown suit came through the door behind him. "I'm here to see Sam Madison."

Sam nodded. "That's me. How can I help you?"

"I'm with the county's Building and Code Enforcement Office. I've been looking over your property here, and I'm going to have to cite you for a couple of violations. I need you to sign here, and I can be on my way." The man shoved a clipboard toward Sam.

Sam took it and glanced over the paper it held. He narrowed his eyes as he lifted them back up at the man in the suit. "Deplorable living conditions?"

The man tugged at his tie and swallowed. "Have you seen your roof? That's only the start of the problem."

"What happens if I refuse to sign this?"

The man cleared his throat. "You sign it, you're given a hundred and twenty days to appeal or make repairs. You refuse to sign, and I can come back here with the police and shut you down now."

Heat simmered under his skin as Sam grabbed a pen off the counter and scribbled his name on the paper. "I get a copy, right?"

The man separated the carbon copies from the top form and gave Sam the pink and yellow copies without making eye contact. "I'll be on my way now…"

The words hung in the air as the door soundlessly closed in the wake of his exit.

Sam pulled in a lungful of oxygen before setting the pink copy on his desk. He folded the yellow one and slipped it into his back pocket.

He gulped down another expansive breath and released it slowly.

"I can come back later if you need me to, Boss."

Sam focused on Gideon for a second before the fog cleared and he could think again. He reached back to the desk and grabbed a blue piece of scratch paper off the top and slid it across the counter.

Gideon read over it, and his eyes grew wide. "This is current?"

"As best as I can tell."

"How'd you find it?"

Sam hooked a thumb in the direction of the computer. "The internet. Public record searches. It took a little while, but I think that's it."

Gideon ran a finger across the paper. "This says she lives not too far from here. She used to live in Washington. What happened?"

"I can't tell you anything more than what I wrote down. Anything you want to know, you'll have to ask her yourself."

Gideon pulled off his glasses and rubbed his eyes. "Any way I can get a ride over to see her? Maybe that's better than calling?"

Skye, who had been studying the computer screen in silence, caught Sam's eye and mouthed, *"Can I help?"*

He looked over at Gideon before turning back to Skye and taking the two steps over to the desk. He squatted down to her eye level. "Gideon hasn't seen his sister in a long time. We found her, and she's over in Waschak Falls. He'd like to go, but I'm needed here today since Lance called in sick."

"I can give him a ride. Or I can keep watch on the guys while you're gone."

Sam pressed his lips together. He should be there for Gideon. But leave Skye alone with the men? He'd left before when she'd been on-site, but another volunteer or staffer had always been around somewhere.

"I can handle it. Give me a chance. Besides, I can't really give him a ride anyway, right? Female volunteers aren't allowed to be alone with a resident."

The rules were starting to get under his skin. Even if they were good ones to have. "Alan..."

"Alan and I get along fine these days, but if he goes off the rails, I have this now." She opened the desk drawer and showed him the air horn she'd brought in with her that morning.

Sam winced. "Careful. That might do more harm than good."

"Oh." Color tinged her cheeks. "I didn't think of that. Would a whistle have been better?"

171

Higher pitched, a reminder of high school gym more than war… "Maybe. It's hard to know. Everybody has their own issues, you know?"

Skye gave a decisive nod and reached for her phone. "I can download a whistle app. Or something. Maybe Alan can help me figure out the best sound."

Sam rose with a chuckle. She'd come a long way in such a short time. Samaritan's Reach would be in good hands. "I guess that's that, Gideon. Meet me at my car in thirty minutes, and we'll head out."

Gideon, eyes rounder than his spectacles, dropped his mouth to half-mast. "Really?"

Sam gave a single nod. "Go, before Skye changes her mind about running the place."

"Think Miss Skye will do okay without you? She's a little skittish sometimes."

Sam kept his eyes on the road. "She is, but I think she's stronger than any of us realize. Including her."

"She reminds me of one of us."

"Me, too, but I don't think she'd appreciate the comparison."

Gideon chuckled. "I don't mean the old, ugly, and homeless part. But the battle scars? Yeah."

The corner of Sam's mouth tried to pull upward. "Speak for yourself. I'm pretty sure Alan is younger than all of us."

"You might be right about that one. I'm not even sure he's thirty yet. It's hard to see someone so young be so damaged."

"Like you said, we all have our battle scars. We just wear them differently."

Gideon hooked a thumb around his seatbelt. "We're almost there, aren't we?"

"It's only twenty miles from the shelter. You won't even have time to change your mind."

Gideon sank a bit into his seat as they crossed into the Waschak Falls city limits.

A couple of GPS-directed turns later, and Sam pulled up in front of a house. "What if nobody's home?"

"I almost hope that's the case."

Sam rested his hands on the steering wheel. "Would you like me to pray?"

"Yeah. That'd be nice."

"You know what we're doing here today, God, and how badly Gideon wants to set right some of the mistakes of the past two decades. Give him the words, Lord, and go before him. Prepare his sister's heart. Amen."

Gideon took a deep breath. "I like that about you. Short prayers. Straight to the point, nothing fancy."

With that, the Samaritan's Reach resident stepped out of the car and started up the walkway.

Sam stayed in the car and continued to pray for Gideon and his sister, all the while watching events unfold. Gideon rang the doorbell. When the door remained closed, he knocked.

The door opened then, and a man stood in the entryway. They chatted for a moment before the man became agitated, his voice rising.

Gideon's hands moved, a sure sign that he was talking.

The other man reached the point of yelling, and Gideon took a step back.

Sam climbed from the car, ready to intervene if needed.

The man's voice carried across the yard. "Worthless, no good bum. Get off my property, or I'm calling the police."

Gideon's shoulders slumped as he turned away from the house.

The man in the door continued to hurl insults as the resident made his way back to the car.

Sam's gut twisted up. He wanted to go set the man straight, but he didn't know the whole story. And Gideon – as well as all the residents – needed to learn to live with the consequences of their choices. The inability to face those consequences was sometimes the very thing that crippled men and kept them on the street long after they would have otherwise returned home.

Gideon reached the car, avoiding eye contact, and climbed in.

Sam sent one last glare at the house's now-closed front door before sliding behind the steering wheel.

He started the car and silently pulled away from the curb.

About ten miles later, he cast a glance toward his passenger. "I'm sorry."

Gideon kept his eyes trained straight ahead. "Thanks, man."

"Don't let this set you back."

The resident looked at him then, and Sam could see it in his eyes. Gideon would survive. Pain was present in spades, but not despair. Guilt, but not shame.

Gideon grunted. "I'm tutoring a couple of the guys in algebra. They need me. That's enough for now."

"Are you sorry you came?"

Gideon shook his head. "No. I did something I'd been putting off out of fear. The rest is up to God."

Silence filled the car for a few miles before Gideon returned to the subject. "You know, if Alan hadn't ever gone after Miss Skye that day, I probably wouldn't be here now. I was thinking about leaving, cutting loose and taking off. Got into your leadership program, then started to feel tied down, and I didn't like it. Miss Skye saw something of value in me, though, and it made me want to…"

Gideon's soft snores filled the car. Sam switched the radio on and adjusted the volume so it played low. The man deserved his rest. Besides, Sam had plans for him. Gideon wouldn't be resting long.

CHAPTER 21

Skye kept the foyer door open so she could hear what was happening elsewhere on the grounds.

She had hoped to figure out the accounting problem sorted out already, but it was proving elusive. Her limited hours at the shelter didn't speed things along, either.

Skye released a sigh through gritted teeth. She needed to go back to the beginning and comb through every single receipt and every single entry since the shelter's opening.

Sam had shown her where the past tax records were, so at least she didn't have to wait. She retrieved the box, hauled it over to the desk, and thumbed through until she reached the receipts.

One by one, she went through each receipt and compared it to the entry in the software.

There'd been no trouble balancing the books during the first couple of tax years, so the problem most likely existed in the current year. Since she couldn't find it, though...

Three months into the first year's receipts, a yell echoed from the courtyard. Skye grabbed the keys and dug around for her phone.

Where on earth had it gone?

Failing to find her phone, she grabbed the air horn and ran, pausing only long enough to lock the glass door behind her.

She skidded to a halt midway across the courtyard. Alan held Rafael in a headlock. Both men had a wild look in their eyes, and curses flew through the air around the duo.

Skye ran as close as she dared and pushed the button on her air horn.

The instant the piercing screech filled the courtyard, Alan's gaze slammed to hers, and he let go of the other man.

Rafael spun, though, and tackled Alan to the ground. Fists flew as Rafael punched Alan again and again.

Matt jumped on Rafael's back and tried to pull him off Alan.

Skye held down the button on the canned air horn. The trumpeting dissonance rang out strong for several seconds before the gases in the can were expended and the sound petered out.

Rafael staggered to his feet, shook Matt off his back, and charged toward Skye.

She screamed and threw her arms up to protect herself.

The blow never came, though, and the seconds-ago rhythm of shoes slapping on pavement finally registered. She opened her eyes. Sam held Rafael pinned to the cracked asphalt while the resident bucked and writhed like a man possessed.

Seconds later, Gideon came running. He squeezed in next to Sam with something black and strappy.

In another minute or so, Sam got up. With Paul's help, he picked the screaming Rafael up, scooted his back against the wall so he was sitting with his legs stretched out in front of him, and backed away. Rafael's hands were restrained behind his back with whatever device Gideon had brought over.

Sam squatted in Rafael's line of sight, got right into his face, and yelled. "Stop! Settle down, or I call the police."

The City Council's regulations prevented Samaritan's Reach from housing anyone with violent tendencies. They also couldn't take in any men actively fighting a drug addiction, another crippling blow to their ability to help people. Everyone knew the rules, though. Sam was clear about them from day one and reminded the men frequently. Skye had heard his warnings and reminders often enough.

As much as she wished he had more leeway in this area, the reality was that he didn't. If he violated the city's regulations, he would be putting the future of Samaritan's Reach in even greater peril.

All violent residents must be reported to the police and taken to the state VA hospital. The City's ruling didn't allow leeway for PTSD or for inept volunteers. If Rafael got hauled off...

Rafael stopped screaming, but he continued to fight his restraints.

Alan sauntered by Skye, his face bloodied, and his fists clenched.

She swung toward him to say something, but the look in his eyes robbed her of the ability to speak. It was the same wild look from the day he'd yelled at her in the laundry room.

She glanced back at Rafael. It appeared Sam was starting to make some progress talking him down.

Her gut flopped in that way that told her she had to do something she didn't want to. She needed to talk to Alan.

She jogged a couple steps after him before finding her voice again and calling out his name.

He waved a hand behind him and kept walking.

She tried again. "Alan, please stop. Please."

He halted his forward momentum but didn't turn around.

Everything inside her said to run the opposite direction. Everything except for that still, small voice that had prompted her to follow him in the first place.

Skye took as deep a breath as her paralyzed lungs would allow, and walked around Alan so she could face him.

He stared at the ground.

"Can you look at me?"

His eyes remained downcast.

"Alan, I need to know what happened."

"It don't matter."

"It does to me."

"Ain't you scared of me?"

"Y-yes. But I'm more scared of who I become if I don't give you a fair chance here."

He glanced up then, and she saw his eyes. The wild was there, yeah, but not as much as that day in the laundry room. And the wild faded more with each second he held her gaze.

"Can you tell me what happened?"

He closed his eyes, let out a breath, and opened them again. "Car drove by. Must've backfired. Rafael went over the edge. Started screaming and circling around and lunging at us. I knew the look in his eyes. I've seen it in the mirror before. He was back there, reliving something. A shooting, maybe an IED. Who knows? It was bad, though. I told Paul to warn you, and I tried to restrain him." His look accused her. "You were supposed to call the police."

Skye glanced over at the office door. "Nobody came for me. I heard a yell and came out. I didn't know... I grabbed the air horn, not my phone. I thought that would be enough. It's meant to shock people, snap them out..."

He grunted. "Snapped him further in, I'd say."

Somewhere between admitting she was scared and listening to the agony in Alan's voice when he'd said Rafael was reliving an IED attack, Skye's lungs had started functioning again. "I'm sorry you got hurt because of me."

Alan angled his head to the side and studied her for a second before speaking. "It ain't you. I knew what he was going through, and I thought I could help. He's got at least fifty pounds on me, though. Should have sent the men to their rooms and come to the office myself. It's hard to fight if no one's around you. He mighta snapped out of it faster then."

"You reacted on instinct."

Another grunt.

"Your instinct wasn't about hurting him. You wanted to protect everyone else. It didn't matter that he was bigger or stronger. You were defending us all."

He lifted a hand to his swelling nose. "I'm not sure how well that worked out."

Skye almost smiled. "Go to your room and get cleaned up. I'll tell Sam where to find you." She fell short of touching his nose. "Do you think it's broken?"

"I know what broken feels like. This is just good and pounded." Then he pivoted and headed back across the parking lot toward his own room.

That was when it hit Skye. When he'd started walking, he'd been planning to leave, to walk right off the property and never come back.

Thank you.

She wasn't talking to God, not really, but she was thankful for whatever had prompted her to go after Alan.

"I have to write him up."

Skye slapped a file folder down on the counter. "It's not right."

"The rules are in place for a reason."

Sam was lucky she wasn't holding anything heavier than a folder. Had she been, she would have been sorely tempted to launch it at him.

"Gideon got written up when he restrained Alan that day in the laundry room."

Skye let out a disgusted sigh. "I didn't think it was right then, either."

"The men know the rules. When they take action like Alan did today, there are consequences. This won't be a surprise to him."

"He was going to leave."

"You stopped him."

"What if I hadn't? What if I'd been too afraid?"

Sam sat down in the desk chair and inspected her. "Is that what this is about? His almost leaving? Or your almost being too afraid to stop him? Because if it's the latter, I'm not worried about it. You'll do what's right regardless of how you feel. I wouldn't have left you in charge if I didn't believe that."

She looked out the glass door for a while before turning back to Sam. "He's come so far, but he almost walked out of here. He almost threw it all away. He would have lost all this progress he's made because I grabbed an air horn instead of a phone."

"It doesn't work that way. You can't be here if you're going to blame yourself every time something goes wrong. Yeah, Alan almost left. Assuming he followed

183

through, I'd have gone after him. I'd have beaten every bush and called in every volunteer until we found him. Not because he's come too far to throw it all away, but because he's one of my men. One of my men runs away, I chase."

"No man left behind?"

"With a little bit of Jesus and the runaway sheep thrown in."

"I thought it was the lost sheep."

Sam's head tilted to the right. "From where I'm sitting, most people get lost when they're too busy running away to pay attention to where they're going."

"Maybe. I still handled it wrong."

He gave his head the smallest shake. "You acted on instinct just like Alan. Could you have done better? Sure. So learn from it. If you want to blame yourself, go ahead. Just remember that blaming yourself is a totally different game than beating yourself up. Don't confuse the two."

Sam was messing with her well-equipped guilt complex.

"Besides, Samaritan's Reach belongs to God. Every man we serve and every person who works here, paid or otherwise — they all belong to Him. He's in control. When something goes wrong, He's the only one with real answers about why and how."

Skye frowned at him. "Shut up already."

He threw his head back and laughed.

She scouted in earnest for something to throw at him this time, but the only thing in reach was a stapler, and she didn't want to chip his teeth and ruin his smile.

Sam got up from the desk, strolled over to the counter, and leaned on it opposite her. "Alan will take his lumps and, if I'm not mistaken, he'll do it with grace."

"Won't he get kicked out if you write him up again?"

"It's been long enough since the last incident that he'll be fine as long as he doesn't go picking any other fights for a while. Now go home."

"You're not going to be too hard on him, are you?"

"I have the men cleaning out the torture chamber as we speak. I was thinking about using the rack this time. What do you think?"

Skye stuck her tongue out at him, picked up her purse, and marched out of the office.

CHAPTER 22

Sam let out a breath that landed somewhere between a sigh and a chuckle.

Skye had stuck her tongue out at him.

She'd come a long way from the timid little mouse he'd met on the airplane. Whether being back home in Montana or her work at Samaritan's Reach had made the difference, one thing was clear.

Skye found her footing — and became surer of herself — with each new day.

As she gained confidence, she grew in beauty, too.

She was a volunteer, which made the thought inappropriate, but still...

Confidence was sexy, and if her confidence continued to grow, she would become downright dangerous.

With a shake of his head, Sam grabbed the paperwork he needed for Alan and headed for the man's room.

His knuckles didn't even make contact with the wood before Alan opened the door.

"Boss."

"Can I come in?"

Alan stepped aside and let him pass.

In contrast to the last time they'd been in this situation, Alan sat on the floor and stretched his legs out, crossing his ankles. He left the chair for Sam.

"I don't like doing this…"

Alan cut him off. "What happened to Rafael?"

Sam set the paperwork down on the table and leaned back in the chair, loosely folding his hands in front of him. "Police took him to the state hospital."

"You called them?"

Sam gave a negative shake of his head. "I hoped to resolve the matter peacefully. It's a fine line, but I would've tried."

Alan scrutinized the world beyond the still-open door. "That could've been me."

"Had you physically assaulted Skye, it might well have been."

Alan met Sam's gaze head-on. "Are you kicking me out?"

"No. Not today. Three write-ups in a month and you're out. Enough time has passed since the last one, so you're safe."

"Good. I'm not ready to go."

The words were a balm to Sam. A time came in each resident's life when he needed to be ready to move on, to go. Alan wasn't there yet, though, and it was encouraging that he recognized it.

"In fact…" Alan studied his hands now. "I was thinking I'd like to get into the same leadership program as Gideon. Or something like that. Maybe. How does it work, anyway?"

Sam sent a silent prayer of thanks heavenward. "You need sixty days without a write-up to be considered for the leadership program. Once you're approved, you'll be allowed to take on leadership roles in various aspects of the shelter.

"We'll start small. Keeping laundry day on track, making sure everyone gets a haircut if they want, things like that. Thirty days later, you sign up for classes. You decide on the career you want, and we line up an online school to support that goal. Slowly, over time, we increase your responsibility as you continue to pursue your degree."

"How long to graduate from all that?"

"Depends on your degree and how seriously you take the classes, but our objective is to have you ready for the world with a job lined up by the time you graduate."

"I'm not book smart."

"I think you'll surprise yourself, but if a college degree isn't the right course, then a certification or trade school works, too. Want to be a mechanic? Fine. Want to go to a technical school? No problem. The point is that we will work to build your leadership skills while you work to build your skillset and resume."

Alan held his hand out in front of him. "These aren't mechanic hands, and I don't have the patience for computer stuff. I want to do what you do. I want to help people like me."

"Dealing with other people's PTSD when you battle it yourself is a hard row to hoe. Are you sure that's the one you want to go down?"

"Yeah. I'm willing to go to counseling beyond the group sessions here, too, if you think I need it. Whatever you say. I…" Alan's gaze skipped around the room. "I don't want to scare people anymore."

God had done an amazing work in Alan's life. He still had a long way to go, but he'd turned an important corner, and Sam wanted to bask in that success for a minute. Instead, he still had to write the guy up. He pushed the paper across the table toward Alan. "Read it and sign it. Your sixty days starts now. No write-ups during that time. And I want you to know, Skye almost took my head off over this. She fought hard to stop me from writing you up."

"Felt sorry for me?"

Sam gave a quick shake of the head. "She sees something in you, something valuable. I can't help but think that she wants to believe you can change, because if you can do it, she can too."

Alan grunted. "At least she wasn't puking out her guts this time. Nothing went the way it was supposed to, but she didn't panic. Or run away. Or lose her lunch."

Sam chuckled. "Sounds like progress to me."

"She came after me today. I was gonna leave. I figured my time here was done, and I hated myself for letting it go down that way. She was scared, too, but she still chased me down." Alan looked at Sam. "She might look at me and see change, but I look at her and see courage. And hope. I see the kind of person I want to be."

Without further words, Alan got off the floor, grabbed the pen off the table, and signed his name to the paperwork Sam had brought.

Half the men at Samaritan's Reach who decided they wanted to go into the leadership program ended up washing out before they even reached their sixty days of qualification. Of the ones who managed the sixty days and started the program, only a third followed it all the way through. Alan could fall anywhere on the spectrum, but praying for his success had just become Sam's priority.

Saturday arrived bright and sunny. Sam breathed in the fresh air as he and a couple of the guys got out of the van.

The week had passed uneventfully since Tuesday's incident with Rafael, and today was yard work day. They were visiting Miss Rebecca to mow her lawn, weed her flower beds, and take care of anything else she needed.

Sam knocked on her front door and hollered through. "Miss Rebecca! It's Sam."

"It's unlocked. Come on in." Her voice warbled with age but managed to sound feisty at the same time. Much like the woman herself.

As he stepped through the door, Miss Rebecca called out. "I'm in the living room, but do you think you could open some curtains on your way in? My house needs more sunshine."

"Sure thing." Sam strode through the kitchen and parlor and opened the curtains. Then he made his way around the edge of the living room and did the same. "Need anything else?"

She pointed to a piece of paper on the nearby coffee table. "I talked to a couple friends of mine who are laid up for various reasons. They could use some help, too, if you don't think your men wouldn't mind. It doesn't have to be today. Their names and numbers are there."

Part of helping the men integrate back into society was teaching them to be civic-minded. Putting in some hours for the benefit of others wouldn't hurt anyone. "Sure. We can do that."

Miss Rebecca beamed at him. "Excellent. I told them each to expect a call from you."

He hadn't stood a chance. "How are you feeling today?"

"Fair to middling. You?"

Sam sat on the chair oppose the couch where Miss Rebecca reclined. "I'm satisfactory."

"I heard the police were out at your place."

He'd been in Rainbow Falls over two years now, but the small-town grapevine still amazed him. "Yep. One of our men had a flashback that got out of hand."

"Violent flashback from what I understand."

"How do you hear so much? You have a police scanner in here I'm not aware of?" He stood and lifted his chair cushion to peek under it.

She waved her hand. "Never you mind. The guy was hauled off in a police cruiser, though. Did they arrest him?"

Sam returned the cushion and sank back into his seat. "Got transported to the state VA hospital instead. They have the facilities to deal with those situations. My operation isn't quite there yet. Besides, the City Council won't allow me to house any violent residents. If the police are called in, there's not much I can do to intervene."

"Hm. I heard the City Council made some changes to the town charter this year."

"Yeah. They made a few."

"Seems like they're trying to run you out of Rainbow Falls."

"Maybe. What do you think I should do about it?"

"Make friends."

Sam stared at the older woman. She was telling him something, but he was too slow to catch on. "Friends?"

She nodded. "You need the kind of friends who are there for you when things get tough."

"I'm not sure where to find those kinds of friends. Most of our donors have pulled out because they assume the city will be shutting us down at the end of the year."

"Pshaw. Donors aren't the same as friends. You ought to know that by now."

What was the woman was getting at? Not that it mattered. He didn't have time to make friends. He had a shelter that needed all his attention. He rose from his seat and started for the door. "I need to go check on the men."

Miss Rebecca didn't say anything until he had one foot out of her living room. "You brought a woman to church last Sunday?"

He regarded her with a nod. "One of our volunteers."

"You know anything about her?"

"She's good with the men, is helping me untangle some accounting issues, and has some ideas for fundraising."

"She a believer?"

"We don't require our volunteers to be believers. We ask them to sign a paper saying they won't say or do anything contrary to the Christian faith while on-site or with the residents. There are some legalities involved in that decision. Why? Is that important to you?"

Miss Rebecca glanced out her front room window before looking back at Sam. The usual snap was absent from her eyes. "Skye Blue."

Like a moth to a flame, Sam was drawn to Miss Rebecca's sadness. "Tell me what you know. Pastor Dennis acted all weird when he realized who Skye was, but he walked off before I could ask why, and I couldn't say anything to Skye. She…" *She's been through a lot. She's been hurt by someone. She doesn't like it when I pry.* There were too many ways to end that sentence.

"Skye was only here in our community for ten years or so."

"I thought she grew up here."

"Not her whole life. Just the worst, wretched years."

"Tell me."

Miss Rebecca gave him a sad smile. "It's her story to tell. It might help you to know that Dennis Diangelo wasn't always a pastor. I doubt Skye realizes who he is, or who he used to be. But he knows her. You could say it's because of her that he's a pastor today."

CHAPTER 23

Skye took a deep breath as she crossed the church's threshold. One of the men held the door for her, so she couldn't very well skip out unnoticed.

Instead of making a run for it, she followed her door-holder to the doughnut line where she picked up a small pastry piled high with chocolate frosting. Okay, maybe not *piled*, but still, it was covered in chocolate, which was exactly what she needed.

She skipped the coffee line since balancing a cup and a plate without a table and also eating at the same time was a skill she hadn't yet developed. The shelter's residents were clustered in a couple of different groups, and at least one man from the church had joined the conversation in each one. Hm. The church seemed to be making a conscious effort to welcome the men.

Yet nobody approached her. Not only that, but everyone gave her a wide berth. What was up with that?

Sam drew near, two cups of coffee in hand. "For when you're done licking your fingers."

"I do not…" Oh, bother. "Huh. Maybe I do lick my fingers. That frosting was delectable." Skye removed all evidence of chocolate with the napkin she'd grabbed from the table before reaching for the cup he held out to her.

"What was it like growing up as one of the Rainbow Girls?" He wore long sleeves today, and the tattoos that no longer bothered Skye were hidden from view. The earring was still there, though, as was the goatee she'd once thought too long to be civilized. Funny how easy it became to judge based on appearance. Sam was far more civilized than most of the perfectly groomed and polished men she'd met.

She sipped the hot coffee. "How do you even know about the Rainbow Girls? You're not from around here, are you?"

Sam shook his head. "A woman in my battalion. Ginger Schneider. She kept us all entertained with stories about her hometown of Rainbow Falls. I probably know more about the history of this town than most of its current residents."

Ginger Schneider. A vague mental picture of a skinny girl with red hair and braces came to mind. "Huh. Small world."

"So if you didn't grow up here, how did you become a Rainbow Girl?"

The past wasn't exactly a favorite topic, but since he wasn't going to let it go… "My mom and I moved here when I was eleven."

"No dad?" He cringed. "Not my business. Sorry."

Hm. Questions usually put her on guard. Or they annoyed her. Somehow, his awkward prying did neither. "Killed in Action. Army. We lived in Boise with my dad's parents while he was deployed. My mom didn't like it there. She didn't get along with my grandparents. When my dad died, Mom took me and left."

"I'm sorry to hear that. Loss is a hard thing."

She met his words with silence. What else was there to say?

"But how did your mom know to name you Skye? You were a ready-made Rainbow Girl when you moved here at age eleven."

A softball question. Those she could handle. "My mom grew up here. She named me Skye because sit reminded her of something. I never quite understood why, but it mattered to her."

Sam rubbed a hand along his scruffy chin. "Must have been hard on your grandparents to lose you so close after losing their son."

Hard? Maybe. Maybe not. "I didn't hear from them again until I was graduating high school."

"Not a word? It's not like they were on the other side of the world."

Music filtering out from the sanctuary rescued her from having to answer. "Guess we should go in."

She dropped her half-empty cup of coffee into the garbage can as she passed by on her way to the sanctuary doors.

The piano was silent and the pastor stood at the small country pulpit before she shook off Sam's questions enough to be able to pay attention to anything being said. Even then, she only half-listened as she traveled down memory lane and revisited her years in Rainbow Falls. The memories, every single one of them, were at best bittersweet. If the Rainbow Girls hadn't adopted her, would she have survived?

"Look at Ephesians 1:7 one more time with me…"

She must have missed the bulk of the sermon because she hadn't looked at the verse even once.

"It is only by the richness of God's grace that we can find redemption, only through his mercy that we can know forgiveness."

Forgiveness was a familiar enough topic in the real world. What about redemption, though? What did redemption really mean?

She thumbed out of her Bible app and went to the dictionary on her phone.

Redemption (noun): the act of regaining something previously lost with payment made in the form of exchange.

Um… *The act of?* That made it sound like a verb, not a noun, but what did she know? She'd majored in business, not English.

"What has God redeemed for you lately? Your marriage, your relationship with your parents? Your sobriety? A price has to be paid, folks, but it's not one you and I can pay. To have any staying power, redemption needs to come through Christ."

Skye frowned at the words on her screen, clicked back over to the Bible app, and tried to at least pretend to listen to the message.

Of course, just as she did that, everyone bowed their heads. The sermon had ended while she'd been fiddling with her phone. Oh well. She hadn't actually wanted to listen anyway. Pastor Dennis kept looking at her, and it was starting to give her the creeps. At least she wasn't scared. That was progress, right? Instead of running from him, she wanted to use a can of pepper spray. On a pastor that Sam seemed to like.

Thank goodness the people in church couldn't read her mind. Otherwise they'd be collecting their pitchforks.

A couple of days later, Skye settled back in at the office. She was close to finding the accounting problem. She had to be.

The shelter's first years of receipts all checked out against the software. No mistakes there. Both years balanced, too. Which made sense. They'd balanced when Sam had done his taxes those years, too.

The error *had* to be from the current year, and she was two months into those receipts. She wasn't leaving until she found it.

"Hey. Mind if I share the desk?"

"Um, sure."

He scooched around to the other side and sat down in the chair that had never been put back out in the foyer. He set down a printout and picked up a pencil.

Skye fiddled with her pen, put it down, picked it up again, and started turning it over in her hands. Some subjects were taboo. She knew that better than most. "Can I ask you something?"

Sam cast a quick glance her way. "Sure."

"Where'd you get the scar?" She winced. It had sounded natural in her head, but out loud, the question came across as invasive and nosy. Which it kind of was.

Sam leaned back in his chair, his blue eyes studying her face before they stared off into the distance. "Firefight. Bullet skimmed the side of my head. Another millimeter or two in one direction, and I wouldn't have a scar at all. The other direction, and I'd be dead."

She'd asked, but now she didn't know what to say. "Was anybody else hurt?"

A whole winter's worth of clouds passed through Sam's normally pale blue eyes. "Yeah. We went in to rescue an Air Force pilot that'd been shot down and was being held by rebels. Our intel was solid, but so was theirs, apparently. They knew we were coming. We got the pilot out, but we lost one man. Two others ended up with a medical discharge. I got off easy. I was patched up and back at work a week later."

"The men who got discharged... Were they okay?"

Sam's gaze snapped back to her face, and he gave her a small smile. "'Okay' is a subjective term, and I don't have the right to determine whether or not another man is okay. I can't peek inside his head."

Skye bit her bottom lip. "That makes sense. I... I'm sorry if I brought up bad memories."

"Don't be. It's a fair question. I'm surprised it took you this long to ask."

"You don't like to talk about it, though."

"No, I don't like to, but I talk about it anyway. It's important to these men that I'm able to share the ugly stuff in my past. It gives them the freedom to share their own nightmares and memories."

She nodded, still at a loss for words. Then she saw the papers he'd brought in and set on the desk. "Calling donors?"

"Yep. That's the plan."

Skye pushed the desk phone in his direction. Hopefully her question hadn't put him off his game. He was going to call those previous donors who had given at some point in the past but had stopped for one reason or another.

He had a different list for the donors that had pulled out since the City Council's crackdown. They were all highlighted in green. When she'd joked and asked if the green was for money, Sam had denied it. "The green is from traffic lights, to remind me to keep going when I'm discouraged. I have a feeling there are going to be a lot of depressing calls once I start on those."

Thank goodness he wasn't working on that particular list today, especially after she'd opened a door into the past that he might have a hard time closing.

With one last glance in his direction, Skye blocked out his conversation and got to work on the accounting.

Thirty minutes later, Sam put the phone down for the umpteenth time, a sigh passing his lips.

"I found it!"

He looked at her, eyebrows drawn together.

"I found it!"

Sam glanced from her to the receipt she clutched in her hand. "You found it?"

A grin split Skye's face. "I found it. You have a food purchase here for $236.89, but in the computer, it's $896.32."

"And that balances everything?"

"It's not quite as easy as that. You let your receipts pile up. I need to enter a three-month backlog to get everything caught up, but I should be able to get to that this coming week. Then we'll see where we stand. I'll go through the rest of the receipts that have already been inputted, too, just to make sure nothing else is off."

Sam stretched his legs out in front of him. "I'd treat you to ice cream or something, but we're a little low on treats these days."

"No worries."

"So, tell me how you know all this stuff? I took classes on running a nonprofit, and I can grasp all the basics, but accounting makes me feel like my brain's rotting. How come it's so easy for you?"

"I studied business in college."

"Yeah, but you run the business. CEOs don't generally handle accounting issues, do they?"

Ugh. Did she really have to talk about the company she didn't want to own? On the other hand, this was a fairly safe enough topic. "No, not on the job, but it was my favorite of all the business classes. Numbers and I clicked. We got along well. I'd rather work on a spreadsheet than write an essay any day."

Sam chuckled. "Isn't it ordinarily the men who struggle with words? I hated writing papers because I could say in two paragraphs what the prof wanted me to take five pages to explain."

"I could have condensed your two paragraphs down to two sentences without breaking a sweat."

"Do you like the business stuff? How can you be a CEO but still have time to help here?"

"What? You don't want me around?"

Laugh lines accented his eyes as he raised his hands in front of him. "I'm not running you off. I'm just curious."

Skye picked at a flawlessly manicured nail. "It's easy to run a company part-time when the company runs well without me and when I don't have any interest in running it myself."

"You don't enjoy the work? Or is it this specific company you don't want to run?"

Gideon ambled into the office then, but stood back as Skye answered the question.

"I don't have any passion for it. I would have gotten an accounting degree if I'd been allowed. My grandfather insisted on an MBA, though. After college, he could have put me to work in the company's accounting department. I would have loved it there where I was happily ignorant of what it took to run the place. My grandfather didn't give me a choice, though. I don't like being in charge of a company when I know every decision I make affects hundreds of employees and their families. It's more pressure than I want in my life."

"Then why don't you sell?"

"I don't know. I should. I just… Every offer I've gotten would end up in at least half the employees losing jobs. I can't do that. Even if I hate what I do, which I don't. I'm apathetic, I guess. But even if I hated it, these are good people. Their futures are in my hands, and I don't want to make the wrong choice."

"You've got yourself a conundrum."

Gideon cleared his throat. "You ever think about turning it over to the employees?"

Skye frowned at him. "What do you mean?"

He gave his head a quick shake. "Some companies are employee-owned. The company shares are all owned by employees, and the employees are the stockholders who make all the decisions. I might be fuzzy on the structure, but it's an employee-owned business, and all the profits are split between the employees."

She drummed her nails on the desktop. "Why haven't I heard of this before?"

Gideon gave a half shrug. "You just didn't ask the right person…?"

Skye shut down the computer one-handed as she reached for her purse. "I'll bake you a cake if this works out, Gideon."

"Whoa!" Gideon backed away from the counter. "You've already warned all us about your cooking skills. No need to threaten me with cake."

She pulled her phone from her purse and gave a mock salute with it in her hand. "How about this? If this doesn't work out, I'll bake you a cake…"

CHAPTER 24

August

Sam was a man of action. He had a straightforward approach to life. See a problem, fix the problem.

People were harder to fix, though. Military service had taught him that. Working at Samaritan's Reach drove the point home further.

Even harder than people?

Politics.

Some problems just needed to be doused in gasoline and set ablaze.

Not that he was condoning — or suggesting — arson.

The thought had at least a little appeal, though.

"Boss, you wanted to see me?" Franco stood in the doorway.

Sam rose from his desk and picked up the cordless phone and his keys. "Come with me."

Franco kept pace as they walked the perimeter of the property. "What's up, Boss?"

"I wish you guys would stop calling me that."

"Then stop acting like one."

Sam shook his head. He'd almost said he couldn't change how he acted. Wasn't that exactly what he was asking them to do, though? And wasn't that a part of the hope they all had in Christ? That He could make them new? That He could get inside and change them from the inside out?

Franco must have taken his silence as acquiescence. "You were born to be a boss, and you're a good one, so we follow you."

Sam stopped walking and looked over at Franco. "I didn't mean to gripe. I get the name, and I'm honored by it. So tell me. How are your classes going?"

"All A's except for that one B in algebra. I still don't know what I'll do with a degree in criminal justice, but…"

"I thought you wanted to work on becoming a parole officer."

"Yeah, but I got to thinking. Who'd hire a former homeless dude to keep track of parolees?"

Sam chuckled. "A smart person, that's who. You know what it's like to be in a bad place. That gives you compassion. Unless it's just a job. Then never mind. If it's more than a job, though, if you actually want to have a positive influence on people's lives, I think you picked the right field."

Franco rolled his eyes. "Thanks for the pep talk, Boss. Always a pleasure."

Sam gave the resident a light punch in the arm before pointing to some underbrush. "What do you see?"

Franco studied the shrubs. "We need rain, and someone's been here. They're all trampled."

Sam nodded. "Pull together some men from the leadership program and start doing random night patrols."

The big man beside him let out a whistle. "You think someone's casing the joint? It ain't like we got much."

"I don't care if they steal something. I care about providing a safe place for these men. For some of you, this is the first safe place you've laid down your head in a lot of years. I won't give that up without a fight."

Franco followed the trail of trampled underbrush. "They didn't come from the street."

"No."

"Inside job?"

Sam chose his words with care. "Maybe. I'm not sure. Whoever was here came from the courtyard, but that's all I know for sure. The real question is *why*. What were they doing?"

"Too bad we can't use Alan yet. Between me, Gideon, and Alonzo, though, we should be able to coordinate night patrols."

"I'm putting you in charge of it. I want a printed schedule, and I want a report each morning from whoever did the patrols."

"Do you want one man per night or rotate in shifts so everyone gets at least some sleep?"

Sam clapped Franco on the shoulder. "It's all you, man. Just get me the schedule before tonight so I won't be surprised if I leave my room after lights-out and stumble across someone."

Franco slogged off without a goodbye, but it was fine. Sam's list of things to worry about was growing by the minute. Delegating something to his leadership team relieved some pressure, and it would be a good lesson for them.

"The accounting's up-to-date, and now I'd like to learn more about the scope of your operation here."

Sam, who was helping Harry unload his barber equipment, gave Skye a quick look. "Hold on."

Once they got the wash sink and everything else into place, Gideon headed off to knock on each door to tell everyone the haircut van had arrived.

Skye's phone chirped, and she took it out of her pocket.

Sam used her distraction to take in her appearance. She'd been coming regularly to the mission for over two months now, and he couldn't imagine the place without her. One of these days, he was going to have a serious spiritual discussion with her. That was sort of his job, seeing to the spiritual, emotional, and physical wellbeing of his residents, staff, and volunteers. Not that he'd say that to Skye. She'd already put him in his place about his attempts to help her. He hadn't stopped, though. Instead, he'd gotten subtler about it.

She stuffed her phone into her back pocket and caught his eye. "Ready?"

"Sure. Mind if we walk while we talk?"

"Um…okay. I was going to take notes, though."

"Don't worry about writing anything down. It's not that complicated, but if you need me to repeat something later, I can."

"All right then. Lead the way."

Sam headed toward the corner of the motel where the picnic table resided. Might as well walk the perimeter while he talked to Skye. "What do you want to know?"

"Everything, but let's start with where you find the men who come here."

"I used to go out and visit all the homeless camps and tell them about Samaritan's Reach, leave information behind, that sort of thing. Anyone who qualified and wanted to come back with me, I'd bring back in the van and process them in. Eventually word of mouth started working in our favor. Most of our current residents found us on their own or through someone they met in or around Rainbow Falls."

"Do you ever go back to the homeless camps?"

Sam rounded the corner by the street and began crossing the front of the motel's property. "Whenever I have time, and when it gets cold. As winter starts to set in, I'll make two or three trips out to each camp. I tell people about us and put up signs. Stapled to a tree or whatever's handy."

Skye stalled him with a hand to his arm. "Slow down. My legs aren't as long as yours."

He was usually more aware than that. "Sorry. Didn't mean to leave you behind."

"So, after you process someone in? Then what?"

"One of the first things we do is make sure they're registered with Veterans Affairs. There are a lot of services these men can gain access to through the VA that they haven't taken advantage of because they've been transient or because they didn't know. They don't all qualify for everything. Some services will vary depending on how long a person served. Regardless, we work to get them covered by the programs they quality for."

"Such as?"

"Everyone gets a physical and sees the eye doctor and dentist. Those are things we can take care of outpatient at the clinic in Peterman Falls. The VA also offers services to homeless vets if the men want to take advantage of those. That's a little more complicated, though, and our guys don't always go for it."

"What's next? After they've had their medical checkups?"

"Each man here is required to attend the daily Bible study and two exercise classes each week."

"Yoga and... What was the other one?"

"Aikido. My version of it, anyway."

"I haven't seen any yoga poses in quite a while. Let alone martial arts. What happened?"

The men might not thank him for explaining. "We used to exercise in the courtyard during the summer months. When you started volunteering, though, the men balked at doing yoga in the courtyard where you could see them. We're not an entirely graceful bunch. So we moved it indoors. We shuffled furniture in one of the empty rooms. It's a little tight, but we manage."

"And you meet at the picnic table for Bible study. What do you do when it gets cold? You only have so many empty rooms, and winter's not too far off."

"We use the Learning Center for Bible study. Since every man is required to attend, the room's available, and the seating is more comfortable. We also have mandatory group counseling sessions, with one-on-one sessions offered as needed. The initial group sessions are mostly for us to figure out where each man is emotionally and psychologically so we can treat him accordingly and get him whatever help he needs. Some residents are suited to a PTSD group. Others aren't. It varies. We try to assess each man and get him into the sort of counseling best suited to his situation."

"Do you lead the group counseling?"

"I do the private sessions when needed. A couple of community volunteers come in and run the group sessions. I fill in if one of them can't make it, but they're an exceptional team. They rarely call out."

"Volunteers? Do you let just anyone lead counseling?"

"Uh... No. That wouldn't be advisable. Our volunteer counselors are all licensed professionals. They have different specialties. Our family counselor doesn't lead the PTSD group, and our PTSD guy doesn't lead our survivor's guilt group."

By this time, they'd circled back around to the picnic table, and Sam sat down on top of it. For a man who was used to asking the questions, being on the end of so many of them had him a little off-kilter. It was time to turn the tables. "You told me what first brought you to Rainbow Falls, but you never told me what pulled you away."

Color drained from Skye's face as she looked anywhere but at him. "I'd rather talk about Samaritan's Reach."

"I'm talked out. It's your turn."

"Fine." Her lips thinned. "My grandparents offered to pay for college if I lived with them, so I went."

"It must have been hard to leave your mom. Were you close?"

"In a way."

The walls were coming up, but they weren't all the way up yet. She could handle one more question. "How did your mom take it when you left?"

"I never saw her again. She OD'd a month later."

CHAPTER 25

Skye slid into the booth. "How are you ladies doing?"

Ruby and Rose smiled in unison. "Couldn't be better. You?"

Their ability to speak as one was uncanny. When Skye had first met them, she'd thought they were robots. That was the only way two people could be so in sync, after all. Never mind that they were distinctly different. One was outgoing, the other shy. One liked kids, the other didn't. One was analytical, the other creative. They often joked that together they made one complete and well-rounded person.

Tawny approached the booth and gave Skye a gentle shove. "Make room. The birthday girl has arrived."

Leave it to Tawny. Skye didn't like people to notice her birthday. Tawny, on the other hand, wanted the whole town to cater to her every want and whim for the day.

Before long, Jette and Sunny joined them. Then Fern.

It wasn't unusual for one or more of the Rainbow Girls to be caught up elsewhere on a Friday night. They'd tried getting together monthly, but too many of them had missed the meal on a regular basis, which prompted them to meet weekly so everyone could make it at least once a month.

They placed their orders, and all eyes turned to the birthday girl.

She gave them that frightening Cheshire grin of hers that said they were all in for trouble. "My birthday wish this year is for each of you to help Samaritan's Reach."

Skye's breath caught. They'd talked about the shelter around Friday night dinner several times, but nobody had ever made any specific commitments. She'd always thought that if she could convince the girls to visit the place, they'd be as committed as she'd become. She didn't have Tawny's pushiness, though, to pull it off.

Tawny pointed to Sunny. "You run the largest second-hand store in Rainbow Falls."

Sunny's eyebrows lifted. "It's the only second-hand store in town."

Tawny shrugged. "You make a respectable living doing it, too. You can help. Provide vouchers for men to receive a free outfit for interviews or something like that. Or hire some of the guys from Samaritan's Reach when you need extra muscle for one of those estate sales you're always going to."

"How many men are we talking about?" Skepticism laced Sunny's voice.

When Tawny prodded her with a well-timed stare, Skye answered. "Usually ten to fifteen. Sometimes a little more, sometimes less. They can house up to twenty-two at a time, more if they put two to a room."

Sunny nodded and pulled a business card from her purse. She slid it across the table to Skye. "Have your guy give me a call. If it's a number like that, I think I can help. I can't afford to give away my entire inventory, but I'm sure we can work something out that will benefit the men at the shelter and please the birthday girl."

Skye took the card and tucked it into her purse. Sunny would benefit, too. She just didn't realize it yet.

Next, Tawny pointed to Ruby and Rose. "You two run the best employment agency in town. Think you might be able to place some vets in decent jobs?"

The twins regarded each other for an entire millisecond before Ruby answered. "I handle the temp agency. Rose takes care of long-term placements. Between the two of us, we can help place some of the men." She shifted her attention to Skye. "They have to look the part, though. Some of the jobs are manual labor. Some are office. We do random drug testing, too. The men need to be…"

Skye understood what Ruby didn't want to say. "Clean inside and out, right?"

Ruby gave a half-shrug. "Yeah, basically. They also can't have… Um… I can't send out anyone if there's a chance they'll go off on one of our clients."

Rose slid two business cards across the table to Skye. "Have him call us. We'd need a face-to-face with him to make sure we understand each other. Will he get angry if we're not politically correct?"

Tawny snorted. "Sweetheart, he's the furthest thing from a metrosexual you'll find."

Skye reached for the cards. "The first day I officially volunteered there, he told me he wanted me to be honest with him. He didn't have to like what I said as long as he could trust it. I don't think PC's a big deal to him."

The twins exchanged another glance before Ruby spoke for them. "We might only be able to offer a small help. We don't know how receptive our clients will be. We'll do what we can, though."

Tawny crossed her arms and stared at Fern. "You and your daddy run a fine garage."

"I thought Forrest worked at the garage." Had Skye missed something? Forrest, Fern's older brother, had graduated high school with Skye. He'd had grease under his nails the entire time she'd known him.

Fern crossed her arms and glared daggers at Tawny. "That's not funny."

Skye was obviously missing the subtext here. "Somebody needs to clue me in."

Jette took pity on her. "Fern's daddy doesn't think girls should work on cars. He lets Fern run the office. He won't let her in the back, which is where she'd rather be."

Ouch. Skye knew a thing or two about being bossed around by a domineering man. "You don't have to…"

Fern waved her remark away. "We don't need more mechanics. Our roster's full."

Tawny leaned on the table. "Yeah, but they're driving around a fifteen-passenger van that looks like it might have been built before Noah's flood. Besides, you guys know better than anyone in town when someone is thinking of selling a vehicle. Help him keep the one he has running and see if you can hook him up with something a little more road-worthy while you're at it."

Fern's arms were still crossed, but at least her eyes weren't sparking fire anymore. "Fine. I'll talk to Forrest and Dad." She looked to Skye. "I don't have a card on me, but I'll call Samaritan's Reach if I can make something happen."

Skye nodded her appreciation. "Have you ever thought of opening your own garage?"

Jaws dropped all around the table. All except Fern's. "Yeah, but I'd have to be prepared to starve since this town would never accept a female mechanic."

"We would." Rose and Ruby answered in unison.

Fern rolled her eyes. "Aside from the people at this table, nobody in Rainbow Falls would bring their car to me. I'd have to be willing to go into competition with Dad and Forrest, too, and I don't know…"

Skye took a breath, ready to argue the point.

Tawny stepped on her toe, though, and cut her words short. "That's a problem for another day. Which brings me to…" She stared at Jette.

Jette raised a black eyebrow. "You're not going to intimidate me, so just spit out whatever you plan to say."

Tawny shrugged. "Had to try. Honestly, I don't know if they have much use for an attorney."

Skye reached toward Jette. "They do."

Jette drained the last of the water from her glass and nodded to Skye. "Give me the short version."

"They've been here over two years. The City Council approved permits so they could launch, but then they started passing rulings to regulate Samaritan's Reach. A review of his business license is scheduled for the end of this year. If he can't meet all their terms — which is virtually impossible — they're likely going to force him to close."

"What are the regulations?"

"I don't know all of them, but he's lost half his donors as a result. Everyone assumes he's going to fail, so they're jumping ship left and right. But the shelter does commendable work, and the men Sam is helping… He's changing lives."

"Does he have an attorney?"

Skye nodded. "Yeah, but I think he's a divorce attorney or something. He used to serve in the Marines with Sam, and he volunteers his time. He's not equipped to help with what's going on."

Jette held her glass up and made eye contact with the waitress as the woman walked by. Then she gave her attention back to Skye. "Let me ponder. I'll let you know if I can do anything."

A fire burned in Skye's chest, and it grew brighter by the second. All the other things would be helpful, but none of them would mean a thing if Samaritan's Reach had to close down. If she believed in God, she'd be praying, begging Him to save the shelter. She was too many years past that schoolgirl fantasy, though. Jette, though… If Jette got involved, the shelter might have a chance.

Tawny nudged Skye's foot under the table. "Anything else you can think of?"

"What? You're not going to rope me into doing something? Oh wait. You already did. You volunteered me to give them three days out of my week."

Her friend winked. "And you don't regret it, do you?"

Skye couldn't argue. "No comment."

"So? Anything else you can think of that they need?"

"Shoes."

"Shoes?" Tawny echoed her words.

She nodded. "I noticed it a while back, but I wasn't sure what to do about it. They all have bright, new socks, but their shoes are a mess. I don't know sizes, either. Are people picky about shoes? Can I buy inexpensive ones, or should I get name brand? I've never bought shoes for a man before."

Tawny choked. "It can't be nearly as confusing as underwear."

Heat raced up Skye's neck and into her cheeks. "You had to go there, didn't you?"

"Get good shoes." This comment came from Fern.

Skye looked across the table at her. "You think?"

Fern nodded. "Some of these men might be around for months. Some might leave next week. Get something sturdy for them so those men who take off out of there will have shoes that'll last. Don't go cheap and buy them something that's going to fall apart the second they hit the county line."

Jette pointed her fork at Fern. "She has a point, but you also don't want the shoes to be so fancy that someone will be willing to kill a man to steal them."

Skye's stomach flopped. "Right. Sturdy, but not…"

"Kill-worthy?" Tawny's attempt at levity helped.

"I don't suppose anyone wants to go shopping with me? I need shoes for the shelter and curtains for my home."

Tawny rolled her eyes. "You still haven't gotten your living room curtains? You're a disaster, you know that, don't you?"

Yeah, she knew. It wasn't such a big deal, either. Her friends worried she would leave again if she didn't set down roots. Their concern was part of what gave her roots, but she didn't know how to explain that. Not having to do all those boring things that were supposed to make her a functional and contributing member of society gave her a freedom she savored, too. Besides, nice curtains didn't make a nice person.

As for how long she was going to stay in Rainbow Falls…

Who knew? That thought didn't need to be voiced, though.

CHAPTER 26

Something about mornings in Montana put a song in Sam's soul, and this Monday was no different. The rugged majesty of the Bitterroot Mountains provided more peace than any other locale he'd experienced, stateside or otherwise.

The calm was broken, though, with the clacking approach of someone in high heels. He made his way toward the driveway to meet the person. Visitors didn't usually come this early in the morning; the sun had barely kissed the sky.

A woman with long, black hair approached. She wore a dark grey pantsuit and a no-nonsense expression. "Are you Sam Madison?"

He held out his hand. "I am."

She handed him a business card in lieu of a handshake. "I've looked into your operation here."

"Oh?"

"I'm an attorney with Tiller, Cromwell, and Erickson over in Peterman Falls. I handle corporate law, mostly. I take on a set number of pro bono cases, and I've long-since filled this year's quota. I told a friend I'd check you out, though, so here I am. Tell me about your problem."

Sam read the name on the card. Jette Black. Had to be a Rainbow Girl. Skye was somehow involved. He would take that to mean he could trust the stranger. It was a gamble, but his gut said to go for it. "City Council passed some new laws. In short, if we're not running at eighty percent of capacity all the time, they can shut us down. If we have more than three residents removed for violent behavior during a year, they can shut us down. If we are not adding quality and benefit to Rainbow Falls, they can shut us down."

"Quality and benefit? Your words, or theirs?"

"Theirs. It's in the paperwork."

"What kind of capacity are we talking about?"

He ran a hand over his head. "The impossible kind. They want us at eighty percent of what the fire marshal says we can hold."

Jette's mouth drew into a thin line. "How long is this list of conditions you have to meet?"

"It started with five points and an addendum that said they could add additional requirements at any time without public vote."

"And have they?"

"We're up to ten points now. On top of that, they cited me for providing 'deplorable' living conditions because the roof's in bad shape, but the company that's willing to give us shingles at cost says they won't do it till everything is settled with the City Council."

"Am I stepping on your attorney's toes by talking to you?"

Sam gave a single shake of his head. "He told me to jump at the chance if I could find anybody else who was more knowledgeable about this kind of thing."

Her mouth tightened into a scowl. "If you're interested in retaining my services, email me. Include whatever paperwork you have from the city. I'll send you the client agreement and release form. I can't do anything until you return the client agreement to me. The release form will allow me to contact your current attorney for information if I need to."

"That's all well and good, but I can't pay you."

"I know."

"You've met your quota of pro bono cases for the year."

She scowled at him. "Don't remind me."

Skye was skilled at talking in puzzles, but this woman had her beat by a mile. "Don't ask me to read between the lines. Just tell me what it's going to cost me."

The hard look in her eyes softened the tiniest bit. "You're going to owe me one colossal favor. I'll let you know when I need to collect. You're also going to give me your word you won't hurt Skye. Because if you do, I might very well help the Council bury you."

He lifted an eyebrow. "Isn't that a breach of ethics?"

Her eyes were back to onyx-hard again. "Don't be a wise guy. And don't take advantage of Skye."

Sam tucked the business card into his back pocket. This kind of loyalty was familiar. Men and women who served in the same unit — who went through battles and risked their lives together — often developed a fierce loyalty like Jette was displaying . He understood this language a whole lot better than the confusing gibberish from before. "Tell me why Skye left Rainbow Falls."

"She graduated high school. Her grandparents offered to pay for college."

"But she never came back, not till a couple months ago when I met her on an airplane."

Jette crossed her arms. "It's her story to tell."

"You're the second person to say that to me, but Skye's not sharing the story."

The hint of a smirk touched Jette's lips. "Then I guess she doesn't trust you."

Sam ground his teeth. "Then why are you helping me?"

"Tawny asked me to."

"Tawny?"

Her smile didn't come close to reaching her eyes. "You thought Skye asked me to help? She hasn't even bought a couch yet. She's not ready to ask for favors. Favors mean you owe people, and owing people means you plan to stick around. She hasn't quite made up her mind about Rainbow Falls."

The creek of a resident's door reached them. "Would you like to tour our facility?"

She gave a single headshake. "Assuming you're interested in the help, email me. Otherwise, your loss. I'm not always easy to get along with, but I give my clients everything I have. And…"

"And?"

"And I wouldn't mind getting to know you better. I'm still trying to decide whether to warn Skye away or push her toward you."

The black-haired enigma turned, and the echo of her clacking heels receded.

Sam sat at the office desk, typing up a progress report on one of the men, when the phone rang. "Samaritan's Reach, this is Sam. How can I help you?"

"My name's Fern. I work at Green & Son Automotive. We understand you drive an old van that might be in need of some maintenance."

What was going on? "Fern…Green, is it?"

"Yes. Can I make an appointment for you?"

"Jette was just here."

"Yeah, well, don't let her intimidate you too much. She's a softie underneath that rock-hard exterior, but she can scare the wrapper off a chocolate heart when she's in a mood. So, about your van…"

"It's due for an oil change, and there's a check engine light that won't go away."

"I have an opening Wednesday at nine. You'll probably want to drop it off, though. We'll give it a thorough going-over and tell you what needs to be done to keep it in business."

"There's a reason I haven't gotten the oil changed…"

"We're willing to comp you on some of the work if you'll give us a receipt for the donation of parts and labor."

"You're sure?"

"Has Skye talked to you since Friday?"

"Um, no. She wasn't feeling well on Sunday and didn't make it in. I won't see her again until tomorrow."

"Ah, well, I'll let her explain. You might want to buckle up, though. You're in for quite a ride. We'll see you Wednesday at nine. Bring your van to Green & Son Automotive on the corner of Huntley and Jam."

"What? What ride?"

The line was already dead.

He'd no sooner hung the phone up than someone came through the foyer door. "Sam, you in here?"

"Hey, Wyatt, good to see you. What can I do for you?"

Wyatt Phelps managed the local food bank and shared Sam's passion for helping people.

The man removed his cowboy hat, ran a hand through his blond locks, and scuffed his boot on the floor.

A stone dropped in Sam's stomach. "What's up, Wyatt?"

"My board wanted me to call you, but I felt I owed you an in-person visit."

Sam sank back into his desk chair and waved Wyatt toward the folding one still there from the week before. "Spit it out."

"Several of the board members have decided it's no longer in the best interest of the food bank to provide vouchers to your men."

Heat climbed Sam's chest as he leaned forward. "You're cutting them off?"

Wyatt nodded, misery in every line of his face. "I fought the board, but they outnumbered me."

"Why would they do this?" The old Sam would have punched something. The new Sam, the Sam who wanted to trust that God was in control, took a deep breath and battled the urge to blow up.

"I'm not sure. Nobody's giving me a straight answer. The members who voted in favor aren't saying a word. I think…"

The unfinished sentence grated on Sam like sandpaper. "You think what?"

"One of them is the new mayor's son-in-law. Another is married to someone on the City Council."

"You think the Council's behind this?"

Wyatt bobbed his head in what could have been a nod or a shake, depending on the angle. "No. Maybe. I don't know. I'm not exactly a conspiracy guy, but they've put you in a tight spot lately. I'll keep digging for answers."

"When are we cut off?"

"Vouchers already issued to you will be honored. It's not much, but it's the only concession I could get.

They wanted me to flat-out ban you and your men from the food bank."

Sam stood and offered Wyatt his hand. "Thanks for doing what you could and for having the decency to come tell me in person. I appreciate it."

"I'm sorry I couldn't do more."

"You did what you could. I'll figure this out. God is still in control, even if it doesn't particularly feel like it at the moment."

"Amen to that."

The door closed behind Wyatt, and Sam slapped his hand on the desk. He was on the verge of making a dangerous mistake. It was simmering just below his skin. But he couldn't very well storm city hall and tell them — at the top of his lungs — what he thought of their actions. He would demand answers, and oh wouldn't it be satisfying to sink his fist into someone's face? Why were people going out of their way to try to destroy his hard work? Samaritan's Reach was a beneficial addition to the community, and it helped people, too.

The sixteenth chapter of 1 Corinthians jumped at him from the shadows of his anger. "...Act like men, be strong. Let all that you do be done in love." Acting like a man and doing-in-love didn't mesh well, to Sam's way of thinking. Not at the moment, anyway. It was God's word, though, so it had to be right. Acting like a man meant doing things in love, not running off at the mouth — or with fists.

Sam took a deep breath and let the air out slowly. Anybody who said walking in faith was easy lied.

God, give me wisdom. I want to yell. I want to tear someone limb-from-limb. If not with my fists, then at least with words. You saved me from that, though. I'm not that person anymore. You're supposed to be strong when I am weak, and right now, I'm weak. So be strong for me. And wise. I could really use that wisdom.

Gideon was talking to one of the newer men when Sam found him. "Be sure to ask, if you have any questions."

The new guy — Jerald — walked off with a wave.

Sam caught Gideon's eye. "Can I have a word?"

"Sure thing, Boss."

"How's Alonzo doing? With his job off-site, I don't see him as much."

Gideon shrugged. "He's just happy he got hired. Doesn't much like the job, but other than that, he's fine. Status quo and all that."

While Samaritan's Reach tried to help the men acquire steady employment, it wasn't always easy. Alonzo's spot as a janitor at a local office building was a coup, even if the work itself wasn't all that exciting.

"Anything else?" Gideon watched him, eyebrows raised.

Sam nodded. Alonzo was just the small talk. "Walk with me."

The two men headed toward the field next to the shelter. Gideon, talkative as ever, kept quiet.

Sam pointed across the expanse. "I want to build a gym here. A workshop, too. An all-around better facility."

"Dreaming's good."

Sam chuckled. "God-willing, it'll be more than a dream. I haven't given up yet."

They took a few more steps before Sam broached the subject on his mind. "I'd like to increase your responsibilities around here, but before I can do that, I need to understand a few things."

"Such as?"

"Your time in the service. How you ended up on the street."

Gideon sucked in air through his teeth. "No soft questions, eh?"

Sam waited. He'd tried to broach the subject before, but Gideon had always sidestepped it. He had plans for Gideon, though. Where were the tripwires located in Gideon's past?

The older man ran a hand along his jaw. "I was Army."

Sam nodded. That was on Gideon's intake form. "Chaplain."

Wow. He hadn't seen that coming. "Chaplain?"

Gideon grimaced. "Hard to believe, I know."

"So what happened?"

Gideon started walking along the border of the field. "I stood beside the beds of too many dying soldiers."

Sam kept pace with him. "That had to be rough."

"The old line of telling these soldiers and their families that God was in control wore thin after a while. I just didn't have the words anymore when people came to me for solace."

They continued walking, but Sam held his silence.

"A lot of men came back from war and had nightmares about getting blown up by IEDs. I had nightmares of soldiers floating in nothingness rather than being embraced in the loving arms of their Father. I had nightmares about the dead coming back to life and accusing me of lying to them. I could never find the words to defend myself, either."

Sam couldn't put a comforting hand on Gideon's shoulder, no matter how much he wanted to. The man's posture wouldn't allow for it.

"I thought I'd be okay once I got back home, but civilian life didn't agree with me, either. The nightmares kept me up all night. I couldn't sleep, and I couldn't function. I was a zombie, and I'd started to believe that I'd led all those soldiers astray. I didn't want to do that to anyone else, so I left. I didn't even tell my sister I was leaving. I just... I disappeared. After a while, it got easier to stay that way."

"Easy isn't always right."

Gideon's bark of laughter was dry. "Nah, it ain't. But it's easy. Somewhere down inside, I think I decided I deserved the punishment of being isolated, of suffering."

"Street life's no picnic."

"Broken ribs, fingers, a foot one time. Living on the street is violent. Every day. Hunger, violence. Judgment. I deserved it. Or thought I did, anyway. Then one day this idiot showed up in my camp and offered me a roof over my head and two squares a day, and all I had to do in return was sit in a Bible class and not get caught fighting. Someone who'd seen bad things, too, but had somehow managed to find faith there rather than lose it."

Sam's throat clogged.

"You saved my life, man. I owe you."

They reversed course and headed back toward the old Silver Heart Motel. There were no words left to say. Silence settled between them, the kind of silence filled with the sound of mutual respect.

CHAPTER 27

"Hey. You're early." Sam took the decaffeinated coffee she offered. "Want to join me for Bible study?"

Skye had done a superb job of making sure she didn't arrive at the shelter until after Sam had concluded his quiet time, but her perfect record was officially blown.

There was no graceful way out of this, not without admitting she didn't like going to church, either.

"Um. Okay." Hopefully she came across as agreeable but not enthusiastic.

His eyes laughed at her as he vacated the desk chair for her. He pulled a Bible off a nearby shelf and handed it to her. "I'm starting the book of Joshua."

Skye fumbled with the table of contents but tried to play it off. "Using my Bible app has spoiled me."

When she got there, he pointed to the spot. "I'll read verses one through five, and you pick up with six through nine. Then we'll discuss what it says."

Sam still had the rough voice of a former smoker. She'd never asked if he used to smoke. Maybe he'd just yelled a lot. Or maybe it was his natural voice. Either way, it was incongruous. People that read scripture were supposed to sound smooth and sweet-as-honey.

Her turn came too soon, and she stumbled over the verses.

When she finished, she folded her hands and rested them on the Bible. "You said you'd rather have the truth about things, right?"

"Always."

"I don't go to church. I don't read my Bible. I'm not particularly interested in God, either."

"I kind of figured."

"If it's a problem…"

"It's not. You're not required to be a believer to help here. You don't even have to be a believer to go to church. Can you tell me why, though?"

Sigh. Of course he was going to ask that. "Huh."

"Huh?"

She stared into ice blue eyes lit by curiosity. "It's weird. I don't like people asking me questions. I'm private. Kind of to the extreme. And you ask a lot of questions. I usually get annoyed, even if I don't show it."

"Oh trust me. You show it." He winked at her.

Skye shook her head. "Your questions don't upset me as much as they used to. I don't know if that means I should answer you or avoid you like the bubonic plague."

He chuckled. "Let's go with the former. I'm not sure I want to be compared to the plague."

She picked up the Bible and ran her fingers along the spine. "Tawny and Jette befriended me when I first moved here. They seemed to understand something even I didn't get. That I was broken. They took me into their group and made me a Rainbow Girl. I would have done anything for them."

"They sound like the kind of friends worth keeping."

Skye tried to smile, but she was pretty sure she failed to pull it off convincingly. "Yeah, the best. When they invited me to church, I went. It was the natural thing to do. Then I started hearing about this God who loves people, who stays with them forever and always, who never abandons them. My dad was dead, and my mom was... She just wasn't around much. I didn't realize how lonely I'd become until Tawny and Jette made sure I wasn't lonely anymore."

She put the Bible down and thumbed through the gilt-edged pages. There was a time when she would have felt guilty about not reading her Bible. No longer, though. Not until recently. "I accepted Christ at VBS when I was thirteen. I don't know what I expected, but I thought life would get better, you know? God wants only good for His children. Or at least, He's supposed to. Life didn't get better, though. It got worse. Still, I held to my faith. I held onto everything I'd heard in church, everything..."

Skye closed the Bible with a snap. "Anyway. I did the best I could, but then my grandparents took me away from Rainbow Falls, and something bad happened because I wasn't here to stop it. I just couldn't see God in that. I couldn't see Him in the pain and loss, in the pointlessness of it all. He wasn't there anymore, and I figured every time I thought I'd seen Him in my life up to that point had been an illusion."

Sam reached across the desk and rested a hand on hers. "I think of it not so much as seeing God, but more like seeing His fingerprints on different parts of my life. That's my evidence, the thing that proves He was there with me."

She shrugged. "I guess I can work with that. It doesn't change the facts, though. God wasn't there anymore, and it seemed like He'd never been there at all. I'd made it up because I'd been so lonely and desperate to have someone there with me."

Sam withdrew his hand, and the absence of his touch allowed the coldness to seep back in.

"Sometimes we go through bad things so God can grow us."

Heat surged through her middle and heated her core. Not the warm-fuzzy kind of heat, either. "I'm all grown up. What more does He want?"

One of the best things about Sam was his steady mood. Whether he felt anger or not, he never displayed it. She didn't fear her own words when she was around him. She owed him the same courtesy, didn't she? He didn't deserve to be on the receiving end of her ragged and torn-up feelings about God.

Sam leaned forward, elbows on the desk. "I have all kinds of answers I want to give you, but I've been where you're at. If someone tried spouting off their theology to me, I'd want to deck them. Nobody needs empty platitudes."

"You're not a platitude kind of guy."

"Only because I've been there. No matter how true a Bible verse is, it feels like a slap in the face if you're not ready to hear it."

Skye laced her fingers together to stop herself from picking at her nail polish. "So if you're not going to knock me around with your Bible, we're at an impasse."

Sam chuckled. "Knock you around, huh? You give Bible-thumping a whole new meaning. I have an idea, though. You might not be too enthusiastic, but I'd like you to consider it."

The same urge that had filled her when she was a kid and had compelled her to do whatever Tawny and Jette asked, compelled her now. "I'm listening."

"What time do you start work when you're not here at Samaritan's Reach?"

"Nine, sometimes a little later."

Sam sat back, linked his hands together, and put them behind his head in a stretched-out post that emphasized his height and made his muscles all the more defined. "I'd like you to give me thirty days of quiet time. Join me during my morning Bible study for one month."

Her breathing stopped, her heart dropped, and her stomach flopped. "Why?"

"You need to find some real answers, and I can't think of a better way to help you do that."

Just when she needed something to throw, there was nothing at hand.

Not only had Skye agreed to Sam's ludicrous plan, but now she was sitting in a staff meeting. One of the perks of volunteering was supposed to be *not* being forced to deal with inner-office politics. So much for that.

"Alright everyone, let's start." Sam's voice rang out in the learning center. "We need to brainstorm some fundraising ideas. The food bank is no longer going to be providing vouchers to our men."

Gasps filled the room. There were only five staff on-site, and two of those were Sam and Skye. The other three shouldn't have been able to gasp so loudly.

"I'll send an email out to everyone who's not here today, but I don't want them to panic, so I'd like us to come up with some ideas I can include in that email."

A hand snaked up, and Sam called on the young man. "You don't need a single fundraiser. You need something that'll be ongoing, a stream of revenue to supply money for food on a continual basis."

Sam nodded. "Definitely. We can do one-time fundraisers, too, but something ongoing would be best."

Skye raised her hand next. "You have a table at the local weekend flea market, don't you? What happens to that money? And the items you sell are all donated, so you have minimal overhead."

"It pays for the rental space, but that's it. The purpose of the flea market hasn't been to raise money. It's been about getting our men out into society in a structured setting so they can gain experience interacting with customers. They need to be able to do that before we can send them out on job interviews."

Skye bit her bottom lip. Did he realize how much he was missing out on?

"Go ahead, Skye. Spit it out."

"What if you actively sought donations and got people to give you stuff? You've been using the flea market to train the men. You haven't actually tried to make money at it. You could, though, if you put in some effort."

Sam drew his hand down the length of his beard, but another part-time staffer spoke up. "The flea market has been Friday through Sunday only, but when I took the men last weekend, the owners said they were expanding their hours to include Wednesday and Thursday. We only do a half-day on Sunday because of church. If we add Wednesday and Thursday and expand Sunday, we could..."

"We're not skipping church. The flea market booth will remained closed so the men can attend services." Sam's voice was final.

The staffer continued, "I understand, but what if you left one man at the table and did it on a rotating basis so it's not the same man each Sunday?"

Sam shook his head.

"What about Wednesday and Thursday, then?" Skye couldn't let his bullheadedness shut down a valuable plan.

"I'm not sure we make enough money at the table to make more days worthwhile. We barely cover space rental as it is."

Skye smiled. Now they were getting into her wheelhouse. "Let me talk to the folks who run the flea market. Maybe I can negotiate a contract with a better rental price."

The guy who had first raised his hand spoke up again . "I can ask at my church to see if anybody wants to donate something. I'll bet a lot of people around town would give items to us if they knew it was going to the men's food. We could hit up all the churches, the senior citizens' center, the… I don't know. There have to be other places, too, right?"

Energy raced through Skye's veins. "Yes! Now that the accounting is mostly caught up, I can work on this. I'll negotiate the rental contract and contact people about donations.

Sam inspected the group. "Sounds good. In the meantime, I want everyone to keep thinking of other ways to raise money. We need at least a couple backup plans.

CHAPTER 28

Sam sighed as everyone filed out of the room. Everyone except Skye, with her long dark hair and flashing golden eyes. She'd come a long way from the timid woman who'd stared at his tattoos as though they might come to life.

She held out some business cards to him. "Here."

"What are these for?" He took them and read over each one before sliding them into his back pocket.

"Rose and Ruby run an employment agency, long-term and short-term. They'd like to meet with you to discuss the possibility of helping to place some of the men in jobs. They have some specific concerns, and I told them you would rather they be honest than politically correct."

He couldn't help but smile at the solemn nod that accompanied Skye's words.

"The other one is from Sunny. She runs the Stuff & Sunshine store over on Third & Huntley. Give her a call. She might be able to work something out with you so the men can get some clothes appropriate for going on interviews. She's expecting a call."

"You're awfully well-connected for someone who's been out of Rainbow Falls as long as you have."

"I'm not sure *connected* is the right word, but we can go with that if you'd like."

"I got a call from Fern and a visit from Jette. I'm pretty sure neither of those would have happened if it wasn't for you."

"That wasn't me. It was Tawny's birthday. This is what she wanted for her gift."

"Why?"

Skye dropped her gaze and fisted her fingers together before releasing them and dropping her hands to her sides. "I think she's afraid I'll leave again. When I left last time, they all lost contact with me. Nobody knew where I was."

"Couldn't you have reached out to them? Social media... Something?"

Her mouth dropped down in a frown, and dark clouds passed over her eyes. "It was easier to deal with my new life if I cut all ties to my old one. I'm not saying it was right, but I coped the best way I knew how at the time."

And when she'd decided to run away from that new life, she ran straight back to Rainbow Falls. Buried in that truth was a lesson about who Skye was. He didn't have time to dig for it at present, though. Instead, he gave her a grin. "Any other friends you want to tell me about? Maybe Tawny's birthday wish included someone who owns a grocery store?"

Skye chuckled, and her eyes cleared to their normal bright golden-brown. "Not to my knowledge, but I'll see what I can do about getting items donated for the flea market."

She started for the office before stopping and turning back to him. "You need to get a sign made for your table, too. Something that says where the proceeds are going. If people realize their money is going to a worthy cause, they're likely to be more generous, don't you think? I'm pretty sure I read that in a marketing magazine somewhere."

"A tabletop sign or a big tablecloth-type-sign?"

She waved her hand through the air. "Never mind. I'll look into it. I have an idea."

Sam watched her go, torn between two worlds. In one, he had a fierce desire to protect her. In the other, he was so proud of the strides she'd made away from the frightened woman she'd once been. What he felt for her went deeper than the normal boss-volunteer relationship. He couldn't deny it any longer. He was treading treacherous water where Skye was concerned.

He'd had relationships before. Sort of. He'd been single, young, and a Marine. He'd never lacked for female companionship, though they hadn't all qualified as real relationships. Regret was easy to come by if he opened the door to it. Those things were part of his past, though. They didn't have permission to cast a shadow on his present.

If anyone is in Christ, he is a new creation. The old has passed away; behold, the new has come.

Still... Temptation smoldered beneath the surface with every breath he took. He found himself tucking his hands in his pockets more and more, and it had less and less to do with not wanting to intimidate Skye. These days, it was all about not reaching out and touching her. Brushing a hand along her cheek, feeling the silkiness of her hair between his fingers, pulling her into a hug, wondering if the base of her throat was as warm and inviting as it looked...

"Done in here, Boss?" Gideon's voice broke into Sam's reverie.

"Done?"

"Your meeting? It's over, right? Can we have the learning center back? Matt has a math test, and a couple other guys have some work to catch up on, too."

Sam took a deep breath to clear his head. "Sure. It's all yours. Let me know if you need anything."

Sam stayed away from the office for the remainder of the day. He needed to let Skye work. Besides, his attention was required elsewhere.

"Okay, guys, listen up. The food bank is going to honor the vouchers you have, but they will not be issuing any new vouchers to our residents. This is a decision their board of directors made. It's not a reflection on the people working at the food bank, so please don't take your frustrations out on them."

The men grumbled. This was their food. Part of the promise of Samaritan's Reach was that they would have a safe place to lay their head and they wouldn't need to wonder where their next meal would come from.

Sam couldn't help it. He wanted to grumble with them. He wanted to rail against the injustice of the whole mess. What kind of example would that be, though? "I don't believe in pointing out a problem without having at least some sort of a solution, though, so here's the plan. We're going to expand what we're doing with the flea market, and the money raised from that will go into a grocery fund. We will work on a weekly voucher system similar to what you're used to from the food bank, but it'll all be done in-house."

"Flea market? We don't make enough money there to feed one person for a week, let alone all of us."

Sam let the attitude slide. Calling the guys on it right then wouldn't help any of them. "The flea market is expanding to include Wednesdays and Thursdays, and we're going to grow our efforts to collect donations. We are undertaking some new fundraising, too, but the flea market is something we already have in place and know how to do. The learning curve will be short on this one, which is exactly what we need."

Half the men nodded their agreement while the other half stared wide-eyed or glared.

"Having said that, I'm open to ideas about other ways that we can raise funds on a weekly basis. I'm happy to hear any thoughts you have, now or later. Find me, bounce your idea off me, and we'll see what we can do. It's to my benefit — and ultimately yours — if you take ownership of this shelter with me."

"What about woodworking?"

Surely he'd misheard. "Woodworking?"

The man shrugged. "I do some whittling. It's not much, but I do it in my spare time and can donate whatever I carve for the flea market. Hiking sticks would probably sell well, especially if I carve a fancy something-or-other for the handhold. There might be someone here who knows how to make bigger stuff. Coffee tables, maybe, as long as they're not ugly. We just need wood."

"I can sketch portraits of people if I have a sketchpad."

"I used to work with leather. I can make bracelets and belts. I just need a few tools."

"Hook me up with some paracord, and I can make chairs. They're simple, not fancy for women, but men like them well enough."

"Take me to a salvage yard so I can get some hubcaps. I learned how to make yard art and picture frames with them. I used to do clocks, too, but I'm a little rusty."

Sam's chest swelled. Pride didn't even begin to touch what he felt for his men in that moment. "Alright then! If we're going to put this plan into action, we need two things — space to make stuff, and space to store it. That means two ground floor residents need to volunteer to move upstairs."

Alan raised his hand. "I can go up."

"Count me in. It's quieter up there anyway. Easier to study." Alonzo followed Alan's example. Besides his off-site job, the quiet man was working on a degree in accounting, so the ability to concentrate mattered.

The motel had twenty-six rooms in all, but some of those were taken up with storage, the learning center, the kitchen, and more. Sam would need to expand if the flea market became a growing enterprise. Either that or risk not having enough room to take in new residents.

He contemplated the field next to the motel. A storage area. A workshop. He could see the buildings where everyone else saw dirt and weeds. A gym with hanging boxing bags was a dream, too. For now, though, they needed to outlive the current year. Everything else was pure fantasy until he survived the City Council.

Sam pointed to three of the men. "Help Alan and Alonzo move. We'll meet back here in an hour to clean out the two rooms we're going to convert for storage and a workshop." He pointed to Franco. "Keep them on schedule." Then to Gideon. "I need to speak with you."

Gideon followed Sam as he strode to the other end of the parking lot. "What's up, Boss?"

Sam tugged on his goatee. "Check in with Skye and see if she's been able to renegotiate our contract with the flea market and ask if she needs help with anything. Offer to assist with calls or rounding up donations or whatever else she's doing."

"Sure thing, Boss." Gideon jogged off toward the office.

Yes.

Sam was a coward.

He could admit it to himself if no one else.

Being around Skye was more challenging with each passing day. If she joined him during his quiet time for the next month — something she'd only grudgingly agreed to — then he'd need to keep his distance the rest of the time.

CHAPTER 29

"Uh-huh… Yes, I understand… Of course… I'm sorry to have bothered you." Skye hung up the phone and waved Gideon in. "What can I do for you?"

"Boss sent me to ask if you talked to the flea market folks yet."

She nodded. "We had to commit to twelve months, but they gave us our same spot on Wednesday and Thursday that we have on Friday through Sunday."

"How much?"

"Only ten dollars a week, and they get to say *Proud Supporter of Samaritan's Reach* on their literature for one year."

Gideon's eyes twinkled. "That's going to give us as much publicity as it gives them, right?"

"Which is why I was happy to let them think they won the negotiation."

He chuckled. "Do you need help making calls or anything?"

"No, I'm good. I'm starting with the grocery stores to see if any would like to make donations of their expiring or damaged stock. Then I'm going to move on to the churches and ask for donations for the flea market."

"Expired groceries, huh?"

Skye wagged a finger at him. "I'm mostly going after their out-of-season items. You know, all the leftover stuffing after Christmas, ham after the Easter rush, those sorts of things. Expired foods are fine too, though. These days they really only put expiration dates on meat and dairy products. Most all nonperishables have a 'best by' date. You can still eat after that date without any danger. It just might not be as delicious."

"Well, don't go trying to poison me with some nasty, old, expired milk." He shuddered. "Now, is there anything I can do to help?"

She waved him away. "I concentrate better when it's quiet. Go do whatever you need to do out there, and I'll work the phones in here until it's time for me to head home."

"You should let us help. Teach us how so we can be useful, too."

Now that was an idea…

The foyer door opened again, and a deliveryman stepped through. "I have several boxes for Samaritan's Reach. Wanted to make sure someone was here before I loaded them all on my dolly."

Skye gave the man a small, welcoming wave. "We're here. Can we assist?"

"I'd love it, but company policy and all that. Gotta do it on my own." He pivoted back toward the steep driveway and his truck idling at the bottom.

If she was right, Samaritan's Reach was about to receive an anonymous donation of shoes, a hundred pair in different sizes and colors. About time, too. She almost wished she'd forked out the money for the expedited shipping.

Her grandfather would roll over in his grave if he knew she'd bought something online with a credit card. He'd always had such firm ideas about paying cash and keeping your account information private. Which was funny considering *his* customers had often paid online and with credit cards.

"Whoa, what's all this?" Sam approached from the left and eyed the four boxes as the deliveryman pulled away from the curb.

Skye tapped one of the boxes with her toe. "He just said it was a delivery for Samaritan's Reach. Guess you'll have to open them if you want to find out what's inside."

Sam slid a utility knife from his belt holster.

Ha. They'd come a long way since that first day on the airplane. A butterfly knife, indeed. Time sure had changed the way she saw Sam Madison.

Before he cut through the tape on the first box, she interrupted him. "Say. I was thinking about training a few of the men to make calls, too. For donations, at least. I'll probably handle the grocery calls myself, but if you're going to grow the flea market, donations will need to become an ongoing thing. So the guys might as well learn how."

Sam gave her a quick glance. "Grab two and train them. If you still have calls to make tomorrow, you can pull them back in or get two new guys."

She nodded and headed for the Learning Center. Maybe someone in there would want to help.

Skye was fifteen feet away when Sam's whoop caught up with her. Men came streaming out of various rooms to investigate the fuss. Pretty soon, the courtyard was filled with whooping and hollering as the men celebrated their windfall. She would have ordered them ages ago if she'd known something as simple as shoes could make so many people happy. She was at Samaritan's Reach every week, but she still had a lot to learn about life, especially life for these men.

One hour and four grocery stores later, Skye hung up the phone and dug her fingers into her forehead. She hadn't had a tension headache like this since…

Hm. She hadn't had one since coming to Rainbow Falls.

She fished a couple of ibuprofen out of the bottle in her purse and tossed them back without bothering to take a drink. Her coffee cup was empty, and whatever was left in the pot was likely burned beyond recognition.

Skye got the pills down with only minor gagging as the foyer door opened and Sam entered.

"You okay? You don't look so great."

She grimaced. "Gee, thanks. Just what every woman wants to hear."

He slid his hands in his pockets and leaned a hip against the wall by the half-door. "How'd the calls go?"

She let out a breath that turned into a yawn that she tried to cover it with her hand, but the laughter in his eyes told her he hadn't missed a thing. "You could at least pretend not to notice when I'm being unladylike."

"Is ladylike so important?"

"Not to me." Matt, one of the men who'd been helping her make calls, stood and headed toward the foyer door. "Give me a holler if you need more help."

Jerald, the other one, rose to his feet, too. "I can do it again, too, if I have to, but I'd rather be outside than in here any day. No offense."

Skye waved both men off. "None taken. Thanks for all your work."

After the men cleared the office, Sam gave her an appraising look. "So? Is ladylike important?

"It was to my grandparents." Thoughts like that would have typically thrown a wet blanket over her mood, but it didn't sting this time. Rainbow Falls had been good for her in more ways than one. Or maybe just Sam. Either way, she was a better person now than when she first boarded that plane and found herself seated next to a man she'd labeled as a criminal before they'd even left the tarmac.

"I'm sorry to hear that. Every girl should be encouraged to bait a hook and play in the mud now and then."

"My dad used to take me fishing before he died. He learned from his grandfather. I had my time in the mud. Who knows? I might make it back there someday. We'll see." She straightened the papers on the desk she shared with Sam. "So, for the damage… The flea market is letting us add Wednesday and Thursday for ten dollars each week, but we had to agree to a one-year contract, and during that year they can say on their promotional materials — or wherever they'd like — that they are a proud supporter of the shelter. It's win-win as far as I can see. We get publicity, and they get to look charitable."

Sam nodded. "That's a pretty sizeable discount off their regular price. I can live with that."

"I talked to every grocery store in town. Two of them said they would put items aside as they clean out their inventory but that we have to come claim them immediately. You need to meet with the store managers to iron out the details of when and where, and a Samaritan's Reach staff member must accompany any of our men who go to collect food. One of them indicated it would be a couple boxes each month, not a ton."

"Alright. Did you set up meetings, or am I supposed to schedule those?"

"Your calendar's on the computer, so I went ahead and scheduled the meeting with the couple-of-boxes store. I entered the appointment, but I also wrote it down for you." She handed him a blue piece of notepaper with the relevant information on it before tapping her fingernail against a note that remained on her desktop. "This other one said it used to support the food bank. We'll get the stuff that would have otherwise gone to them."

Sam's eyebrow took flight. "I'm not sure I want to take away from the food bank."

"I got the impression they were expecting your call. It was kind of weird." She passed him the blue paper that held the details. "He didn't want to make an appointment, though. He just said you should stop in when you get a chance."

He scanned the paper and frowned. "They were expecting a call from us?"

"Like I said — weird. When I introduced myself, he said he was glad I called and saved him the trouble."

Sam folded the papers and slipped them into his shirt pocket. "I'll check it out when I meet with him. What else do you have for me?"

"The men found three churches that are going to collect items from their members. One is going to announce it one Sunday and have people bring it in the next Sunday. Another is doing a couple weeks, I think, and the last one is going to do a month-long drive-type collection thing. I put follow-up dates in the calendar. The churches all said they'd give us a ring when the items are in, but I figure it can't hurt for us to call them if we don't hear back. We still have a few more churches on the list, too, so we're not done yet. I was wondering, too, about contacting convenience stores."

"Convenience stores?"

"Yeah, like they have at gas stations."

"What can they offer?"

"They might have grocery items they need to get rid of. A lot of them serve breakfast sandwiches and things like that. If they don't sell, do they just throw the food out? Why not donate it instead? I wanted to run it by you first, though, before I made those calls. There's a coffee shop in town, too, that does pastries and fresh breads. I'm sure they have bread left over at the end of the day. I could line up some places like that, but you'd need to be able to send people out to make rounds pretty much every day to collect from various sites."

"Let's hold off on that until we know what we'll be getting from the grocery stores. I don't want to end up with so much food that it ends up going to waste."

That made sense. "Fair enough. I don't mind putting in the legwork to make it happen, but only if you can follow-through. The gas alone might make it cost-prohibitive."

The corner of his mouth tilted up in the most seductive way. "We wouldn't use the van, don't worry."

Wait a second. Seductive? Had she just had that thought? "Um, gotta run."

She grabbed her purse, pushed away from the chair, and started to leave. Only, to get from the office to the foyer, she had to pass by Sam. Sam, who was leaning against the wall between the two spaces and leaving her only about twelve inches through which to squeeze herself. Maybe if she sucked it in…

Sam backed out of the way and held the half-door open for her. "Have a good afternoon, Skye, and thanks for coming in. For all your help on this, really. I've, uh, been a little more panicked about it than I want the men to know."

"Sure thing. No problem. Bye." She made it all the way down to her car at the curb before she stopped to breathe. Talk about an embarrassing exit. That might be her worst yet. Worse even than her sophomore homecoming when she ended up in the men's restroom on accident. She'd blathered apologies as she'd tried to flee the room with one hand over her eyes. She'd bumped into the wall and at least two boys before she'd gotten out of there. Still, somehow, this was worse.

Skye clicked her seatbelt into place, took a deep breath, and started her car. Tomorrow was a new day. It would be better. And she wouldn't have to see Sam again until Thursday.

Except.

Oh yeah.

She'd agreed to join him for his morning quiet time for the next month.

She leaned forward and caught herself just shy of banging her head against the steering wheel. With her luck, she'd smack the horn with her face or make the airbag deploy. Instead, she hit the gas harder than she meant, peeled out into a U-turn, and headed for the safety of home.

CHAPTER 30

Sam opened his Bible and looked across the small desk to Skye. She'd been avoiding eye contact since arriving. Based on their discussion the previous morning, he might have been tempted to think it was because they were going to be reading scripture. After her abrupt and tire-squealing exit yesterday afternoon, though, who knew?

Women were confusing, confounding, and contrary. Maybe contrary was too harsh. Complicated? Yeah. Complicated.

"Are we going to start?"

Sam blinked. "Of course. Sorry. Um… Ecclesiastes. I wanted to check out chapter three. Someone said something yesterday. I don't remember who or what, but at the time, it made me think about these verses, so I wanted to go back and study them." He ran his finger down the page in his Bible. Maybe what he wanted would jump out at him. "Aha. Here. Nine through twelve, but mostly eleven. Do you want me to read it, or do you want to?"

"Go ahead."

"He has made everything beautiful in its time. Also, he has put eternity into man's heart, yet so that he cannot find out what God has done from the beginning to the end."

Skye looked up from the Bible she'd brought with her, one so new the pages were still stuck together. "That's all? Yesterday you read a bunch of verses."

"It's like that sometimes. This verse came to mind yesterday, and I've been mulling it over since. What do you think it means to make everything beautiful?"

"I don't know. It's the Bible, so I'm not sure beauty means what we think. I doubt it's about flawless skin or the latest fashion."

Exactly. "I had the same thought. When we think *beauty*, we think of people or sometimes nature. When God talks about beauty, though, I'm not always sure. The verse says everything, right? So people, things, situations. It's not like I was a murderer or anything, but I did stuff before I knew Christ, stuff He didn't approve of. If He makes everything beautiful, does that mean He turns my past into something of beauty, though?"

"I — I don't know. Like you said, what about murder? That can't be beautiful."

"I'm not sure we get to tell God what is and isn't beautiful. He sees things beyond anything you or I will ever understand in this lifetime. Even if God's ways are often a mystery to me, I can say for certain that He redeemed my past. He took me out of it and saved me, sure. That was only the beginning, though. He transformed my past into something that allows me to reach men others can't." A fire started burning in his soul, the kind that told Sam he was on the right track and heading in the direction God had intended when He'd brought this verse to mind.

Skye looked around the room, her eyes delivering the message she wouldn't – that she wanted to change the subject. She didn't voice it, though, so Sam kept going. "I can help these vets because I know where they come from. I can minister to them — whether it's a Bible study or a hot meal — because of my past. I understand the things they battle, the demons and the temptations. God took a past I could have been ashamed of, and He made it into something that helps me do the things He wants me to do. He redeemed it by making it useful, and in its use lays the beauty."

Skye stared at him, the expression in her eyes falling somewhere between argument and question. "For something to be redeemed, a price has to be paid. I looked it up in the dictionary."

Sam nodded. "I've never thought of it, but that makes sense."

"You're going to tell me Jesus paid the price for your past, that He's the one who redeemed it."

He thumbed over to 1 Corinthians and found chapter seven. "Here, look." He slid the Bible over so she could see it and pointed to verse twenty-three. "You were bought with a price."

She gave her head the slightest shake.

Either she wasn't interested or didn't agree. He pulled the Bible back to his side of the desk and let her have the space she seemed to crave. "Let's go back to our original verse. See where it says God 'has put eternity into man's heart'?"

Skye followed along with her finger on the page of her Bible. "What does that mean?"

"A desire for God was built into our DNA. At least, I think so. He built us to crave eternity, but eternity means nothing without God, right? So He must have built us to desire Him, to want to be in His presence for all eternity. That's the only thing that makes sense to me, but I'm open to suggestions. Do you have any thoughts?"

"I don't buy it."

A tap at the front door pulled Sam from the desk before he could respond to her remark. Oh, right. Conway was coming by that morning. "Hey man. Did you just arrive?"

Conway shook his head. "Nah. Water heater's all fixed. It should hold for now, but you'll need a replacement before too much longer."

No surprise there.

"My shingle guy's still on the hook, too, if you can sort things out with City Council."

Sam shrugged. "I'm working on it."

Conway nodded as he made his way back out the door. "I figured. Let me know when you make some headway."

Sam settled into his seat again. "So what don't you buy? The part about eternity?"

She waved his words away. "The beauty thing. God can't make everything beautiful."

Skye was a complex communicator. So, what was she trying to communicate this time?

"He can't make drugs beautiful." Her chin jutted forward.

Ah, she was asking him a question disguised as a gauntlet-throwing challenge. But what, exactly, was the question?

I know I keep asking, but wisdom please.

Sam took a deep breath. He could do this. He could walk blindfolded into the minefield. For her. For Skye.

"God could wave a magic wand and change the whole world into a perfect utopia, sure. Who does that help, though? He wants us to learn and to grow, not to be automatons. We each have the power to change the world by showing mercy, love, and grace to the people we come into contact with. We change the world by letting Him change us first. Then we get to be a part of what He's doing by impacting the people around us. That's where the beauty lies. And if we all do it, it spreads."

"And the world is changed."

Okay, so it wasn't as easy as that. "I think so, if we lived in a perfect world. But we don't."

"So why bother, then?"

"I can't tell you why *you* should bother, but I can tell you why I do."

She tipped her head toward him, and he took it as her consent to keep talking.

"God didn't just save me from my past. He saved me for something, too, and He's at work in my life every day, growing me toward that thing, whatever it is."

"What is he growing you for?"

"I don't know yet. To tell you the truth, I'm not even sure if it's something in this world or the next. The thing is, though, God gave me this amazing gift. He saved me from myself, from a future much different from the one I'm currently living. If He did all that for me, how can I go through life and not want to tell other people about Him and about what He can do for them?"

She frowned but didn't tell him to stop.

"That's why I bother. Because He changed me for the better, and I want other people to have the same chance, that same hope."

She broke eye contact, and Sam sat back. He'd said what God had wanted him to say, and there was a special joy in that. Skye didn't appear to be interested in what he'd said, though. The glint in her golden eyes mocked the care he'd taken with his words and the part of his heart and soul he'd poured into his answer. Joy and dejection all rolled into one? He'd been there before, but it had never been quite so bittersweet.

"I'm glad that works for you and makes you happy. That doesn't mean it's for me, though."

Oh, how he wanted to argue. She was shutting the door, though, and Sam needed to let her. He couldn't muscle his way in. It didn't work like that. So he did the gracious thing and gave her a way out of the conversation. "I'm taking the van over to your friend's auto shop this morning. Want to come with? You ever seen where she works?"

Skye met his eyes again. "Her name's Fern, and you can't call it her auto shop while we're there. Her dad's kind of particular about that. I'd love to see it, though, and I'm not sure I can come up with a viable excuse otherwise."

"Why would you need an excuse?"

"Fern has a brother. He works there, too."

"That's a problem...?"

"We sort of dated in high school."

"Yeah, but... That was a long time ago, right?"

She rolled her eyes. "You don't know anything about small towns, do you?"

CHAPTER 31

Skye followed in her car while Sam drove the van to Green & Son Automotive. That man was infuriating. He talked about God with such a calm voice, as though everything he said was supposed to be perfectly reasonable.

So God worked in individual people, huh? What about her? Where had God worked? What about her mom? Nothing beautiful came out of her mom's death. Or her dad's. Nothing.

The weird thing, though, was that at the same time she wanted to pick up a book to throw at Sam, she also wanted to soak in his every word. Something inside of her responded to what he was saying. It was almost like she craved those words. She didn't like them, and she didn't want to hear them. Yet she was compelled to listen. Talk about not making any sense.

Then again, nothing in her life had made sense recently... and it had been more than a decade since she'd felt so alive.

Maybe one of these days she would tell Sam about her mom.

If he tried to tell her it was all beautiful, though...

Skye's jaw was clenched tight by the time she climbed out of her car and walked through the door Sam opened for her.

"Hey, Skye, I didn't think I'd see you this morning." Fern's greeting was a warm balm to her irritated soul.

Sam held out his hand. "Sam Madison. I brought the van in."

"Keys in it?"

Sam nodded.

"Give me a second." Fern disappeared through a solid brown door and came back a few minutes later. "We had an emergency brake job that's going longer than expected. It'll be at least an hour before we pull the van in, and since they're going to go over it bumper to bumper, it'll be a few hours after that before they're ready for you."

"Sure. Skye came along so she could give me a ride back."

Fern pushed a paper across the glass countertop. "Fill this out. We'll call you when we're ready to talk about what needs doing. Be sure to include your email address. You'll give us verbal authorization on the phone to proceed with whatever you want done, but then I'll follow up with an email going over those same points, and you'll need to reply to the email with a confirmation."

Skye grinned at Fern. "How's that working?"

"Outstanding, actually. When someone asks why, I just tell them we need a paper trail, and they're fine with that. Mr. Harchett's the only one who's gotten crotchety about it. He demanded to know why a paper trail matters, so I told him the truth. Some people give permission over the phone then refuse to pay the bill by claiming they didn't give permission. He's probably still complaining about it, but at least he's upset at whoever cheated us and not at Green & Son."

"How'd your dad take to the change?"

Fern leaned across the counter. "I haven't told him yet."

Skye winked at her friend. "Your secret's safe with me."

A few minutes later, Sam was climbing into Skye's compact car, and she was pulling out of the garage's gravel parking lot. When she took a turn a couple streets before the one that led to Samaritan's Reach, Sam cast a sideways glance at her but didn't say anything.

Until she pulled up in front of a house.

"Is this where you live?"

Skye scowled at the house. Could she go through with this? She forced her fingers to unlock themselves from the steering wheel and pull on the handle to open her door. She would just show him the place. She wasn't ready to do something about the idea floating around in the back of her mind.

Sam followed her, his solid presence at her back.

With feet like cement, she trudged up to the front door and slid the key into the lock. Once inside, she started flipping on light switches in every room until no shadow could find a resting place within those walls.

She circled back around to the living room and stood, hands on her hips. "I brought you here to show you the garage, but if that's all I show you, you'll ask all sorts of probing questions because that's what you do, even when you're trying not to. I don't want to deal with that right now. So I'm going to tell you a few things. It's not the whole story, but it's all I'm willing to give you today. I know I'm being cryptic. I just…"

"It's okay. Tell me what's on your mind. If I have questions, I'll save them for another time."

Skye was swallowed up by the look in Sam's eyes, a look filled with so much more there than she wanted to see. Integrity and honesty, faithfulness and compassion. His eyes, the ones she'd previously classified as icy, reflected the understanding of someone who had battle scars of his own. And for whatever reason, he looked *right* in her childhood home, like he belonged. Too bad she wasn't convinced that was a good thing.

She nodded and swept an arm to encompass the room they were in. "I lived here with my mom when I was younger. We stayed with my paternal grandparents while my dad was deployed. When Dad died, something went wrong between my mom and grandparents, so we ran away. We came here. My grandparents bought this house for us to live in. I didn't realize they owned it, not until I was going through their papers after they died."

She touched a picture hanging on the wall. Her tenth birthday. She posed with both her parents, and they all looked so happy.

Skye turned away from the picture, and her gaze sought Sam. "The house has a two-car garage, and I thought maybe Samaritan's Reach could use it for flea market storage. No one lives here, though. Nobody's lived here for a long time. It might become a target for thieves if people realize the garage is full but the house is empty. You can't afford to have stuff stolen."

"We converted one of the rooms at the shelter to use for flea market storage."

"I know. But if you want to grow the flea market and turn it into a real income stream, you'll need a place to store the items that don't move quickly. You can't sell winter coats in July, and you can't sell kayaks in November. Samaritan's Reach doesn't have enough space for that sort of thing. Or you could look into getting a trailer and keeping everything in it so you're not constantly loading and unloading the van."

Sam stuffed his hands into his pockets. "It's hard for you to be here."

"No questions."

The corner of his mouth twitched. "It wasn't a question."

Skye sighed and made her way through the house again, flipping off the lights. Her gut clenched with memories of the past and dreams of the future. The words were there, trying to make their way past her gritted teeth. If she could just loosen her jaw... "Would the shelter have use of a three-bedroom house with a two-car garage in the center of a middle-class neighborhood?"

"Honestly?"

She stared at him. "That's the type of relationship we have, right? Honest."

"I'd do almost anything for a home like this. When our guys graduate the leadership program, we throw them right back out into the world, and they flounder. I always wanted to have something like this. A kind of halfway house, where they came to be out from under the control of the shelter but still room with one another until they get their feet on the ground and have the confidence they need to stand on their own and succeed. A house like this would be perfect. Provided we had men in residence, we could use the garage for storage, and it would be safe."

Skye flipped the last light switch and left through the front door.

A halfway house.

Could she do that?

Could she let go of the bad memories and release this house to Samaritan's Reach? Could she give her childhood home a chance to become a place of hope? Was she strong enough to let go of the pain that held her anchored to this place?

Skye got into her car and waited for Sam to latch his seatbelt. As she pulled away from the curb, she said the words clogging her throat. "Would Samaritan's Reach want to buy it, or would I remain the owner and landlord?"

"Are we talking theoretical here, or concrete?"

She swallowed. "I'm not sure."

Skye kept her eyes trained on the road ahead, but Sam's presence still nearly overwhelmed her. He was far too big for her small car, and she didn't mean just his long legs and wide shoulders.

"I'd love to buy it, but we don't have the money. I sold my home to buy the old Silver Heart motel. I'm tapped out. I don't have anything else, and you've seen our books."

The steel bands tightening around her chest eased up, and Skye was able to take a breath. "I might not be prepared to sell it yet anyway, but I think I'm ready to see the house used for something positive."

Sam was silent for a minute before his soft words filled the space between them. "That's kind of like redemption. I don't know the details, but it's obvious the home has bad memories for you. You're willing to use it to do something meaningful, though. You're redeeming it. You're redeeming the years you spent there."

"Redemption comes with a price. Who's paying this price?"

"By the look on your face, I'd say you are. Jesus is willing to pay it for you, though, if you let Him."

CHAPTER 32

Sam watched Skye drive away after dropping him off at Samaritan's Reach. With each passing week, it was harder to watch her leave. He was getting closer and closer to danger where she was concerned.

There was something about her, though. Her strength. Her resolve.

Yep. He was in trouble.

Alan and Jack were waiting for his help to fill out their financial aid paperwork so they could start their online college courses during the upcoming term. He was going to have to put them off for a bit longer, though. He needed to clear his head.

He popped into the supply room, where Lance was doing inventory. "I'll be back in an hour."

Lance glanced up long enough to blink. "Sure thing, Boss. All's quiet on the home front."

Sam collected the gym bag from his room, tossed it into the backseat of his car, which he kept parked behind the shelter, and headed to the nearby boxing gym.

He pulled into the gym parking lot and jogged inside. Before the ink was dry on the sign-in sheet, he was gloved up, in his southpaw stance, and throwing some warm-up light jabs at the patched and worn bag.

There was something about the smell of sweat, leather, and testosterone that reminded him of his time in the Marines. He hadn't liked every part of his job, but he'd thrived in the environment of male camaraderie. The shelter provided a similar atmosphere, except he was the one in charge. Everyone looked to him to lead, and by default, that put him outside the circle of camaraderie. It had been a hard adjustment to make and was one with which he still sometimes struggled.

Ten minutes in, sweat poured down Sam's face. His head was starting to clear, too, allowing him to go back over the morning.

Those pictures on the walls of the home were something else. Skye and her family. Skye had been out of Rainbow Falls for over a decade, but the pictures still hung on the wall. The place could use a good cleaning. A thick layer of dust covered every surface, giving it an abandoned feel. Like everyone left for work one day and never returned, a museum piece of a now-extinct family.

And the look on Skye's face…

Agony.

It was the only word that came close to describing the pain in her eyes as she'd tried to matter-of-factly explain the house to him.

He hit the bag hard, let his gloved hand rebound back to him, and stood, deciding whether or not to swing again.

"Done already?"

Sam glanced around. Pastor Dennis was watching him. "Yeah, I think so."

"Want to talk about it?"

Sam would have rather punched the bag again, but he could use his grown-up words if forced. "You ever want to fix something, but you don't know how because you can't tell where it's broken?"

The pastor gave a somber acknowledgement. "More times than I care to admit, and it's almost always a person. I can replace a flat tire, but there's not much I can do to mend a broken past, a hurting heart, or a deadly addiction. Far as I can tell, those are all God's department, though. Not mine."

Sam rested gloved hands on his hips as he walked around in tight circles to cool down from the exercise he hadn't properly warmed up for to begin with. "No argument there, but this is one I wish I could fix on my own because I'm not sure she's willing to take help from Him."

Something passed over the pastor's face. Remorse? That didn't make sense. He must have misread it.

"Women are complicated creatures, no two ways about it."

Maybe it hadn't been remorse, but something was definitely off about the pastor. Everything had been fine until he'd mentioned... The pastor had a problem with him wanting to fix a woman? Or maybe not a problem...

Remorse. What had it meant?

Something had been off with Pastor Dennis for a while, and now was as good a time as any to try and get some answers. "Skye took me to the house she lived in with her mom back in the day."

All color drained from the pastor's face. Whoa. He'd hoped for a reaction, but he hadn't expected anything like this.

Pastor Dennis blinked several times, turned around and stalked out of the gym without a word.

Sam took two steps after him before stopping.

Should he run after him and demand answers?

No.

He was back in the same situation he'd found himself in too often with Skye. Standing in the middle of an unmapped minefield.

He needed a clear head before he traipsed out there into the middle of that mess. Metaphorical though they were, explosives were dangerous business.

Instead of chasing after the pastor, Sam showered, dressed in some fresh clothes, and headed out to his car. He needed to squeeze in a visit to a grocer.

Ten minutes later, he pulled into the parking lot of Lucky Luke's Grocerama. Who named their grocery store Grocerama? Every time Sam saw the name, he thought *gross*... Oh well. Nobody had asked him, right?

Sam made his way over to Customer Service. "Hi there. Name's Sam Madison, and I'm with Samaritan's Reach. I was told your manager wants to talk to me."

The pregnant twenty-something girl behind the counter picked up the phone at her elbow. "Somebody from Samaritan's Reach is here for you." Her eyes widened. "Sure thing." She rested the phone back in its cradle while looking at Sam with new interest. "Luke'll see you. Go straight past dairy, take a right at the bathrooms, pass them, and circle around to the locked door. There's a doorbell. Ring it with two short bursts, and he'll let you in."

"Thank you for your help." Sam headed through the maze of pasta, produce, and pet food. He turned at the restroom sign when he got to dairy and followed the hallway till it dead-ended at a dark brown fire door with a doorbell button half-hidden behind a fire extinguisher.

He snaked his finger in behind the extinguisher and gave the button two short pushes. Before he could get his finger back out from behind the extinguisher, the door opened.

"Sam, right?"

"Uh, yeah." Sam shook the man's hand. Why had he always thought of grocers as short and stout? This guy rivaled him for height and had nothing to him but skin and bones.

"I'm Luke. Follow me back."

Sam did as he was told. "I believe you talked to someone from our office about grocery donations."

Luke glanced back over his shoulder. "Skye, right?"

Sam nodded as Luke indicated an office.

As soon as Sam was through the door, Luke closed it tight and pointed to a chair. "Have a seat."

Just like a movie that had been playing last night on television. Sam was now buried in the bowels of a grocery store, and the only people who knew where he was were Luke and the girl from the Customer Service counter. The office door was closed tight, which either meant Luke wanted privacy, or he was up to something nefarious…

Sam needed to cut back on late-night horror movies.

"So…Luke? As in Lucky Luke's?"

The scarecrow of a man settled behind his desk and nodded. "My grandfather started the business, and since he slapped his name on it, the name had to be passed down. At least that's the way he saw it. My dad, too."

"Not many family businesses around anymore."

"Especially grocery stores. Too many big chains trying to take over."

"How do you fight the competition?"

"We sell a lot of locally sourced produce and specialty items. People have come to think of us as their year-round farmer's market, in a way. As grocery competition heated up between the local stores, we plugged into a niche market, and it ended up fitting us pretty well."

Sam leaned back in his chair. "Skye tells me you'd like to help out Samaritan's Reach."

"We would, but there's a little more to it than that. It's political, if you must know." Luke grimaced. "I can tell you what's going on, or you can stay in the dark. Either way is fine with me. I figured you deserve a choice, though."

"Honesty works for me."

Luke tipped his chair back and twirled a pen in his left hand. "This is more about transparency than honesty, but the point's valid. So…" His chair *thunked* forward again. "Wyatt's a distant cousin. We've been helping the food bank since he first took over and pitched it to me as a promotional win-win. And it has been. Our niche market likes that we help those in need, especially when it means none of our produce ends up in the dumpster out back."

"Sounds like a respectable use of resources." Sam leaned forward, elbows resting on his thighs.

"Wyatt came to me about what the City Council is doing. He asked me to shift my donation from the food bank to Samaritan's Reach."

Of their own volition, Sam's legs stretched, and he stood. "What? Why? The food bank needs the help just as much as we do."

Luke was virtually unflappable. Sam's sudden movements didn't even make him blink. "That's pretty much what I said, but he blew me off. Said this was the right thing to do, and I couldn't change his mind. Also told me to make sure you don't say anything about it. If word gets back the City Council, the food bank might end up in their sights, and Wyatt doesn't want that."

Sam sat back down. "He's putting his neck out for my guys."

"Yeah, well, I've got his back. I'll take full responsibility for it if word gets out that I moved my donation. I won't let it splash back on Wyatt."

"Because he's family?"

"Because he's right. The family part is a bonus."

Sam took a deep breath. *Thank you, God.* "Tell me what I can do to help you."

Luke squinted at him. "Send one or two of your men over to do trash collection around the outside edge of the parking lot every couple of weeks. You know, where people's junk gets stuck in the weeds. The east side is the worst."

"Consider it done."

"Otherwise, just come each Tuesday at 5am with a big enough vehicle and enough men to haul out what we've put aside for you. Pull around to the loading dock in the back and ring the buzzer there."

"Is that one hidden behind a fire extinguisher?"

"You'd think that'd deter people, right?" Luke snorted. "That's why we had to set up a ring code. I was spending half my days running over to the door to see who was there only to catch the backside of some kid running away. Or Mrs. Peterson. She's a hundred if she's a day, and even with those glasses, she can't see a thing, including the four-foot-tall picture of a woman on the door to the lady's restroom."

That must have been a hassle-and-a-half.

"Anyway, most weeks it's produce and dairy. The last week of the month is a lot of nonperishables. Some other things are hit and miss, but that's the basic rundown. So I'll see you next Tuesday at five in the morning."

Luke held out his hand, and the men shook. Then the grocer opened the office door and led Sam back to the brown metal door.

Before long, Sam was in his car again and heading back to Samaritan's Reach.

God was faithful. It had felt like touch and go lately, but God had never turned away from their need or from the men He'd called Sam to help.

He couldn't wait to tell the guys.

Sam held his Bible open to the book of Hebrews. He was ready to start his morning Bible study, but the words wouldn't come. Skye sat there, hiding behind her coffee cup and trying to act as if yesterday hadn't happened. At least, that's how it came across.

"What chapter?"

He snapped his gaze down to the page in front of him to see where he was. "Four."

"Which verses?"

The highlighted ones, of course. Because everyone knew that when you had no idea what you were doing, you went to the highlighted verses, the ones that had meant something to you at some point in the past even if you couldn't remember when or for what reason.

Then again, maybe that was just Sam's shortcut. Either way… "Fifteen and sixteen. You want to read them?"

Her hesitation lasted only a second, long enough for her to flinch and try to act as if she hadn't. "For we do not have a high priest who is unable to sympathize with our weaknesses, but one who in every respect has been tempted as we are, yet without sin. Let us then with confidence draw near to the throne of grace, that we may receive mercy and find grace to help in time of need."

Sam drew in a deep breath and slowly released it. Now he remembered why he'd liked those verses enough to highlight them. "What does it mean when it says Jesus was tempted like us?"

Skye bit her bottom lip before answering. "You can't live life on this planet without being tempted in some way, shape, or form. Whether we're tempted to lie, lash out at someone, or hide from things that hurt — we all face temptation."

"You're not the same person now as when you first came to Samaritan's Reach. Do you remember that first day?"

"Don't remind me. Not my finest moment."

"You were scared."

She gave a single nod.

"You were scared before the incident with Alan."

Another nod.

"Do you think fear's a temptation?"

Skye sucked in a big breath, held it for a long time, then gave another single nod as she released the air. "Not for everyone, but for some."

A knock at the foyer door interrupted them. Man, he was going to need to put up a *Do Not Disturb* sign at the rate they were going. What happened to the good ol' days when nobody bothered him before he propped the door open in the mornings?

Sam rounded the counter. A young woman stood on the other side of the glass door. People didn't usually end up at Samaritan's Reach on accident, but it did occasionally happen. He pulled the door wide. "Can I help you?"

"I, uh…" Her words faltered, and she chewed on her bottom lip while staring at her hands. "I'm looking for my uncle."

Sam's heart clenched. Not many family members came around. Most of the men traveled far from home before landing at Samaritan's Reach. If she was someone local looking for a lost relative… "What's his name?"

She met his gaze, and her eyes pleaded with him. "Gideon Sharpe."

He did his best to keep his face blank, but had she given him a front kick to the solar plexus, he couldn't have been more surprised. "Gideon?"

"Is he still here? I know sometimes…um…homeless people… They move on a lot. But I need to find him. It's important."

"All guests sign in." He stepped aside, allowing her to enter the foyer. Then he pointed her toward the clipboard on the counter.

She wrote her name. *Gabbie Pierce*. She pulled out her wallet and copied her driver's license number onto the form without a word.

Sam got a look at the picture on her license. It matched her face. And Gideon's sister's name had been Pierce.

The girl put the pen down and swung to him, her fingers clasped tightly together in front of her.

"Follow me." Was Gideon ready for this? Things had gone so badly at his sister's house. Did he even know he had a niece?

They reached Gideon's door before Sam got far enough through his thoughts. If his brain had been a little more in gear, he'd have started praying as soon as they exited the office. Instead, he'd been worrying.

It was too late for anything wordy, but he could still get in a few words.

Please help.

Sam took a deep breath and knocked.

The door opened. "Hey, Boss. What's up?"

"There's someone here to see you."

Gideon's eyebrows shot up as he tried to peer over Sam's shoulder.

Sam blocked the whole doorway on purpose, though. He wanted to give the resident a second or two to adjust to the idea. "Your niece is here."

The eyebrows shot higher still, so high they looked like little waves surfing over the tops of his spectacles. "Niece? I didn't know... I have a niece?"

"Looks like it."

When Gideon reached out to push Sam aside, the bigger man shifted out of the way.

"Remember the rules. Your door has to stay open." The words were probably wasted on Gideon. He wasn't listening to Sam. He only had eyes for his niece.

"Hi, Uncle Gid. I'm Gabbie."

Tears welled in Gideon's eyes, and Sam took that as his cue to leave.

He returned to the office. Skye sat where he'd left her. "Is that really Gideon's niece?"

"Seems so."

"Is he okay?"

Sam shrugged. "I don't think we'll know that till after she's gone."

He settled back at the desk and looked at the passage they'd been talking about. "So...fear."

A grin shaped her mouth into something...

No. Not kissable. That was *not* where his mind had been heading. Uh-oh, no way.

Skye lifted an eyebrow. "Yep. Fear and temptation. Unless you'd rather talk about Gideon and his niece."

Sam shook his head as he yanked together the wandering ribbons of his thoughts. "I don't see fear in you anymore, not for a while now. Did you overcome it?"

She picked up a retractable ballpoint pen and started screwing and unscrewing the base that held the ink cartridge in place. "It's not there all the time now, but it still shows up now and then. Certain things make it worse, but even then, it's not controlling me. I used to have all-out panic attacks and this constant anxiety that kept my blood pressure high and my enthusiasm for life low. It's no way to live."

"What changed?"

Before Skye could answer — or avoid answering, as her thinned lips and flared eyes indicated — a knock sounded on the foyer's glass door.

Pastor Dennis stood on the other side, a strained look on his face.

CHAPTER 33

Pastor Dennis walked in, took the knit cap from his head, and nodded to them.

Skye stood to go. "I can leave you gentlemen alone."

"No." The pastor shifted from one foot to another. "It's you I need to speak to, Skye, but it affects Sam and the shelter, too, so I'd like him to stay if that's alright."

Every time the pastor had looked at her oddly flashed through Skye's mind. "What's this about?"

He waved toward the desk. "Sit. I think better on my feet. Must be all the preaching."

Skye sank back into the desk chair, but Sam continued to stand with his arms crossed as he stared at the pastor.

"I, uh, wasn't always a pastor."

Why did Skye have the feeling she wouldn't like where this was going?

"In fact, I used to deal drugs here in Rainbow Falls."

Skye jumped up from her chair and grabbed her purse. "I need to leave."

Sam looked back and forth from her to the pastor before closing his eyes for a second. He was praying. She was sure of it. He was hurt, too. It was plain as day in the strained lines of his face and the way his shoulders had curved forward at the pastor's words. She should have just told him about her mom and her childhood in Rainbow Falls. Weeks ago. Or even that morning. Anytime.

By not telling him, though, she'd been able to pretend — in a weird, small, bizarre way — that life was different. She could ignore the past if nobody dared bring it up to her. Except that it still ate at her on the inside, which was why she kept pushing others away, including Sam. Including God.

"I need to say this." Pastor Dennis' plaintive words stalled Skye's exit.

She sank back into the desk chair, slapped her purse down on the desktop, and crossed her arms, mimicking at least part of Sam's posture of moments ago.

"I was your mom's dealer back in the day."

Bile rose in Skye's throat.

"She texted me and asked me to bring something by. When I reached the house, she was dead. I'm the one who found her body and called the police."

Skye tried to breathe, but the breath wouldn't come. Everything closed in around her, and darkness lined the edge of her vision.

"Skye. Skye, look at me. Are you okay?" Sam kneeled in front her, his work-roughened hands holding her in place as she fought to pull air into her lungs.

She blinked slowly, trying to force herself to act normal, but every movement — even that of her eyelids — felt hampered by a heavy, smothering weight. "I'm…fine…"

Sam stayed there in front of her, his eyes glued to her face, as the pastor continued talking.

"I'd never seen a dead body before. I was young, I guess. Certainly dumb. I didn't realize how much damage I was doing. I could have fled, but I called the police instead, and I waited for them. It was a mistake at the time, but it ended up being the best thing for me."

Her pulse thundered in her head, but not quite loud enough to drown out his words.

"Several months into my sentence, a chaplain came to visit me. I started going to church services in prison. I only went so I could get out of my cell for a little while, but it eventually made sense, and Jesus saved me. I don't know why it was that day and not the day before or the month before. I don't know why it had to be in prison instead of before I started dealing drugs. I don't understand all that, but I know He saved me, and I'll spend all eternity being grateful for that."

Skye swallowed and forced her eyes open. Sam was right there, and she stared into the vivid blue of his eyes. They were filled with so many things she'd never allowed herself to see before. Emotions from sadness to joy and from worry to love pooled in his eyes, but they were all colored by the raw pain etched on his face, a face she'd previously found frightening.

The irony wasn't lost on her. When she'd first seen Sam, she'd thought he looked like someone who had been in prison. Instead, the pastor — who looked like one would expect a pastor to look — had passed time behind bars.

Pastor Dennis continued. "When I got out of prison, I wanted to start a church. None would have me, of course. Who wants a pastor with a record? I had this vision, though, for a church that would open its doors to the undesirables, to the wretches, the poor, the homeless…"

She had to get out of there. She couldn't sit a minute longer and listen to this man talk about church as though what he said held any weight with her.

"How I ended up at the church I now lead is a long story, and I won't go into it. I needed to tell you, Skye, how sorry I am for the actions of my youth, for the choices I made that ultimately contributed to your mother's death. Not a day goes by that I don't look in the mirror and remember who I was and the damage I did." His focus migrated to Sam. "As for Samaritan's Reach, I hope that you will continue to bring your residents to New Hope, but if you decide you can't, I understand." He picked up his knit cap from the counter and nodded to them both. "I'm sorry."

A second later, he was gone, and Skye held in a scream. Every emotion she'd locked up tight in a little box and thrust to the back of her heart had been ripped out of its hiding place. It was too much. It was all just… too much.

She shoved as hard as she could, and Sam toppled backward.

She grabbed her purse, and she ran.

Skye got to her car, but it took forever to get the keys out. When she finally did, her fingers fumbled, and she dropped them to the asphalt.

She reached for them, but Sam was there with his steady, strong presence. He picked up the keys, stuffed them in his pocket, and put his arms around her.

The pain, grief, and guilt consumed her. Was she in her right mind? Not hardly.

She pounded both fists against his muscled chest, but he only pulled her closer with his gentle arms.

She screamed into the cotton of his t-shirt, but he didn't let go.

She choked on her sobs, and he rubbed her back while whispering words in a hoarse voice, words that barely penetrated the typhoon of emotion threatening to capsize her whole life.

"It's okay... You're safe... It'll be okay... You can do this... It's okay..."

Only, nothing would ever be okay again.

"I killed my mother. It's my fault she died."

CHAPTER 34

I killed my mother. It's my fault she died.

Sam's hand, which had been rubbing Skye's back, stalled.

He'd misheard her. He had to have misheard.

He started rubbing her back again, but she pushed him away.

Tears ran down her cheeks, and her amber eyes were bloodshot. "Your platitudes don't change anything."

He knew what it was like to push someone away because you didn't think you deserved to be comforted. He understood more about what Skye was going through than he wanted her to know, but he also knew she wouldn't believe him. Nothing he said would matter to her. He needed to show her.

Sam took a step closer to her, but kept his voice just above a whisper. "Tell me about your mom."

She looked away from him, wrapped her arms around her middle, and started talking. "I graduated high school. My grandparents came to Rainbow Falls and offered to pay for college if I went to live with them. I welcomed their offer. I didn't know how else to cover the cost of college. I hadn't won any great scholarships… It seemed like the best way. And I was tired of living with my mom. I knew she loved me, but the up and down of never knowing from one day to the next how she was going to be… It was old, and I was tired. The constant worry wore me down. She loved me, but her love for me wasn't enough to make her kick the habit. Which is a child's perspective, but that's what I was — a child. Sometimes I'd come home from school and find her unconscious. Sometimes laying in her own vomit. She missed Dad so much. It's like her whole world fell apart when he died. She didn't know how to function anymore. I wasn't enough for her, and… Like I said, I was tired. So I took their offer."

Oh, how he wanted to reach out to her. To pull her into a hug and hold her and take away all her hurts. She didn't want to be touched, though, and no matter how much he wanted to make this better, no matter how much it was wired into his male DNA to want to fix things, this one was beyond him. The only person who could get inside her heart and heal this wound was Jesus. Sam needed to remember that and to help Skye see it, too. Without pushing her away, if he was lucky. So he stood there, and he didn't touch her even though it was ripping out *his* heart not to. "What happened?"

"Mom didn't handle my leaving too well. She would call me all the time and want to talk to me, but I had school, and I got tired of the slurred conversations. I was eighteen and selfish, and I wanted a fresh start. During my first month at college, I got the call. Overdose. She was dead, and I was to blame. She'd called three times that morning, but I sent her to voicemail every single time because I didn't want the downer of talking to her. Every time we spoke, the conversation hung over me like a cloud for the rest of the day, and I

was sick of it. So I didn't answer, and she died, and..."
She swallowed. "And the guilt has been killing me ever since."

"You're not responsible for your mom's choices."

"My brain says you're right, but my heart doesn't agree, and I don't think it ever will."

"What about your grandparents? What did they say?"

Her mouth turned down, and her chin quivered. "Good riddance. They were my dad's parents. They'd never liked my mom, and they thought the world was better off without her. They were heartless, cold, unfeeling people. Maybe they hadn't always been. I don't remember them being like that when Dad was alive, but I was young. Who knows? By the time I went to live with them, though, they were old and bitter. Every time I got a B on a college exam, they would remind me that I didn't want to turn out like my mom. When I graduated and wanted to take some time to figure out what to do next with my life, they put me right to work in the company business because idleness was temptation wrapped in a pretty package, and I might be tempted to turn out like my mom. A few years later, when I wanted to leave the family company and strike out on my own, they said I was just like Mom, ungrateful for everything they'd given me. I didn't have the energy to fight them. I was still tired, too tired to stand up for myself. So I stayed."

"Skye..."

She offered a weak version of a sad smile. "Don't worry. I didn't kill them."

Sam didn't return the smile. He couldn't. Her pain tore at him until he was sure he'd see blood if he looked down at himself.

"They hit an icy patch of road this past winter. Their car spun out of control and went over an embankment. There were witnesses, and the police were called immediately, but by the time the rescue workers could get to them, they were already dead. Suddenly I had a big, empty house in the city and a company I hadn't ever wanted to work for, let alone own."

"But you didn't sell. You put your employees first, even though it couldn't have been easy."

"If things had been different, my dad would have inherited, and he'd have done the right thing. He never would have sacrificed people for a profit." Her eyes — eyes that normally made him think of honey — flashed like liquid gold in the midmorning sun. "Besides, it wasn't their fault. Everyone I've ever met at Treasure Valley Chux has treated me well. They've shown me more kindness and compassion in the months since my grandparents' death than my grandparents did in all the years I was with them. It's always been that way. They're upstanding people."

"You're upstanding people."

Skye held out her hands. "Keys?"

Sam slipped them from his pocket, put them into her hand, and closed her fingers over them. He didn't let go, though. The minute she drove away, she might drive straight out of his life, and he wasn't ready for that. "What are you going to do with the company?"

She tugged her hand free. "Jette is finding an attorney for me. I wanted to keep it under wraps until I can make the announcement, so I decided not to use the company's attorneys. I'm heading back to Boise for several meetings over the next few weeks. Our annual picnic will be taking place, too. I've been working on my speech. I hope they'll appreciate it. I hope they'll understand that I want to do what's best for them."

"Just be honest. Let them see your heart."

"I'm not very good at that. The whole heart thing."

"Skye…"

Centimeter by agonizingly gradual centimeter, she raised her eyes to meet his. "I need to go."

"You said you killed your mom, that she OD'd, and you never saw her again. When you told me those things, your voice broke on only one of those phrases."

She watched him as though trying to figure him out.

"When you said you never saw your mom again — that's where your pain was. Not with the rest of it."

"What does that have to do with…?"

"Don't run away from the friends you have here. Otherwise, someday you may be saying those same words — that you never saw them again — following some other tragedy. And it'll tear you up."

She glanced at the car, at her keys, and even at Samaritan's Reach. Not at him, though. "I need to go."

Sam reached out and brushed his fingers against her cheek. "I'll be praying for you."

She closed her eyes and leaned into his touch. For a split second, he thought she might stay. It wasn't to be. She opened the car door, and pulled forward on the street to make a U-turn. He stood there, hands by his side, and watched her drive away and out of his life.

She didn't want to face her past. She didn't want to face the emotion. And she especially didn't want to face God. Until she could do those things, she wasn't going to want to face him.

Shoulders hunched, Sam climbed the steep driveway up to the shelter's entrance. The men were up and about and no doubt wondering where he'd gone off to.

"Everything all right, Boss?" Franco called from the doorway to the room where they did their yoga.

No. Everything wasn't all right, but he couldn't say that. These men needed him to be rock-solid and steady. They depended on him for that.

Sam headed toward Franco, but movement to his right drew his eye.

Gideon's niece was leaving. Her face was blotchy, and her eyes were red-rimmed. She met his gaze, though, and didn't flinch away. "Thank you for taking care of Uncle Gid, for looking out for him like you have."

Then she was gone, like a wisp of wind. When a motorcycle roared to life, he looked out toward the street and caught sight of Gabbie Pierce snapping the strap on her helmet.

Sam veered away from Franco. His long legs ate the courtyard up and, in no time at all, he was once again knocking on Gideon's door.

"Come on in."

Sam pushed the door open and found Gideon sitting in his one chair, his hands resting on the small, scarred table. "Want to talk about it?"

Gideon had the same red-rimmed eyes as his niece. "Shelly died two weeks before I showed up. Ovarian cancer."

Stones tumbled in Sam's stomach. "I'm sorry."

"Me, too. She died not knowing I was okay, that I was finding my way back."

"Her husband…?"

"Dan. Gabbie thinks the world of him. Says he was just grief-stricken. She might be right. I don't remember much about him from before, but Shelly wouldn't have married a jerk."

"He may not have welcomed your visit, but he told Gabbie you'd come by."

Gideon nodded. "Yeah, there's that. He wouldn't tell her where I was, though. Until he found out she was driving to every homeless shelter she could find looking for me. Guess he decided he didn't want his little girl putting herself in danger like that."

"He's a good dad."

"She wants to come back and see me again. She…" Gideon's words broke off again.

Sam sank to the floor and stretched his legs out, settling in for as long as it took.

"She says Shelly always loved me, that she understood how much the war messed me up. She…" He blinked several times. "She didn't blame me for running."

"That has to feel good."

"Maybe. Eventually. Right now, it mostly hurts. She named Gabbie after me."

Sam lifted an eyebrow.

Gideon looked back down at the table. "My folks couldn't decide between Gideon and Gabriel. Since Shelly couldn't think of a girl version for Gideon, she named her girl Gabriella. In honor of me."

"She loved you."

"More than I deserved. She was pregnant when I left. I never even knew."

"Would you have stayed if you'd known?"

Gideon shrugged. "I don't know. I might've tried, but I don't think it would have stuck. I was a mess."

"So what do you do from here?"

Gideon lifted his gaze again. "She wants to get to know me. Wants to be a part of my life. I don't know… What if I end up hurting her the same way I hurt Shelly?"

Sam leaned his head back against the wall. "Are you that same man?"

"No."

"Then you probably won't make the same choices."

"How can I be sure?"

"I don't suppose you can, but we serve a God of second chances, a God who believes in restoration and redemption. You might feel like selling yourself short now and then, but don't sell Him short."

"Do you believe He wants to redeem the mess I've made of my life?"

"Not a doubt in my mind. The question is, are you willing to let Him?"

"If I got that business degree I was talking about, do you think you'd have any use for a used-up old man like me around here?"

"As in paid staff?"

Gideon stared at his hands as he nodded.

"A business degree isn't bad. Neither is a nonprofit business degree or a counseling degree. We all wear a lot of hats in a small operation like this. Regardless of the degree, you finish the leadership program all the way through and, as long as I haven't been shut down by the city, I'll find a place for you here. The pay's lousy, and the hours are long, but the work is worth it."

Gideon flexed his hands, clenching them into fists and releasing them a couple of times before setting them back down on the table. "I want to be in Gabbie's life, and I want to be worthy of that honor. The way I see it, God's the only one who can make that possible. But me doing something with my life that matters is a start."

CHAPTER 35

September

Nearly two weeks had passed since Skye had left Sam in her rearview mirror.

She wasn't going back, either. Not yet, anyway.

Someday…

Sam had made a valid point. Never seeing her mom again was an open sore that had festered too long. Was she brave enough not to repeat that mistake? Maybe. Maybe not.

She didn't want regrets, though. Even if she never returned, she'd stay in touch with the friends who'd loved her through her previous long absence.

As for Bible study… She hadn't honored her commitment to meet with Sam for thirty days, but she'd still managed to crack open her Bible every morning and read something. At least that way, she could tell herself she'd kept her word.

"Miss Blue, Juan Clarion is here to see you."

Skye glanced from the tree-filled Boise view to the intercom on her desk. She pushed the appropriate button. "Send him in."

The attorney, older than she'd expected him to be, with silver liberally threaded through his wavy black hair, entered the office she'd taken over from her grandfather. "Miss Blue."

"Mr. Clarion, it's nice to meet you." Skye rose and reached her hand across the mahogany desk.

His grip was warm but not that uncomfortable sweaty warm. An excellent start. "Jette asked me to help in any way I can, so here I am. And please, it's Juan."

The two settled back into their seats as Skye contemplated the man across from her. "Jette said you met in law school."

He flashed a smile. "Study partners whenever we shared a class."

"I expected you to be younger."

Laughter sparked in his dark eyes. "Yeah, well, it took me a while to get my act together and figure out what I wanted to do with my life."

"What kind of law do you practice?"

"I specialize in immigration law, but I also work with businesses that are unfairly discriminated against by the government because of ethnicity."

"What I need you to do is different than you're used to."

Juan acknowledged her words with the dipping of his chin. "I wouldn't have made it through law school without Jette. I owe her. She'd have done this herself if she was licensed to practice in Idaho."

Silence fell between them as Skye continued to appraise the man Jette had sent to her. He wouldn't have made it through law school without Jette… What was she supposed to make of that?

"If it helps, I've written up similar documents for two other businesses, both smaller than your enterprise, but still, I have some experience. Jette reviewed those cases and decided I was qualified."

Skye gave a single nod. "I figured as much. Jette's a lot of things, but a slouch isn't one of them. So, is there any way we can keep this quiet? I'd like to announce plans at the company picnic, and I don't want my people getting wind of it beforehand."

"Generous and sneaky. I like it. We can meet at my office, or we can discuss details over dinner or coffee whenever you'd like. We'll keep it away from the prying eyes and ears of your employees for as long as you like."

This was going to work. She would pull it off. Then she'd be free of the noose left to her by her grandparents.

Her soul breathed easier.

Skye got home later that night, kicked her high-heeled shoes off, and padded through the den of the too-big house she'd inherited. When she reached her grandfather's desk, she sat down, booted up the laptop she'd forgotten there that morning, and picked up the house phone to dial Jette's number.

"What did you think of Juan?"

"Why, I'm fine Jette. Thanks for asking. And how are you?"

Her friend snorted. "If I weren't fine, I'd say so."

"Right. I'm not so sure I believe you."

"Seriously. Stay on topic. Juan?"

Skye gave in. She liked to needle Jette, but only so far. That woman had some impenetrable walls. Skye still didn't know what had put them there, but she knew from personal experience that walls were generally unbreachable until the person was ready. "Juan was great. I expected some young hottie when you told me you went to law school with him. He's old enough to be my…"

"Don't you dare say father. He's not *that* old. I don't think. Besides, what does that have to do with anything?"

Skye chuckled. "He said he's done something similar before and that you inspected those documents already."

"They were both smaller, but his work is solid. He'll be able to help you, and he'll keep it on the QT like you want."

"I figured. I was actually calling about something else, though."

"Such as?"

Skye drew in a deep breath of air, held it for a couple seconds then released it. "I'd like to hire you for a legal matter there in Rainbow Falls."

Jette's momentary silence was heavy on the line. When she spoke, her hesitation was clear. "What do you need?"

Skye moved the laptop out of her way, propped her elbows on the desk in direct defiance of everything her grandfather had ever drummed into her head, and closed her eyes. "You remember my mom's house, right?"

"Sure."

"My grandparents kept it after my mom died. I inherited it."

"Wow. I had no idea."

"Yeah."

"So what's my role?"

Skye forced the air in and out of her lungs. "Clear it out and put everything into storage. Then I need you to draw up paperwork. I'm going to lease the house to Samaritan's Reach."

"For storage or for people?"

"Both. Men from the leadership program will be in the house. The garage will be storage."

"Is Samaritan's Reach leasing it, or are the men?"

"Um…" Did she know the answer to that? "I'm not sure. Which is best for the shelter?"

"The men leasing directly from you would remove liability from the shelter, but having Samaritan's Reach listed as the official tenant would give you more protection."

Skye, phone clutched between ear and shoulder, and elbows still on the desk, started picking at a cuticle. "I can absorb the liability better at this point, but the shelter's also going to use the garage to store items for the flea market. The last I knew, only one of them in the leadership program has a paying job."

"You need to tell me what to do."

Men might be moving in and out as they graduate through the program. Changing lessees every few months would be a pain. "Okay. Set it up so that there are four tenants listed on the lease with Samaritan's Reach as one of the tenants since they'll be using the garage. Give them the first three months free."

The sound of pen scratching on paper came across the line. "Rental rate?"

"I have no idea. Find out whatever's normal for Rainbow Falls and then cut it by ten percent."

"Anything else?"

Skye was excited about this part. "I have a plan for helping the men reduce their rent. A trade for volunteer hours. I want these men, as they leave the shelter, to remember to give back. I also know Sam's a little worried about them going out into the world and falling back into old ways."

Jette's pen fell silent. "By giving them a reason to stay connected to Samaritan's Reach, you're putting them back into Sam's sphere of influence so he can keep an unobtrusive eye on them."

"Something like that."

"You're a good person, Skye."

"Eh. Don't go getting all mushy on me."

"When pigs fly and donkeys learn how to roast marshmallows while dancing the waltz."

Skye still had a few more things she hoped to get to that evening, so she let Jette go. "I'll mail the key first thing in the morning."

"I'm allowed to hire people to pack things up for storage, right? You're not expecting me to do it all myself?"

"As long as they're strangers. Don't ask me why. I just don't want people I know going through our things…"

"I can handle that. I'll let you know if I have any questions."

They hung up, and Skye pulled her laptop close again.

After searching for over an hour, she settled on a fitted, open-backed table cover on which she could get the shelter's name and logo imprinted. She could have gone her whole life without needing to know how expensive personalized table covers were. Samaritan's Reach, though… It had wormed its way into her heart and had her stepping out of her comfort zone more than she ever thought possible.

Not that ordering a table cover online was terribly far outside her comfort zone. Thinking about other people — and wanting desperately for them to succeed — on the other hand, kind of was.

Skye tapped the *submit* button before wandering toward the kitchen. She was hungry. And she wanted to celebrate.

In one day, she'd managed to put the sale of Treasure Valley Chux into motion while also starting the process of renting out her mom's house. Those were big steps, both of them.

But she had no one in Boise with whom she could share her excitement.

The big city had never felt so lonely.

CHAPTER 36

"Boss! You in here?"

Sam pulled himself out from under the sink and sat up. "Over here. What's up?"

"Some guy here to see you. Miss Fern just drove up, too."

Saved from working on the plumbing. He could live with that.

Sam got up and wiped his hands on a nearby rag before heading into the courtyard. He waved to Fern as she headed toward the picnic table to cut through to where the van was parked.

She waved back. "We're cleaning the carburetor today."

Sam's steps stalled out. "Is that a one-day job?"

She laughed at him. "Have a little faith. It's early still."

Sam moved in the direction of the office. Fern looked out of place every time he saw her with a tool in her hand, but the second she started talking about what she was doing, even he was hooked, and he had zero desire to work on an engine. She wasn't just a skilled mechanic. She was gifted in sharing her passion with others. She should open her own garage. Maybe start an apprentice program. He'd mention it to her one of these days.

"Sam Madison?"

The man standing outside the office wore khakis and a short-sleeved button-up shirt. At least he hadn't thrown a tie on with it. So, not an attorney. Not a process-server, either, if he had any say in it.

"That's me. Can I help you?" Sam held out his hand.

The man shook his hand then tipped his head toward the foyer. "Think we can go inside?"

Sam glanced around. He couldn't see anybody, but that didn't mean residents weren't peering out from their windows. "Sure."

He unlocked the door and ushered the overdressed man back to the office, but the guy didn't sit. He stood at the counter and eyed the space that used to be tidy.

Sam looked around. Yep. His office was a disaster area. Without Skye around to keep things organized, it looked like a tornado had come through. Followed by a hurricane, an earthquake, and a tsunami.

He trained his eyes back on the man invading his territory. "You know my name, but I'm afraid I don't know yours."

"Can I depend on confidentiality?"

Seriously? He didn't have time today for strange men and cryptic questions. "You must have me confused with your doctor."

The guy rolled his eyes before nodding. "Max Wizkonzky."

Max... *Oh.* "What can I do for you?"

"You've sent people my way occasionally, but we've never officially met. I thought it was time."

"Why now?"

Max shifted on his feet and studied his fingernails before answering. "I'm going to lay my cards on the table. Or, the counter I guess."

Sam crossed his arms. "Be my guest."

Max shifted again. "I got competitive when you came to Rainbow Falls and opened another homeless shelter. I've been running one here for almost a decade, and I've been doing a competent job of it. We've helped a lot of people."

"I wasn't competing."

"I know, but everyone kept fawning over the new veteran's shelter, and I let it get to me. Which is why I never came by to welcome you to the community. It was childish, and I can admit it."

The timing was too coincidental with everything the City Council was doing. "So why now?"

"I know the city's gunning for you. I mean, I had an idea. It wasn't until my cousin Luke started yelling at me that I got it."

"Lucky Luke?"

Max gave a half-smile. "One and the same. He heard about it from our distant cousin Wyatt. We had a family reunion last weekend, and Luke let me have the what-for, told me I had my head in the sand."

"So, why does it matter now?"

Max looked at Sam, really made eye contact, for the first time since Sam had greeted him. "If the City

Council succeeds in taking you down, they'll come after us next. Nothing else makes sense. This has to be part of a bigger plan. All those anti-vagrancy laws they put into place. Last week they passed a new ordinance about loitering. Enforced to the letter of the law, it makes it impossible for us to go around town and reach out to people on the street. They claim that's not the intent, but… The whole thing is out of hand."

Sam eyed the man who looked like he played more video games than basketball. "So what do we do about it?"

Max shook his head. "I don't know. I don't have any answers. After Luke tore me a new one, though, I realized my silence on the matter might seem like… Might be misunderstood. I want you to know I had nothing to do with any of this. And now that I grasp how serious it is, I want to help, but I'm afraid it might be too late."

"Prayer's always appreciated."

The man from the other shelter nodded. "Of course. The thing is…who's next, you know? Once they knock you out, they'll come after me. Then they'll go after the food bank. Pretty soon, they'll be shutting down any of the churches that offer a soup kitchen or help to shut-ins. All because they want our city to appear clean and well cared for. Sure, we get tourists here, but it's not like we're a tourism hotspot. I don't get it."

"But we're on our way, and I think that's exactly what the City Council wants. People are starting to come from all over the country to enjoy our hiking trails, river rafting, and waterfalls. We get skiers in the winter and campers in the summer. There's even talk about a hot air balloon business coming to town to cater to tourists. I'll bet they're trying to spit-polish Rainbow Falls so they can take it international. Start bringing in tourists from other countries. Discover the unblemished wilds of Montana. That sort of thing."

Max's lips thinned. "Our city doesn't need those kinds of tourists. We need people who fall in love with Rainbow Falls the way it is."

Sam didn't argue. In the relatively short time he'd been in Rainbow Falls, he'd come to consider it not just his home, but his community also. That didn't make tourism evil, though. Money-hungry councilmembers, on the other hand...

Max must have been a nervous sort; he shifted on his feet again. "Anyway. I wanted you to know I'm not behind any of this and that I'm sorry for the way I've behaved up till now. I hope you'll be around long enough so I can make it up to you. Maybe we can have a joint fundraiser someday. A way to show solidarity within the community."

Skye's words from long ago came back to Sam. She'd told him he was scary. Maybe that was Max's problem. Sam purposely relaxed his post, uncrossed his arms, and slipped his hands into his pockets. "I'd like that. We can do even more good if we work together. We can learn from each other, too. You have experience I lack."

Max offered his first genuine smile. "And you have ingenuity and enthusiasm that I may have lost somewhere along the way."

Sam situated himself back under the sink.

He missed Skye. More than he would have thought possible. It'd been six weeks since she'd left, and life wasn't the same without her.

No time to dwell, though. The sink trap — or u-joint, according to Matt — under their kitchen sink needed his attention. No matter how much pressure he applied with the wrench, the coupling simply would not come loose.

Sam shifted to the side and put his weight on his left shoulder. This freed up his right arm to force the wrench and hopefully free up the coupling.

Right as he pushed the wrench with all he had, the door opened. The *clickety-clack* of high heels registered as the wrench finally moved. The wrench spun so hard that the coupling came lose, the sink trap fell away from the other pipe, and black sludge slid out of the hanging now-open-ended pipe and splattered all over his chest.

That was close. Had he still been lying flat on his back, the sludge would have oozed straight into his mouth. He shuddered.

At least now he knew why the sink hadn't been draining well.

Sam shoved his way out from under the sink. Skye wasn't a high-heeled kind of gal anymore. She'd gotten comfortable wearing her lace-up sneakers.

"Mr. Madison." Jette Black stood there looking at him in all his sludge-covered glory.

He had to give her credit. She didn't shudder. Of course, she didn't offer to shake his hand, either.

"What can I do for you, Jette? And it's Sam."

The corner of her mouth moved up the tiniest bit. "Yes, well, I'm here representing somebody else, so formality seemed in order."

Sam reached for the rag again. After wiping his hands clean, he tried to get the worst of the gunk off his shirt. "If not me, then who do you represent?"

"Skye."

Sam's eyes snapped to Jette's. She couldn't have captured his attention any faster if she'd claimed the City Council had backed down and was going to let him live in peace. "Skye?"

Jette nodded, and something close to sympathy passed through her eyes. "She wanted me to draw up papers allowing Samaritan's Reach to lease a home from her."

"She should wait till our case against the City Council is resolved. Everyone else is."

The smile touched her mouth again, a little more this time. "Skye's not like everyone else."

"You can say that again. How's she doing?" He'd told himself not to ask. He was hungry for news of her, though. Too hungry to keep quiet, it seemed. She'd gone away and cut him out of her life. Not a single call or text returned. He'd even stooped to looking for her on social media, all to no avail.

Jette lifted a shoulder. "I'm here on business."

Sam admired her discretion, but that didn't mean he had to like it. "Very well. I'm afraid I can't sign a lease with Skye. I can't make any long-term commitments."

Jette stepped forward and handed him some papers. "She's leasing a three-bedroom house to Samaritan's Reach. The home can house up to four tenants, three from your leadership program and then Samaritan's Reach itself."

Sam lifted an eyebrow.

Jette waved away his question. "The garage. For the flea market."

Ah. That made sense.

"Each of the bedrooms will be occupied by a tenant as determined by Samaritan's Reach. The tenants can be graduates of the leadership program, current members of the program, or any mix thereof."

Sam waved the papers. "This doesn't change the fact that we can't afford to make any long-term commitments right now. The funds for this…"

Jette stared him into silence. "You'll see the rent listed on page two. How you choose to split it between the four tenants is your choice, but Skye's wish is that whoever resides in the master bedroom pay a larger share than the other two men. Additionally, she stipulated that the first three months be rent-free. At the end of three months, Samaritan's Reach can back out of the lease without penalty. If you stay, the rent you see listed will go into effect."

"She can't give us three months free. We're not a…"

"What? Not a charity case? But Samaritan's Reach *is* a charity, and you can't deny someone's attempt to be charitable toward it."

Sam clenched his jaw. Why couldn't Skye have called and told him all this herself?

"Each of the three living tenants — the ones occupying rooms rather than a garage — will be given the opportunity to work off part of their rent. For every hour they volunteer here at Samaritan's Reach, Skye will reduce their individual portion of the rent by ten dollars. You'll need to keep a sign-in sheet, of course, and make sure the men are being productive during that time. At the end of each month, you can fax or email a copy of the sign-in sheet. The discount will be applied to the following month's rent."

"Will the men be paying her directly, or will they be paying us?" All this talk was making him believe they might actually be around long enough for it to be an issue.

"Skye would appreciate it if you could coordinate that. It doesn't matter if it's cash, a single check, four checks, a check and three money orders, or rolls of pennies. She'd just like to receive the four payments together at one time."

Sam skimmed over the papers. "She won't return any of my calls."

Jette bit her bottom lip, the first hint of indecision Sam had ever seen from her. "The Rainbow Girls are on your side. We're doing what we can to help Samaritan's Reach. And Skye's a Rainbow Girl. She hasn't forgotten that. She's just...on sabbatical for a little while. I still believe she'll come back."

"Back to the town, to you all, or to me?"

"I don't know yet."

A short time later, Sam was watching Jette as she *clickety-clacked* her way toward the front of the property.

He'd seen Fern and Jette today, but neither was a replacement for the Rainbow Girl who held part of his heart. He missed her, and he didn't even know any more if he had a right to.

CHAPTER 37

October

Two months had passed since Skye's departure from Samaritan's Reach.

As with every other day since, she battled the temptation to remember what it had felt like to be held in Sam's arms.

She wasn't ready to go there, though. Not yet. Some things needed to be settled first. Even then... She wasn't convinced that her return to Rainbow Falls was the right thing for anyone.

The intercom in her office buzzed. Man, she was tired of that sound. "There's someone here to see you, but he's not on your calendar."

Normally Charlotte would have just sent the person away if he wasn't on her schedule. Something must be going on for her to ring though. Skye pushed the button on the antiquated intercom. "Who is it?"

Charlotte's voice held more of a question than a statement. "He says he's a pastor? Pastor Dennis Diangelo."

Skye's stomach twisted up. She gritted her teeth and spoke into the intercom. "Send him in."

Her office door opened, and Pastor Dennis strode through. He was dressed in faded jeans and a wash-worn polo shirt. It made him look almost... human.

"Thank you for seeing me."

Shaking his hand was out of the question, so Skye remained in her seat.

After an awkward moment, he settled into a chair, too. "I hoped that I could speak to you."

"Isn't that what you're doing?" If her voice had been a tangible thing, he would have been bleeding from its razor-sharp edge.

"I've been thinking a lot lately about why God led me into ministry."

He was smart enough not to ask her permission to continue. She'd have told him no.

"At first, I thought it was a penance. Or punishment. I thought God wanted me to atone for my sins."

Some things could never be atoned for.

"It took me a while to figure out that Jesus had already atoned for my crimes and covered my debt in full."

Not to Skye. The debt had not been paid to her.

"I needed to learn some things, though, and one of those things was about redemption. God doesn't just save us from our past. He saves us to our future. He takes every bad, ugly, ungodly thing we did before we knew Him, and He redeems it. He turns it into something He can use for good."

Pastor Dennis was a reminder of the worst day of her life. A living, breathing, slap-in-the-face-reminder of how she'd let her mother down. He wasn't allowed to talk about redemption the way Sam did.

"I work with kids in a juvenile detention center over in Butte."

Butte was two hours from Rainbow Falls in the best of weather. If nothing else, the man sitting before her was committed.

"I go every Thursday. And every week I tell those kids about who I used to be, about a woman who died because of it, about a girl who has no mother as a result, about the time I spent in prison, and about the Jesus who saved me."

He owned it. He owned his past. That meant something… but what?

"You might think it gets old. Who's crazy enough to relive their past over and over again when it's the sort of past most people would rather forget?"

Skye couldn't seem to stop reliving her past, either.

"The thing is, every time I tell that story, I'm reminded of how God transformed me. I couldn't have done that on my own. No way. I might have felt guilty enough to call the cops when I found… when I found your mom. I would have gone back to dealing as soon as I got out of prison, though. By the end of my first week, I knew I'd go back to that life. It was the only thing I knew, the only way I'd ever have money in my pocket. When you're in prison, you spend a lot of time thinking about the things you want but can't have… and then almost as much time thinking about how to get those things."

Skye's hands fisted in her lap.

Pastor Dennis ran a hand through his hair. "I don't mind talking about the past because, bad as it is, buried in the middle of the bombed-out rubble that was my life is the story of a savior who takes the ugliest parts of who we are and recreates them into something more beautiful than we can imagine, more beautiful than we deserve. The story of my past is the story of who Christ is and how He took my ugly, messed-up life and turned it into something useful. It's not a work of art, but it's sturdy and usable, something it wasn't before."

Could she honestly sit there and listen to him talk about a God who redeems, who turns drug dealers into pastors?

Before she could throw him out of her office, Pastor Dennis stood. "I got a ride with Miss Rebecca's nephew's best friend. He was coming down to Boise to pick his daughter up from college. I came because... Because I needed to tell you... I wanted you to see..." He let out a whooshing breath. "I have an idea what you think of me, and I can live with that. I deserve it. What you think of God, though... I wanted to tell you my story so you could see God at work in it. What you think of Him matters more than you realize. I blew it in the past. I messed up my life and hurt a lot of people. I don't want you to be another casualty of my past choices."

He nodded to her and let himself out of her office.

She was left staring at the closed door.

Skye reached for the intercom box sitting on the desk, picked it up, and hurled it with all her strength. She wanted to relish in the sound of metal on wood as the box crashed into the door. Instead, it fell to the soft carpet three feet from her, tethered by the cords that gave it power and allowed it to do its job.

There was a message in there somewhere, but she wasn't sure she wanted to hear it.

Maybe she was directing her anger at the wrong person. Or maybe anger was the altogether wrong emotion.

But wasn't she justified?

Except, she'd been eaten up by guilt for so long. She hadn't been angry then at the unknown drug dealer. She'd been angry at herself. It didn't make sense to start blaming Pastor Dennis now. It was easy, and it might even be defensible, but that didn't mean it was right.

Skye picked up the now-cracked intercom box and placed it on her desk.

She would need to think about the things Pastor Dennis had said, but not yet.

First things first. Today was the company picnic.

Skye made sure everyone was out of the office before she left. The corporate offices closed early on picnic day. Everyone from sales reps to accountants to janitors attended. This would be the first picnic since her grandparents' death, and she hoped it was well-attended. She needed to be able to look these people in the face as she told them about their futures.

Skye circled the park complex a couple of times before finally finding a parking spot. It was for the best, too. By the time she climbed out of the car, her anger had cooled, and she was ready to face the people whose futures she held in her hands. She stood by her car and looked across the green expanse. The sprawling lawn of the park was packed with tables and chairs and clusters of people who ended up on the grass because the chairs were all taken.

Good. Everyone, or close to it, had come.

The air tasted of fear. She knew the taste because she was so familiar with it herself. This wasn't her fear, though. It belonged to her employees. Virtually every person she interacted with mentioned how much they valued their job, that their family depended on their income, that they had a sick relative or a child in college.

Yeah. She knew fear, and it was palpable here today.

She needed to get her speech over with before the people's fear grew. Fear fed by more fear would mutate into terror. She had experienced that, too.

Skye climbed the steps, nodded to the teenager running the soundboard, and picked up the microphone.

"Hi, everyone."

The electronic squeal shot out across the gathered crowd. Thank goodness they were in an open space. It would have ricocheted back at her otherwise. Still, she winced along with every person present. Her speech was off to a rousing good start.

The teen at the soundboard played with a knob before giving her a thumbs-up.

She tried again. "Hi, everyone."

Her voice carried out across the crowd without interference.

"I'm so glad you could all make it today."

A smattering of applause met her words.

"That's one of the things I like about Idaho. If you pick your day well, you can still have a picnic in October."

Silence met her words.

Skye scanned her notes. She had several pages of remarks, but that wasn't what these people were there for. She folded the papers and set them down on the stage by the base of the microphone stand.

"I have a lot I want to tell you, but I know you're anxious to hear about my plans for Treasure Valley Chux, and I can't blame you. Before I get into that, though, I want to first and foremost tell you how much I appreciate your hard work, your dedication, your acceptance of me both before and after my grandparents' death, and the genuine goodness every single one of you has displayed to me time and time again in the years that I've known you."

The applause was a little stronger this time.

"While I care deeply about each and every one of you, this company has never been in my heart. I don't have a passion for the product, the industry, or for being a CEO. You all are depending on me to do right by you, and that's not a responsibility I take lightly."

Silence.

"I'm selling Treasure Valley Chux."

Dead silence.

"I'm selling it to you. I've had all the paperwork drawn up to convert this company from privately owned to employee-owned. You all will be the ones making the decisions. The transfer of ownership will take a couple of months, and you all have a lot of work ahead of you, but once we get through this period of transition, Treasure Valley Chux will be owned by the people who work for it. You will be corporately responsible for the decisions, including the appointment of a new CEO, but the effort will be worth it because, at the end of the day, the profits will be split by you, too."

More dead silence.

Then, just to the left of the crowd's middle, Mike Hollingsworth stood. Mike worked on the manufacturing floor, and he always reminded Skye of a grizzly bear — tall, broad, hairy, and with a ferocious growl. He would have been head and shoulders above everyone else if they'd all been standing. With everyone else sitting, though, he was a giant among dwarves.

Mike started clapping with those mammoth mitts he called hands.

Then Lucia from sales stood and joined him.

Lisa, the office janitor.

Gerald Paulson, the Operations Director — and her recommendation for CEO should they ask her opinion — followed.

The rest of the employees rose as one, and Skye stood breathless on the stage.

Gerald made his way through the crowd and up to the platform. He took the mic from Skye's frozen hands and waved everyone into silence. "Skye, I think I can speak for all of us when I say, 'Thank you.'"

The applause roared to life again.

Gerald switched the mic off and leaned toward Skye. "This is for real? A done deal?"

"The employees have to vote on the terms. There may be things they decide to change, but yes."

"What kind of terms?"

"Sale price, for one, but also the division of profit. My attorney and I drew up something we think is fair. We modeled it after similar successful arrangements other companies have made and that have been sustained long-term."

"How much time are we talking about?"

"Three to six months, depending on how quickly everyone moves on this. If the employees stall out over any part of it, the process will drag out longer."

Gerald waved the crowd back into silence as he clicked the mic back on. "The transition will take three to six months, and every single one of you will have a say in how we move forward and what direction we take. There will be items that will need to be voted on, and if you decide not to vote, it can drag things out longer. Check with Human Resources tomorrow to make sure the email address in your file is current and valid. Then expect to see information coming out to you via email beginning early next week."

The crowd settled back into their seats as Gerald released the microphone back to Skye.

She looked out over the sprawling group of people. They had a lot of work ahead of them, but Skye wanted to dance in celebration for them. "Thank you, everyone, for being part of the Treasure Valley Chux family all these years and for welcoming me into the fold when I came along. Working with you has been an honor, and I know you're going to do fabulous things. Now please, if you haven't eaten yet, grab a plate and pile it high. Enjoy the dessert. Spend time together and start thinking about all the things you can do to help make this company — your company — better, stronger, and even more competitive than it already is."

Skye shook what must have been her thousandth hand of the day.

Most everyone had left for home now. The catering crew was cleaning up and putting things away. Balloons were still scattered here and there, tied to chairs and tables. Streamers that had decorated the space hung limply from the surrounding trees.

She sank into a plastic folding chair and thought about taking her heels off. Her feet hurt, and her toes felt like they'd been pinched within an inch of amputation. She'd gotten used to wearing tennis shoes during her time at Samaritan's Reach. What would the next chapter of her life look like? Would it require strappy heels or lace-ups?

"Hey girl. Outstanding speech." Tawny sprawled out in another nearby chair.

Jette was a bit more ladylike, but she pulled a plastic chair close and settled in as well. "You did good up there. These people are going to remember you for a long time."

"So when are you coming home?" Tawny reached out with a sandal-clad foot and gave Skye's chair a light shove.

"Rainbow Falls isn't the same without you." Jette was as understated as Tawny was obvious.

Skye gave up the fight and pulled her heels off. As she massaged her feet, she looked at the two friends she'd walked away from more than once. "You guys have turned this into a one-sided friendship. I'm not sure you get out of it nearly as much as I do."

Tawny twirled a long lock of her hair. "You taught me to think about other people. You showed me how valuable life is. I wouldn't have learned those lessons nearly as well without you."

Jette lifted a sculpted eyebrow. "You don't try to make me talk. It's hard to find friends who are comfortable with silence."

"What would I do if I came back to Rainbow Falls?"

Tawny shrugged. "Does it matter? Do you need a job? Don't you have some huge inheritance to live on?"

Skye chuckled. "I think I'm supposed to be a productive citizen."

Jette crossed her legs gracefully — no small feat in those flimsy chairs. "What will you do? You'll live your life, and you'll do it with friends. You'll find your path, figure out what you want to do, and you'll help the people you come into contact with. You have a lot to sort out, but you might as well come home and do it among friends, right? How is doing it all by yourself any better?"

Tawny hooked a thumb in Jette's direction. "What she said. Besides, Sam needs you."

Jette shushed her friend.

Too late. "What about Sam?"

Jette sighed, threw a glare at Tawny, and answered Skye. "There's a hearing tomorrow. The District Court will listen to arguments to determine whether or not the City Council overstepped the legal boundaries of its authority. If it finds in favor of Samaritan's Reach, the Council's recent regulations will be overturned and their stranglehold on the shelter will be finished."

Skye's breath caught in her throat. "How does it look?"

Tawny crossed her arms. "Jette's had all the Rainbow Girls praying like crazy since she got the hearing date. The Council has brought in a team of attorneys.

Jette's on her own. Her firm didn't want her touching this one. They're letting her, but they're not backing her up."

Skye looked back and forth between the two women. It wasn't her business. She wasn't needed. Still. The future of the shelter hung in the balance. Gideon, Franco, Jack, Alan, the others. Not to mention the men like Rafael who would end up in jail instead of in a VA hospital if they didn't have someone like Sam fighting for them. Sam. Samaritan's Reach was his life. It would destroy him to lose it.

Maybe not destroy. He was stronger than that. He wasn't a quitter.

But if he lost the shelter and left Rainbow Falls, she might never see him again.

And that would destroy her.

CHAPTER 38

Sunny had made sure every man from Samaritan's Reach had an interview-ready outfit. Sam needed to thank her. The men looked solid and professional.

Sam stood silently as the men filed into the van. He shut the side door before climbing into the driver's seat. It was time for their hearing. Jette would meet them at the courthouse. He could only hope that a gallery full of well-dressed men would help sway the judge.

Parking was a tangled-up mess, and they ended up two blocks away from the municipal complex. Sam fed the meter with every coin he could find before leading his silent entourage of men down the sidewalk.

He arrived at the front of the courthouse to find Rose, Ruby, Sunny, Fern, Tawny, and a couple others he didn't know, waiting for him.

Tawny's wave encompassed the entire group of women as she nodded to Sam. "The Rainbow Girls are here to support you. You haven't met us all yet, but we'll be in the back row holding a little prayer vigil." She shook the hand of each of the shelter's residents. "We want you to know you're not in this alone. We're pulling for you, but more than that, we're praying for you."

Before long, they were through security and inside. Sam sat next to Jette at a table while the attorneys for the City Council clustered around the other table. The courtroom wasn't as glamorous as the ones he was used to seeing on television, but then, few things were.

Both sides made their arguments, but the points each attorney made were lost on Sam. The fate of Samaritan's Reach and his men was out of his control. It all rested on the words spoken by lawyers and a decision made by a single judge. Jette had already warned him. If the judge found against Samaritan's Reach, there would be no point in appealing, and there was no way her firm would let her take on that kind of case pro bono. *Technically*, he could appeal. The chances of it doing him any good were slim to none, though.

"Permission to approach the bench, Your Honor."

Sam glanced to his side. Jette was going off-script. She'd given him a blow-by-blow of what to expect, and this wasn't part of it.

"Permission granted."

Jette walked with a don't-mess-with-me swagger as she approached the judge. As she spoke to him in low tones, the judge scanned the table filled with City Council attorneys until he finally pointed to one and waved him forward. The whispering between the judge and the two lawyers continued until that attorney raised his voice.

"I object. She should have entered it into evidence if she wanted it to be admissible."

More whispering. What on earth was going on?

"Objection!"

The judge rolled his eyes. "This is a sidebar. You can't object."

While they didn't raise their voices again, the two attorneys whispered over each other at a rapid-fire pace.

Was this good or bad? Jette should have clued him in ahead of time.

The judge lifted a hand. "Enough. The court calls Paul Erickson to the stand."

Paul? He'd moved on ages ago. What did he have to do with anything?

A door to the left opened and Sam watched as Paul, one of his former residents, entered the courtroom dressed in jailhouse orange.

He swore on the Bible and took a seat before Jette approached the stand. "Please state your name for the record."

"Paul Erickson."

"Mr. Erickson, are you familiar with Samaritan's Reach?"

"Yes."

"Were you a resident of Samaritan's Reach?"

"Yes."

"Have you ever served in the military?"

Paul's gaze flicked to Sam then back to Jette. "No."

No wonder they'd never been able to get his Veteran's benefits straightened out.

"If you're not a veteran, can you tell me why you went to Samaritan's Reach?"

"I was hired to do a job."

Sam's breath caught in his throat.

Cool as ice, Jette continued her questions. "What kind of job?"

"Surveillance, mostly. Taking pictures, looking for things the city could cite as violations."

The underbrush… The feeling that someone was snooping…

"And did you ever do anything more than surveille?"

Paul shrugged. "I was instructed to sabotage things, to try to prevent the employees and volunteers from being able to do their jobs."

Jette tapped her toe. "Give me an example."

"There was this one guy, Rafael. A car backfired, and it set him off. I was supposed to go to the office and get Miss Skye, but I didn't. So the situation escalated, and the police were called."

"Were you aware that if the police had to repeatedly come to Samaritan's Reach, the shelter would be shut down?"

He nodded. "Yeah."

"So you willfully set out to make it appear that Samaritan's Reach was a blight on the community?"

"When you put it like that…"

"Just answer the question. 'Yes' or 'No.'"

"Yes."

Sam sat back in his chair. There had been times when he'd felt like he was being sabotaged, but he'd never considered that someone might actually be… He'd just thought he was getting paranoid.

Jette crossed her arms. "Who hired you to surveille and sabotage Samaritan's Reach?"

Paul pointed to one of the attorneys at the City Council's table. "That one there."

Jette's eyes flicked in the direction of the clustered attorneys. "Let the record show that the witness indicated Michael Rothchild, the City Attorney for Rainbow Falls, Montana."

"Objection!" The rest of the attorneys all jumped to their feet at once.

"Overruled. You'll get your chance to cross examine."

Jette asked a couple more questions about how Paul was hired and paid.

The attorneys for the other side tried to tear his testimony apart, but by that time, Sam had tuned out the proceedings. He'd had a plant right under his nose for months and hadn't realized it. His pride wasn't going to let go of that one anytime soon.

The judge cleared his throat, and Sam's attention returned to the courtroom.

"Alright. I think I have everything I need to make a ruling. However, we have a full house here today. While statements from community members cannot change the law and therefore will not affect my decision, I will open the floor in case anyone would like to speak."

Fern made the short trek to the small podium. "My name is Fern Green. I've been helping out at the shelter. I'm a mechanic, and I've been keeping their van running and giving a few of the men pointers. They're a commendable group of men, and they want to rise above the stigma of being homeless. Shutting down Samaritan's Reach will rob them of that opportunity. Thank you."

Ruby and Rose approached the podium, but only one of them addressed the court. "My name is Ruby Rhed, and this is my sister Rose. We run an employment agency in Rainbow Falls. We have successfully placed several men from Samaritan's Reach into temporary positions and have received positive feedback from those businesses. We would like to place them into long-term positions as well, but folks are reluctant to hire them when the future of the shelter is so uncertain. If you rule against the City Council, we'll be able to assure these employers about the longevity of Samaritan's Reach. Thank you."

The sisters retreated to the back.

Sam kept his eyes trained forward. He wasn't superstitious, but even so, he couldn't help but worry that looking back at the crowd behind him would somehow jinx everything.

Harry the barber voiced his praise of Samaritan's Reach next.

Then the flea market's manager.

Pastor Dennis even got up there to speak. "The people who attend New Hope Church of Rainbow Falls are enriched by the attendance of the men from Samaritan's Reach. I've seen genuine spiritual growth in some. Mild curiosity in others. Regardless, though, as believers, we are called to be the hands and feet of Christ, and having these men in our midst has helped my congregation embrace that concept and turn it into a reality."

He glanced down at his notes before continuing. "Because of the positive impact Samaritan's Reach has had on our congregation, we now have an afterschool club for grade-schoolers three days every week so parents don't have to worry about their kids going home to an empty and unsupervised house. Meanwhile, those students get tutoring if they need it, help with their homework, and an opportunity to play games and be kids. We've also started a voluntary carpool service of sorts where we can come to the aid of the elderly or those without transportation to make it to the doctor or other appointments. There's more we want to do, too, and all because Samaritan's Reach is here in Rainbow Falls doing its part to make our community better."

Miss Rebecca, with the help of her walker, came next. "As you might can tell, I'm not in the best of shape. I haven't had to worry about a thing around my house, though. These men have taken care of my yard and even fixed some things in the house that needed repairs. It was all their idea, too. Sam called me one day and said he had a proposition for me, and the next thing I knew, my house was in better shape than it had been in for years. When I realized how serious the men were about helping, I gave Sam a list of other shut-ins and seniors who could do with a visit."

She put her hands on her hips — despite the walker — and stared the judge down. "Over the next month, Sam brought a team of men to each and every one of those people and took care of everything they needed done, plus some. They did all this without any expectation of compensation. They did it because it was good and right and because they want to be contributing members of society. By upholding the Council's foolhardy and overstepping regulations, you'll be depriving this community of a valuable asset." Pastor Dennis helped her turn her walker around. On her way past his table, she winked at Sam.

Then Gideon. The men had nominated him to speak for them. "Your Honor, thank you for giving us a chance to be heard. I am speaking on behalf of all the veterans at Samaritan's Reach, and I want you to know that we are all better men for having the experience of living there. Sam Madison didn't just give us a roof over our heads. He gave us hope. He is helping to educate us, integrate us back into society, and turn our lives around not just for a day or a week but for a lifetime. Every man who has spent even a day at that shelter will tell you, he owes Sam his life. If you shut down Samaritan's Reach, you're robbing every single one of us — and all the men to come — of a future we can be proud of."

Jette glanced over her shoulder and nodded at someone. She'd gone over the list of speakers with Sam, and as far as he could tell, they'd all spoken. He couldn't turn around to see who it was without being obvious, and he couldn't even peek over at the podium easily because Jette was sitting between it and him.

"Thank you, Your Honor, for allowing us an opportunity to speak."

Sam's head snapped up while his heart turned inside out and beat a rushing pulse in his temples.

"My name is Skye Blue. I first met Sam Madison on an airplane. He scared me a bit. He's an intimidating guy to look at. When he talked about Samaritan's Reach, though, I realized that I'd done the worst possible thing. I'd judged him by appearance. Underneath that somewhat daunting exterior, he's a wonderful man who loves God and who fights every day to help the men in his care build better lives for themselves."

Sam drank in the sight of her. His mornings had been empty without her, and his days... Nothing had been the same since she'd gone.

"I visited the shelter one day, and I did something that triggered a PTSD episode in one of the men. He didn't assault me or anything like that, but the experience still terrified me and left me shaken. That man is now sitting in this courtroom. He's registered for college classes, is in counseling for his PTSD, and is stepping up to help lead new men coming into the shelter. His journey is far from over, but the progress he has made with the support of Samaritan's Reach has turned his life around."

The professional polish fell away from Skye's voice as she continued. "The changes in him didn't come from a haircut and a toothbrush. They came from inside. They came from being in an environment where he felt safe, where he could speak freely about his experiences, and where Sam Madison and his staff work tirelessly to find and build on the strengths of each resident so they can grow in confidence and ability."

Skye smoothed her hands down the sides of her business suit before picking up where she'd left off. "Despite my experience that first day — or maybe because of it — I kept going back. I couldn't see what it was, but I knew there was something valuable going on there. And even though it scared me, I wanted to be a part of it. What's happening at Samaritan's Reach goes beyond the facts. It's about more than the number of men they house, the amount of money they can raise, or the contributions they make to this community. Those are all important pieces of information to have, but you need to understand that this shelter is transforming lives, and no set of data can tell you what that means or how much a single changed life can touch the world. Let alone a whole group of changed lives. I know your decision today has to be based on law and not emotion, and I want you to know that nobody here will react in anger if you make a ruling we don't agree with. Our hearts will, however, be broken, as will the dreams of these men."

Sam fought the urge to go to her. She was here for Samaritan's Reach, maybe even for the men. She hadn't come back for him, though. He needed to remember that.

Skye thanked the judge for his time and returned to her seat. Her eyes passed over Sam, and the touch of her gaze scorched him.

Don't go, Skye. Don't run away again.

CHAPTER 39

Skye sat there, tucked in between Fern and Tawny, in the back row of the courtroom gallery. The other Rainbow Girls were praying. She knew that, but what was *she* supposed to say to God?

She had to try, though. For Sam. If there was a chance God was real, she needed to try.

Okay, God. This the part where I'm supposed to promise I'll go to church every Sunday for a year if You keep the shelter open. I can't do that, though. Going to church doesn't matter if I spend every second of it wishing I were somewhere else.

As if they'd coordinated the whole thing, Tawny and Fern each reached over and gripped one of her hands. Skye squeezed their hands in return and continued her one-sided monologue.

So here's the thing. I'm not even sure You're real or, if You are, that I want anything to do with You. I won't make promises about going to church. But I'll promise to be real with You. I'll be honest. I'll tell You what's on my mind, and I won't pretend to think, feel, or believe something I don't. If You are what everyone else seems to think, then You already know what Samaritan's Reach means to me. You know how I feel about these men, and... about Sam. You know. Please help them. Don't let the City Council shut them down. It means too much to too many people, and it's not just helping the homeless vets. It's helping everybody. I'm a better person because of Samaritan's Reach. Without it, who knows? I'd still be sitting at my kitchen counter

349

running a company I don't want, from a laptop I refuse to update because I was too afraid of change. I'm not that person anymore, and it's because of Sam…

"The court finds in favor of the plaintiff. The Rainbow Falls City Council acted outside its legal rights to impose unfair and unreasonable regulations on businesses within the community. What's more, they appear to have targeted a single business, an act reprehensible in an entity whose purpose is to represent and protect all the town's citizens. I hope the voters of Rainbow Falls remember this when it's time for re-election. Case closed."

The judge banged his gavel, but everyone else sat there in silence. He cleared his throat and looked over his glasses at the people in his courtroom. "This is the part where you cheer. Samaritan's Reach is staying open."

Tawny jumped up. Since she still held Skye's hand, Skye got yanked up out of her seat too. She returned Tawny's hug, then turned to hug Fern.

She was dragged out into the aisle, and one by one, the Rainbow Girls hugged her. Each of the men from the shelter pulled her into a hug, too.

Alan scuffed his toe against the floor. "You know I'm sorry I scared you that day, right?"

Out of the corner of her eye, Skye watched as Sam shook Jette's hand and made his way through the small gate and toward his men. "It's over. You don't need to apologize anymore."

"Hearing you talk about me today…"

Skye put her hands on Alan's shoulders and stared into his eyes. "You aren't that man anymore, and the truth is, a year from now, you won't be this man standing right here. You're going to keep moving forward, growing, and becoming the man you want to be."

"The man God wants me to be, I hope."

Sam was getting closer, and she needed to leave before he reached her. "That, too."

Skye turned to go, but Alan stalled her with a hand on her arm. "I finished my sixty days and started the leadership program. The Boss pulled some strings and got me a job on a paint crew. It's only a couple days a week, but it lets me work on my studies the rest of the time. I'm gonna earn a degree or something."

"I'm glad. You're going to do fine in the program. Better than fine." She meant every word.

He gave her arm a gentle squeeze before dropping his hand to his side. "It ain't been the same around there without you. We're all survivin', but it's not the same. Neither is the boss. You hurt him bad when you left."

She blinked back the sudden pressure behind her eyes. "I'm sorry. I'm sorry for all of it, but you guys will be safe now. Everything's going to work out."

Jack gave Alan a congratulatory slap on the back, momentarily pulling his attention away from Skye.

She took the opportunity to escape the courtroom. She wasn't ready to face Sam yet, not with so many people watching, not when she was so unsure of what she wanted to say or how she felt.

So she ran away. Out of the courtroom, out of the courthouse, and all the way down the street to where she'd parked her car.

Skye stood by her car. She'd gotten out of it, so that was something, right?

The court hearing was in the rearview mirror, and Samaritan's Reach was safe. In the days since the hearing, she was wrestled with her conscience and the way she'd left things with Sam. Seeing him again…

Could she make a life for herself in Rainbow Falls? What would Sam say?

So she stood by her car in the church's parking lot. The part where she actually entered the double doors… That was something else altogether. She had to try, though, because she'd learned some things during her weeks at Samaritan's Reach.

For starters, fear held people back. It never propelled them forward. And she was done being held back.

She sucked in a deep breath, scowled at the high heels pinching her toes, and walked through the doors into the vacant foyer.

The singing in the sanctuary was muted by the next set of doors. She was halfway across the foyer when a voice reached her.

"Well hello, dear. Welcome. I'm sorry. I was trying to tidy up a bit before going in."

Skye tried to offer a polite greeting and brush past the woman with the walker.

"Here. Have a doughnut. It has chocolate on it."

Skye didn't want one. She didn't want conversation, either. In fact, she wasn't even sure she wanted to be there.

The woman held the doughnut directly in front of her, though. Short of slapping the hand away, there wasn't a polite way out of the situation. Then again, slapping a feeble old woman's hand might not be considered entirely polite. So she gritted her teeth and took the pastry. "Thank you."

"Do you think you could take this one, too?"

The woman held another doughnut out to her.

"No, really, one is plenty."

"Oh, that's not for you, dear." The woman chuckled. "It's for me. I need both hands for this walker. Follow me this way."

The woman maneuvered her walker down a long hallway and to a heavy metal door. Definitely not the sanctuary. With more upper body strength than her slight frame implied, she pushed through the door and out into the sunshine. A wooden bench sat against the exterior of the church building, and the woman sank down onto it.

Skye, who had every intention of handing the woman her sweet treat and escaping, found herself pulled down to the bench next to the woman. "Wow. You have quite a grip."

"I crotchet. Builds up the finger muscles."

"Oh."

"My name's Rebecca, by the way."

Skye handed the woman her doughnut and took a taste of her own without replying. No point trying to run for it now. She could hear the organ playing. If she went in now, she'd be noticed.

"You're supposed to tell me that your name is Skye."

"How do you know my name?"

Rebecca took another bite. "You were at the hearing for Samaritan's Reach."

Oh. That's where she'd seen her. "You spoke, too."

Rebecca nodded. "Sure did. Sam and his boys have been such a blessing to me and to so many of the elderly folks from this church and elsewhere in our community. They're good people."

"Yes, they are. Good people."

"Pastor Dennis is good people, too."

Skye took a big bite of doughnut and faked an I'm-sorry-but-my-mouth's-full-so-I-can't-talk smile.

"I used to teach at the high school here in Rainbow Falls. I was a teacher back in 1978."

'78? That was the year...

"Your mom graduated that year, didn't she?"

Skye looked at Rebecca and nodded.

"So did Emmaline White." Then she frowned. "Sort of. Did your mom ever tell you about her graduation? About Emmaline?"

Skye stared straight ahead. "Emmaline was supposed to graduate with my mom, but she got sick. Leukemia, I think. She couldn't finish school. Everyone knew she was dying. She wanted to speak at graduation, though, and the superintendent let her. And somehow as a result, my name is Skye Blue."

"Your mom never told you why she named you Skye?"

"She didn't want me to see the world in black and white... I think. It's been a long time. I don't remember it all."

Rebecca swallowed her last bite of doughnut and brushed her hands across her polyester slacks. "Emmaline is a shade of white. Did you know that?"

Skye shook her head.

"She talked to her fellow classmates that night about how fleeting life can be and how they needed to seize it and live each day to its fullest potential. She told them — more or less — not to settle for living life in black and white but to instead live out their lives in full color. Celebrate every moment, the joyous and the sorrowful. Celebrate life in all its glory, in all its color. It was a beautiful speech from a beautiful girl."

"She died not too long after, didn't she?"

"Two weeks later."

"So people around Rainbow Falls started naming their kids with colors."

Rebecca chuckled. "From Amethyst to Wisteria. There were some crazy names running around our small town. But it was good. It reminded us all of Emmaline... and to embrace each day and live it well."

"Sounds like Emmaline White was something special."

"Oh, she was. From the day she was born, that girl was destined for greatness. I just didn't expect it to come through suffering and death."

Skye stared at the woman beside her.

"Rebecca White, Emmaline's grandmother." She offered a watery smile.

Skye's breath froze in her chest. Words clamored to escape at the same time that she had no idea what to say. Her breath thawed and began to move again as the right words fell into place. "I'm sorry for your loss."

"As am I, but thank you. Now let's talk about your loss."

Skye crossed her arms. "I'm not sure your granddaughter and my mother had anything in common."

Rebecca moved her walker an inch to the right. "They were both dealt a raw deal, and they both did the best they could."

"My mom did drugs and died because of it. Your granddaughter never did anything wrong."

Rebecca chuckled. "Emmaline wasn't a saint. She was a kid faced with the immediacy of her own mortality. Prior to her illness, she could be a spoiled brat with the rest of them. She wasn't that way often, but she could be. She wasn't perfect and shouldn't be remembered that way."

Skye shook her head. "I don't understand, then. Why are we talking about your granddaughter?"

"Emmaline was going in one direction. Leukemia came along and changed the entire course of her life. Your mom was headed one way, but she married into a family that didn't approve of her, and her life changed direction. Then her parents died. Followed by her husband. Your mama was a fine woman who had too much hurt inside her. She didn't know what to do with it or how to cope, and she didn't know how to ask for help. The people she should have been able to turn to were all gone."

"She had me."

"You were what, eleven, at the time? And she was your mom. It was her job to protect you, not burden you."

"I'm not sure she protected me."

"Maybe not in the way you wanted her to, but she brought you here. She brought you to the one place in the world where you would fit in and be loved for exactly who you were. She brought you to a town where people had learned the hard way not to take their children for granted and to live each day as though it could be their last."

A minivan with a dog hanging its head out the window meandered along the street in front of them.

"I don't understand."

"We all failed your mom. We saw how troubled her heart was, and we thought we were helping. We embraced you. We encouraged our children and grandchildren to welcome the newest Rainbow Girl. We kept an eye out to make sure you weren't out after dark and that you were doing your homework and working hard at school. We got you into church and did our best as a community to simply love you. We didn't do the same for your mom, though. We judged her. We knew about the drugs, and we ignored it. So she's dead now, and every single sensible person in this town feels guilt about that."

Tears clawed their way to the surface, but Skye swiped them from her face.

"God redeemed that past, too."

"I'm beginning to hate that word."

Rebecca chuckled as she patted the wall they were leaning against. "You shouldn't. We have this church here that welcomes all kinds of people. Homeless, addicted, anger issues, whatever. If you don't fit in anywhere, this is the place that wants you. And this church is here because your mom died."

Skye sucked in a breath so quickly it whistled.

"I'm not sayin' God let her die so we could have this church. I'm saying we all failed her, but God took our failings, and He turned them around. He turned them into something He can use for His kingdom. Just like He redeemed that pastor in there. Just like He redeemed your friend Sam. Just like He wants to redeem you."

Skye wiped at more tears that insisted on showing themselves.

"Think about it. That's all I ask. If you ever want to talk some more, you can find me in the phone book."

Rebecca rose from the bench and moved away, slowed by her advanced age and cumbersome walker.

Skye watched her go without saying a word. She had none to offer. All she had left were tears. She'd made such a mess of everything.

CHAPTER 40

Sam's long legs ate up the distance to the van. He unlocked the door, hopped in, and started the engine.

It purred to life, and Sam gave a content sigh. Green & Son had taken care of the imminent repairs, but having Fern on board as a volunteer at Samaritan's Reach had proven far more beneficial. The van hadn't run this smoothly in all the years he'd had it.

"Hey, Boss. Isn't that Miss Skye's car?"

Sam scoured the parking lot before Franco even finished climbing into the van.

Over there. Ahead and to the right. Skye's car, but no Skye.

Was it her car? The right make and color.

He'd never memorized her license plate.

"Sure is. She has that little rainbow crystal thing hanging from the rearview mirror." Gideon pointed just as the sun hit the prism and shot a blinding beam of light in their direction.

Baxter yanked the driver side door open. "Go on. Go find your woman. I'll see to it that they're all returned to the Reach safe and sound."

"She's not my…"

"Right." Baxter snorted. "You ain't convincing any of us."

Sam glanced back at the men in the van. A few of them were new. They'd never met Skye. The rest, though… They looked at him with a mix of hope and fear. They missed Skye, too. In a different way, sure, but they missed her nonetheless.

"No promises, guys. But I'll try to bring her back."

Gideon nodded. "Do your best, Boss. That's all anyone can ask."

Sam climbed out of the van and headed back toward the church's entrance. He arrived in time to open the door for Miss Rebecca, who was coming through. Her friend, Irene, was giving her a ride home since the doctor still hadn't cleared her to drive.

"Good afternoon, Miss Rebecca."

She shuffled past. "There's a long hall to your left, ends at a brown metal door."

"Pardon me?"

She turned to him. Her body might be frail, but her eyes were eagle-sharp. "If you're looking for someone, there's a long hallway to your left. It leads to a brown metal door. There might be someone sitting on a bench on the other side."

Sam didn't stick around to thank her. He slipped into the church's foyer and let the door swing closed behind him. As soon as his eyes adjusted to the interior lighting, he sought out the hallway she'd indicated and followed down its length. Classroom doorways lined the hall.

He reached the door, wiped his hands on his pants, and pushed.

There she was. Skye. She was wearing a blue dress, just like the day he'd met her on the plane. Her head was bowed, and she hadn't looked up at the sound of the door.

Sam took the three steps that put him at the bench, and he sank down next to her.

Silence filled the space between them.

"The first time I saw you, I thought you'd look at home flipping a butterfly knife."

So she *did* realize he was there. "How do you even know what a butterfly knife looks like?"

Her red-rimmed eyes met his. "I watched movies. I wasn't always sheltered, either."

More silence, but this time it wasn't quite as painful.

Skye knotted her fingers together in her lap. "I owe you an explanation."

Emotion surged through him, almost too strong to contain. "Part of me says you owe me a whole lot more than an explanation. And part of me wonders who I am to think you owe me anything at all."

"Honest, even when it's awkward. Right?"

He nodded. "That's always my preference."

She untangled her fingers and braced them on her thighs. "I'm broken. I have more things wrong with me than you can shake a stick at."

"Or a butterfly knife?"

Laughter tickled the edge of her mouth and softened her voice. "Yeah, or one of those."

"I'm willing to listen if you want to talk."

She stared straight ahead, hands clasped together in her lap. "I was at my home in Boise, and the pieces were all falling into place. I was going to be able to turn the company over to the employees, and I'd started things rolling so I could rent the house here to Samaritan's Reach. I was on top of the world, and I wanted to celebrate."

"Sounds like something worth celebrating." Even if her tone of voice said the opposite.

"I had no one to celebrate with, though. I was all alone in a city that I'd lived in for more than a decade. I should have had friends. I should have had somebody I could call, but there was no one."

"Loneliness is hard."

She glanced his way, and her eyes were clearer than he'd seen them in a long time. "You're right. Loneliness is hard. My problem is that I'd brought it on myself. I pushed away everyone who ever cared about me. I'm not sure when it started. I don't know if it was my dad's death, or my mom's drugs, or the way my grandparents always kept me at arm's length. And I'm not sure it matters, either. But somewhere along the way, I started pushing people away, too. I didn't let anyone close enough to my heart to cause me pain. The Rainbow Girls. God. You."

"Loneliness is its own pain, though."

"Exactly. I wasn't saving myself from pain. I was just causing a different kind of pain. Have you ever given God the silent treatment?"

"The first twenty-eight years of my life, if that counts."

She offered a shy, sad smile. "Yeah, it counts."

He'd kiss away her pain if he thought it would help anything. "So where do you go from here?"

"Did you ever hear the story of Emmaline White?"

"A little. Ginger gave me the highlights one time."

"Emmaline died, and people grieved for her. They experienced pain. They also had joy, though, because she'd been in their lives. I want that, too."

"Joy?"

"People. Relationships. The kind of life that has both joy and pain."

Sam caught himself reaching out to brush her hair behind her ear. He pulled his hand back. "It sounds like a good life."

"I think I finally understand this whole redemption thing, too."

Sam locked his hands together behind his back. The urge to pull her close was getting harder to battle.

"It's not about the past being gone. It's about it being used. Our lives aren't written in sand on the beach. The bad stuff doesn't disappear when redemption rolls in. Maybe the shame is washed away, but not the acts themselves. Because God wants us to use those."

She'd come a long way. "Sounds like you have a handle on what redemption means. The question is whether or not you want God to redeem you."

Her eyes shone. "He did. A long time ago. I just... I just didn't want to talk to Him anymore. After Mom died, I got kind of numb, you know? Numb, but angry. Which doesn't make sense. I was mad enough to distance myself from the only One left who seemed to care about me."

"Ah. So this is where giving God the silent treatment comes in."

Color tinted Skye's cheeks. "Something like that. I'm ready to get over it, though. I'm done acting like a spoiled brat who didn't get her way."

"So what does redemption look like going forward?"

She lifted her shoulders. "Not a clue. I'm sure God already has it sorted out, so I'm trusting Him with the details."

"Will it keep you here in Rainbow Falls?" He held his breath.

She gave him a smile. A broad, beautiful, one-of-a-kind Skye smile. "That much I know. I'm not leaving again. I'm done running away. I can't promise I won't ever be tempted to..."

"You didn't need to run from me." Her presence in Rainbow Falls was encouraging, but the way she'd vanished and refused to return his calls still hurt.

"I did, though. Don't you see? When we build walls up around our hearts, those walls can only be breached when we allow it. You were a danger to my walls, and I was about to let you in. So I ran. I thought that was better for both of us."

This time he did reach out, just enough to touch her. He pulled away the strand of hair that kept blowing in her face and hiding her from his view.

"I told myself it was about the business and tying up loose ends, but if that was the case, I would have returned your calls."

"But you didn't."

She shook her head. "You're as dangerous to me as I thought when I first saw you. Only, it's not because of your earring or those tattoos. It's because of your heart. You have one of the most beautiful hearts I've ever seen in another human being, and… It makes me want things. Things I didn't think I deserved to have."

CHAPTER 41

Skye soaked in Sam's presence. "Where do we go from here?"

He smiled, and those blue eyes she'd once thought of as icy heated her skin. "I know a place. Great ambiance. Good people. You might even get lunch out of it. You'll have to drive, though. My ride left without me."

"You're letting Franco drive the van now?"

Sam snorted. "Not hardly. Baxter came along today."

Skye chuckled, but then her laughter faded, and all those insecurities that had kept her twisted up for so long came rushing back in. "What if I push you away every time you start to get close?"

He reached out and took her hand, threading his fingers through hers. "One day at a time, okay? We're not buying diapers for our grandkids today. God has everything between here and there already figured out."

"Between here and there implies a there. With diapers and grandkids. Now you're kind of freaking me out."

His hand, warm against hers, squeezed ever so slightly. "Lunch. We're talking about lunch. After that, who knows? Maybe we'll go shopping and buy you some curtains. Or a couch."

"How do you know about...?"

"A couple of colorful little birds told me."

Skye held tight to his hand. "I'm not sure why it's been so hard to furnish my house."

Sam turned to face her. "You've had a lot of decisions to make in your life recently. Sometimes we get so caught up in those really big decisions that we don't have anything left to offer the everyday decisions."

"Like couches and curtains?"

"Couches, curtains, relationships." With those words, Sam released her hand and cupped her face. "If you're not ready for a couch and curtains, we could try a kiss."

Skye leaned into his touch. He was casting a spell over her, pure and simple. "I'd like that."

Laughter flared to life in his eyes but was almost immediately doused by an emotion that darkened their blue and made his pupils dilate. Want. Passion. Desire.

Sam dipped his head until his lips met hers. His kiss was silk against satin — soft and warm. Skye's toes curled while her imagination took flight. With his lips against hers, diapers and grandbabies didn't seem like such a far-off thought. It felt real, solid. Like Sam.

He pulled away but dropped another kiss on her cheek, then her forehead.

Skye smoothed the front of his shirt where she'd been gripping it. "That wasn't bad for 'next.'"

A smile shaped his mouth, and he leaned in to place another kiss on her forehead. "I'm glad you enjoyed it."

"I want there to be a lot of nexts. I'm going to disappoint you eventually, though. I know that."

"I'll disappoint you regularly. I'm human. So are you. We'll both get exercise in forgiving."

He made it sound so simple. And she wanted him to be right.

Skye stood, tugging Sam with her. "Well then, let's go. I believe you promised me lunch."

A short time later, they pulled up to the curb in front of Samaritan's Reach, but it wasn't the same Samaritan's Reach Skye remembered.

"Where'd the roof go?"

Sam scratched his head. "It was there when we left for church this morning."

"Are you being punked?"

Sam reached for her hand and tugged her with him as he climbed the steep driveway. Two commercial-sized dumpsters sat in the middle of the courtyard. They were filled to the brim with old, faded, worn out shingles.

"Madison!" A woman's voice rang out, but Skye couldn't pinpoint its source. Someone shimmied down a ladder, though, and it clicked into place.

"Madison, look at you!" She gave Sam a tight hug then extended a hand to Skye. "Ginger Schneider. I used to serve with this big lug."

Skye took in the petite woman with blunt-cut fire-engine-red hair. A well-used tool belt hung low on her hips, with a pair of worn leather work gloves waving at her from one of the belt's compartments. "You're the one who told him about Rainbow Falls."

She grinned. "Guilty as charged."

A twinge wormed its way through Skye's middle. She wasn't going to let insecurity win, though. She wrapped her arms around Ginger and gave her a hug. "Thank you for telling him about our home. If it weren't for you, Samaritan's Reach wouldn't be here, and I never would have met Sam."

Color climbed Ginger's neck. "Don't go making a federal case out of it or anything."

Before Skye could say anything else to Ginger, Gideon strolled out of the kitchen carrying two plates. He shoved them both at Sam and pulled Skye into a hug. "It's good to have you home, Miss Skye. This place wasn't the same without you. The boss wasn't the same without you, either."

Some of the men she'd only met in passing. Some of them, though, had burrowed into her heart when she'd been busy looking the other way. She hugged Gideon back. "It's good to be home. I missed you, too."

He pulled back. "You need to meet my niece. She's around here somewhere."

Something a lot like pride lit his face, so Skye didn't bother telling him she'd met Gabbie briefly the first day she'd come looking for her Uncle Gid. Instead, she pointed to the young woman making eyes at a broad-shouldered member of the construction crew.

"Gabriela Pierce, you get over here right this instant!" He ran a hand down his wiry beard. "I tell you, I had no idea having a niece was going to be this hard. That girl has a mind of her own. Just like her mama did."

Skye and Gabbie shook hands before Sam's voice pulled her back in his direction. "You remember Conway, right?"

Skye shook another hand. "Do we have you to thank for our missing roof?"

Conway pushed a cap back on his head. "As soon as the judge made his ruling, I made a call. Got the shingles lined up and figured we'd do our best to give Sam a nice surprise when he got home from church today. 'Course, it looks like he got a nice surprise *at* church, too."

Skye wrapped her fingers around Sam's forearm. "I guess it's a day full of surprises."

Conway nodded. "I suppose you're right."

Sam pushed one of the plates toward Skye. "Here. Go eat. There's room over at the picnic table. I'll join you in a minute. I want to go over a few things with Conway. Like making sure he got all the proper permits."

Skye carried her plate over to the lone table and hoped nobody saw fit to throw shingles, nails, or anything else in her general direction. She sat on top and inspected the bustling courtyard as she took a bite of what turned out to be a turkey sandwich, no mustard.

Two bites later, Alan climbed up to sit on the table next to her.

She took another bite.

More than anyone there — except for Sam — she felt like she owed Alan an apology. Finding the words, though, was proving harder than she'd expected.

"Remember when you came after me that day? Back when Rafael went off the rails?"

"Yeah."

"You stopped me from leaving because you knew I needed to be here."

"You deserved to be here."

"You try to run again, I'm gonna return the favor. You need to be here, too."

How could she take another bite with tears clogging her throat so she could barely breathe?

Alan wasn't done, either. "You have family here. This is a safe place to be."

Skye set her plate down. He'd just bestowed a great honor on her, and she wanted to treat it with the respect it deserved. "I'm privileged to call you my family."

He gave her a nod and headed back to the courtyard, passing Sam in the process.

Sam took her hand. "Come with me. Quick, before anybody else interrupts."

She followed him as he led them behind the building, over near where the van was parked.

He brushed the back of his hand against her cheek before circling a finger under her chin and tilting her face to look at him. "We've had lunch. More or less. So it's time to think about what comes next. After the last next."

"So the *next* next?"

He leaned in, and the air between them grew heavy with charged electricity. His lips brushed against hers, the barest hint of a caress, before he moved to kiss her forehead. "I told myself I wouldn't rush you, that I'd let you control the pace."

The compulsion to reach out and touch him robbed Skye of coherent thought. She rested her hands on his biceps, and his muscles bunched under her fingers. She slid her hands upwards until they danced along the collar of his button-up church shirt. When her fingers brushed against his skin, he sucked in a hissing breath.

He leaned his forehead against hers. "You're playing with fire."

Maybe I want to get burned. She swallowed the retort and circled her arms around his neck and held him in a loose embrace.

"Are you going to kiss me now?"

With a growl deep in his throat, Sam pulled her close and seared her soul with a kiss. His earlier words floated along the edge of her consciousness. *Playing with fire…*

Skye's knees melted, and she went from a loose embrace to holding on for dear life.

"Come on, people! Give them some privacy."

Sam broke off the kiss, and they both looked skyward. So much for being out of the way of prying eyes.

"Guess I forgot there was a roofing crew up there." Sam's hoarse whisper tickled her senses.

"That's probably for the best." Skye hadn't been prepared for the intensity of Sam's kiss this time. It had taken months for their relationship to go from stationary to a snail's pace, but in the course of a single day they'd shot from snail's pace all the way up to flying on the Autobahn.

Conway yelled from the rooftop at the bottom of the u-shaped structure. "You should have gone inside if you didn't want any of my crew to witness it. We can see the whole property from up here."

Ginger's voice floated down from the roof closest to them. "Awww, I think it's sweet."

Kissing noises showered down on them.

Note to self: Don't make out with a guy within sight of a construction crew.

Sam cupped her face with his strong hands. "I know I said we'd go as slow as you want, and we will. I got carried away with the kiss…"

Skye grazed his jawline with her fingertips. "Slow is kind of a relative term."

"I don't want to have to imagine my life without you."

She slid two fingers up to his lips, gently memorizing their shape as she traced them. "If I have my way, you'll never need to."

Then she moved in, stepped all the way into his space, keeping a hair's breadth of distance between her lips and his. "I'm pretty sure I'm in love with you."

"That makes two of us." He winced. "In love. Not in love with me. I'm not in love with myself."

She closed that last tiny little span of air and kissed the man who had made her think of a thug when she'd first seen him, the man who had taught her so much about preconceived notions, selflessness, and beauty.

He pulled out of the kiss before she lost too much of herself in it, but his eyes held the promise of more to come. More kisses, sure. But more tomorrows, too. Tomorrows filled with love, laughter, diapers, and grandbabies.

Funny how she'd first come to Rainbow Falls to escape the life she thought she'd been born into. And in the process, she'd renewed old friendships, discovered a new purpose, and found the strength to forgive herself and others. More than all that, though, she'd found her way back to the God who had been waiting for her all along.

"Hey, Boss!" Franco's call came from around the corner of the building.

Sam dropped another light kiss on Skye's forehead. "Duty calls."

She pushed him away. "Go see what he needs. I'll be right behind you."

Sam disappeared around the corner of the building, and Skye stared after him. She rested a hand on the cool cinder block wall of the shelter. "Thank you, Mom." Her whispered words disappeared in the Montana breeze. "I wouldn't have met Sam if I hadn't had a place to run away to. Thank you for giving me this town and these people."

No matter where life took Skye, Rainbow Falls would always be the place where life was meant to be lived in full color and where hope was filled with every shade of the rainbow.

THE END

Author's Note

Thank you for spending time with me in Rainbow Falls. I hope that, like me, you are looking forward to getting to know these characters more. I have it on relatively good authority that Sunny's story will be next and that Tawny's happily-ever-after is going to be a bit of a surprise. As for Jette... It's going to take a special kind of guy to get past her reserve. One thing is for certain. Life is never dull when you live in a town filled with colorful people.

If you can, please take a minute to tell others about this book by leaving a review on Amazon and Goodreads. I wouldn't mind if you told all your friends about it, too. Or took out an ad in your local paper... although that might get costly. In all seriousness, though, reviews are golden, and I appreciate every single one of them.

As any writer will tell you, gratitude is a way of life in this line of work. I am beyond thankful that God gives me stories to share and the words with which to tell them. He has allowed me to do something I love, and it's a blessing every single day. Writing isn't a solitary journey, though, and I want to thank the people who have helped pull this story together and make it shine.

Thank you to everyone who cheered me on while catching all my dangling modifiers and missing antecedents: Elizabeth Maddrey, Shari Schroeder, Kay Springsteen, and Lynellen Perry. You're each invaluable.

About the Author

Heather loves coffee, God, her family, and laughter – not necessarily in that order! She writes approachable characters who, through the highs and lows of life, find a way to love God, embrace each day, and laugh out loud right along with her. And, yeah, her books almost always have someone who's a coffee addict. Some things just can't be helped.

She takes joy in creating characters that, much like her, are *flawed...but loved anyway.*

You can sign up for Heather's newsletter by going to http://heathergraywriting.com/newsletter

Other Books by Heather Gray

Informal Romance
An Informal Christmas
An Informal Arrangement
An Informal Introduction
An Informal Date
An Informal Affair
An Informal Reception (coming summer 2019)

Rainbow Falls (contemporary Christian romance)
Skye
Sunny (coming winter 2018)
Rose (coming summer 2019)

Other Contemporary Christian Romance
Ten Million Reasons
Nowhere for Christmas
Bella Notte

Ladies of Larkspur (Christian Western Romance)
Mail Order Man
Just Dessert
Redemption

Regency Refuge (Christian Regency Romance)
His Saving Grace
Jackal
Queen

PREVIEW

An Informal Date
Informal Romance Book 4

Chapter One

Here he comes again.

Kimi pretended to organize her muffin assortment as Dr. No-Name approached. She could set her clock by him. Every Monday, Wednesday, and Friday at 7:05 in the morning, he came for his large half-caff triple nonfat medium whip white mocha. Even though she knew what he would order, she waited for him to arrive. One day not too long ago, she'd started his drink as soon as he'd stepped into view. She'd had the steaming beverage ready and waiting for him. The poor guy had been so flustered he'd knocked over the fruit basket and taken out half the cookie display in the process.

She'd learned an important lesson that day. Two, really. Patience paid off. And some people don't handle change well.

Dr. No-Name glanced to the side and tripped over a covered cable that ran along the floor. He kicked the toe of his loafer into the top of the cable's molded rubber protector, lost his balance, hopped a couple of times on his left foot, swung his arms like a grade-schooler doing the windmill in PE, and finally got his right shoe back down on the ground. Despite the theatrical gymnastics, nobody but her appeared to be watching the show. She had to give him points for the landing. Not a brown hair on his head was out of place, and his lab coat hung from his shoulders with straight lines in complete denial of its recent whirlwind of activity.

The same cable had been positioned across that floor for as long as Kimi could remember. The doctor had to know it, too, but unless his eyes were trained directly on it, he seemed to forget. She'd witnessed his footwork often enough to realize that much, at least.

Kimi turned her back on him lest he catch her spying. Despite his oddities, she enjoyed Dr. No-Name's visits to her kiosk and didn't want to scare him off by staring or — heaven forbid — laughing.

"Um, excuse me."

She turned around, her smile in place and hopefully no pity in her eyes. "Good morning! The usual?"

Dr. No-Name nodded. Most doctors wore their name embroidered on their official white lab coats, but not this one. Plain white, no fancy frills, and no embroidery. Either he wasn't important enough for a name on his coat or he was humble enough not to care. She secretly hoped it was the latter.

Kimi set to work on his drink and tried to make conversation. "You always order a triple shot, but you want half-caff. Most people who want to go easy on the caffeine avoid the triple."

She caught his shrug out of the corner of her eye. Getting this guy to talk was harder than pulling a barking dog's molars with a pair of tweezers.

"There must be a reason. What about the triple shot do you find inviting?"

He blinked a couple of times, masking the bright blue of his eyes, before answering. "I like the taste of the triple, but I don't want a caffeine high."

She'd figured as much. As a coffee aficionado, she could understand. She loved the flavor but wasn't always interested in the calories or the caffeine. Like him, she'd learned to improvise.

She handed over his drink, and Dr. No-Name passed her three ones, two quarters, one dime, and one nickel. That was the other reason he remained a no-name. Had he ever paid with credit card, she would know his name by now. He always paid in cash, though. The exact $3.65 including tax.

"There's going to be a price increase later this month. I don't know the date yet or the new prices, but I thought I should warn you."

His turn away from her kiosk stalled. "Why?"

"Why am I warning you, or why the change?"

He reached for a napkin and wiped off the spotless customer side of the counter. "Why the increase?"

It was her turn to shrug. "The late summer rains have been too heavy. Flooding ruined a good part of South America's coffee crop. Our owner expects to see an exponential hike in bean prices over the coming year, so he's trying to get ahead of things with a small increase now. He hopes doing that will allow him to postpone a larger increase."

"Supply and demand." He was a master at being succinct.

"Pretty much. Kind of the same reason why some pharmaceutical drugs are so expensive."

He shook his head. "That's an erroneous comparison. Coffee crops depend on nature to thrive. Pharmaceuticals are almost all manmade these days. If a company wants the price of their drug to go up, they can choose to make less of it. Decisions like that happen in boardrooms. Nobody chose to ruin their coffee crop."

Kimi wiped the imaginary crumbs off the small counter near her cash register. "Excellent point. Do you think pharmaceutical companies actually do that? Make less so they can charge more?"

A shadow passed over his face, transforming his normally blue eyes into an obscure shade of grey. "Some do. It's a fact of doing business. There are others, though, that I think... I hope... maintain integrity." With a brisk nod in her direction, he turned and headed back the way he'd come. He stopped before he came to the site of his previous trip. Kimi would have loved to see the look on his face as he took a higher-than-usual step over the rubberized cable protector.

Dr. No-Name fascinated her, but she still hadn't figured out why. She didn't get many doctors in her part of the hospital. Near the surgical waiting room, her kiosk put her in a position to deal almost exclusively with family members. Doctors didn't usually come this way — at least not for coffee. What's more, Dr. No-Name always approached from her right, which meant he came from within the hospital, not from the parking garage. There had to be other kiosks more convenient to his location than hers.

Oh well. She'd gotten him to talk more today than any day previous. Maybe he'd still be talkative come Friday. If so, she might even be able to pull a name out of him.

All for the sake of making conversation and putting her customers at ease, of course.